BRING BACK THE SINGING

Beneath the materially brilliant façade of the home which Hugh and Clare Eagleton had established were loneliness, fear and insecurity. Clare, partner to a top-ranking dress-designer, was confident that she had made a successful synthesis of career and marriage and could not conceive the possibility of either her husband or her children seeking love and security in any other sphere.

By the same author

TURN OF DAYS
SHADOW OF WINGS
THE CONVOYS PASS
GARDEN OF PARADISE
HE TOO WAS A GALLANT GENTLEMAN
AND WE SHALL BUILD
LISTEN BELOVED
OUT OF TOMORROW
THE BRITTLE GLORY
THE UNFAMILIAR NAME
SOURCE OF THE RIVER
THE UNRELENTING DAY
JAN
THE EVERLASTING ANSWER
THE STRONG ARE BOUND

BRING BACK THE SINGING

BY

STELLA MORTON

Everyone's voice was suddenly lifted,
And beauty came like the setting sun.
My heart was shaken with tears, and horror
Drifted away. . . . O, but every one
Was a bird; and the song was wordless; the
    singing will never be done.

SIEGFRIED SASSOON
"Everyone Sang"

THE ROMANCE BOOK CLUB
121 CHARING CROSS ROAD
LONDON W. C. 2

THIS EDITION BY ARRANGEMENT WITH
HODDER AND STOUGHTON LIMITED

*Printed in the Netherlands
by N.V. De Arbeiderspers, Amsterdam*

Acknowledgments

The author is indebted to Mr. Siegfried Sassoon and Messrs. William Heinemann for permission to quote from "Everyone Sang" on the title-page of this novel, and to Mrs. Yeats and Messrs. Macmillan, publishers of *The Collected Poems of W. B. Yeats*, for the lines cited from "The Cloths of Heaven".

Chapter I

In the early evening light, Bellhammer had a Continental appearance, as though it had been designed for the blue and white sea-board countries of the Mediterranean rather than for the thin intermittent sunshine of southern England; the kind of house that might possibly have been seen with a background of olive trees and distant mountains a couple of kilometres out of any town from Naples right up the Portuguese coast to Vigo.

"I want," Clare had said to Giles Roache, the architect, "first and foremost to catch every ray of the sun. That's the most important point. Secondly, I want the exterior to be white with strong, uncluttered lines and curves, giving the feeling of"—she hesitated, but only for a moment—"of blue seas and high hills, of a"—she considered again, her eyes narrowed—"of, I think, a Spanish house we saw last year outside Torremolinos, I'll sketch it for you later. And, thirdly, I want to incorporate every modern"—she smiled slightly and inserted "don't ask me to use the word 'contemporary'—device, both interior and exterior."

It was a job after Roache's own heart and he had captured pretty faithfully the idea Clare had transferred to him and, on this particular April evening when the oblique rays of the sun were giving what was, in some lights, its too stark whiteness a softer, more English appearance, it had a simplicity that was near beauty.

The piece of land on which it stood had been chosen and rejected and chosen again with the most minute consideration, and there was little doubt, now, that Clare's insistence had been right, for Roache had built it on what was a small plateau, a little hillock with the top sliced off so that it had the appearance of being 'raised', sailing free, while the ground sloped gently away, on the south and west to the wide sweep of the river, on the north and east to the triangular arms of the beechwood.

Possibly the Continental air was emphasised by two features in particular: one, that on the west side, Roache had incorporated a loggia as part of the actual building, extending the upper storey into a separate guest-suite, with its own bathroom and small sitting-room. Paved with black and white tiles, enclosed on the north and east with removable glass windows, furnished in spring and summer with scarlet wicker chaise-longues and Swedish-design chairs and tables, with the successful 'Clare Eagleton' rose, which Hans Calenfals the Dutchman at the Nurseries had brought into being seven years ago, thrusting its strong green leaves up the square pillars, and in summer putting out flame-velvet blooms, it gave a gay, 'holiday' atmosphere to the whole place. The second feature was the wrought-iron screen at the main entrance at the centre of the house. Here, Roache had contrived that the double doors could, in summer, be opened wide, leaving the interior—the splendid proportions of the white-panelled hall with the blocked-in curve of the ascending stair-balustrade—visible through the wrought-iron screen. In keeping with the main idea he had the design of the screen copied from a seventeenth century Andalusian house, and when the light was bright and clear and the shadows sharply defined, when there were always bowls of roses and lilies from the Nurseries against the walls, the feeling of the Latin influence was strong.

To some people though, and in particular to Mark Sheridan, the artist, Clare's cousin, who had moved into The Nythe Farm when Hugh and Clare had left it for Bellhammer, the effect was too theatrical, too, in Mark's own words, 'darned clinical' for a home.

"You can't *live* in a place that's a cross between a ballet décor and an operating theatre." he scorned. "A home worth the name is a place where you can wear your carpet-slippers and knock your pipe out on the grate—there isn't such a thing in the whole place—and leave your gum-boots at the door if you feel like it. A place where there's a sign of life, conflict if you like, but *life*. A line of washing blowing in the wind, and rain-water butts and bicycles and even an old saucepan or two that the kids are making mudpies in. All that perfection! My God, if any of Clare's children left an old saucepan hanging about that pseudo-Spanish contraption there'd be hell to pay. Only it isn't likely because there wouldn't be anything so homely as an old saucepan available, and even if there were, either Clare herself or the nurse or the gardener or one of the tribe would whisk it away long before anyone could scoop up a handful of good solid mud to put in it. The whole thing's sterile, aseptic, a modern museum-piece."

"Just because you don't like it," Patty his wife answered, her needle interweaving the strands of wool on the heel of the sock stretched over her left fist. "But if they'd never built it, we wouldn't have had the Nythe."

"You wretched, prim, *reasonable* little woman!" Mark replied, his singularly red lips in his greying beard parted in a slight smile. "My self-appointed conscience and ready-reckoner," he added as he slid back behind the paper again.

"One man's meat is another man's poison," Patty remarked, biting off the wool with her teeth, but Mark only rattled the news-sheet in reply.

The Nythe hadn't been so much 'poison' to Clare as a cross, a burden. The nooks and crannies and beams and upper-floor sloping ceilings which enchanted Mark, giving him a feeling of security, of continuity—of roots reaching back to some richer, truer, more gracious living—to her were little more than symbols of decay, other people's decay at that. And although, when she and Hugh lived there, she made the best of the place—because it was her nature to make the best of any situation; to tackle and wrestle and subdue it to her will—there was always at the back of her mind an awareness of woodworm and dry-rot, of crumbling plaster and damp walls; of the impression of something tattered and worn, the discarded remnant of people long dead. At first, when there had only been herself and Hugh and Annabel, and before she had gone back to her work with Daniel Forest, she had managed to banish the sense of decay and impress her own vitality and energy on to the house. But when she had returned to Forest, and when Annabel had been joined by Piers, and after Piers, David, the nooks and the crannies and the dust and the antiquated kitchen and the suspicious plumbing had, so to speak, come into their own again and Bellhammer had taken shape, first in her mind, then in Giles Roache's plans and finally in bricks and mortar.

By that time, four years ago now, Hugh had re-established Eagletons after the disastrous war years, and the little Nurseryman's business, which his grandfather had started in the field behind The Nythe, was by then not only nationally, but internationally known.

Eagletons, the rose specialists. Eagletons, the carnation specialists. Eagletons' freesias—thousands of bunches packed for Covent Garden every day. Eagletons' mushrooms—hundredweights delivered weekly to the soupmaking factories alone. Eagletons' turkeys and chickens from their specialised farms going off by the hundred to the hotels and the canners. The one word 'Eagletons' appearing on the firm's writing-paper, on the five hundred pay-roll envelopes, on the fleet of battleship grey lorries. Eagletons, the new post-war Eagletons, was sailing out on a full tide and Bellhammer became, in part at least, financially possible. And while Hugh steered Eagletons into the new age, Daniel Forest with Clare at his right hand, climbed—not perhaps as fast as he should have done and certainly not as fast as Clare had hoped he would—up the ladder of style and fashion and elegance and originality in the wake of Dior and Balmain and Givenchy and Jules Coré, so that Forest, too, though indirectly and through Clare, had his part in Bellhammer as, brick by brick, it grew and developed and took on form and identity on the little sliced-off hillock where once Cromwell's men had gathered and from which, too, in the year eighteen hundred and seventy, William Eagleton, horticulturist, had surveyed the land about him, the dream of a flame-coloured rose in his eyes.

So Bellhammer was born, and the present generation of Eagletons, Hugh and Clare and Annabel and Piers and David passed out of The Nythe, and Mark and Patty with their four children passed in to the first settled home they had ever possessed. They had been there two years when Clare produced the Baby as efficiently as she produced most things, and within a month was back with Forest again in good time for that year's spring show.

It was the first of his advanced shows, and it brought him within hailing distance of the big designers. With him went Clare, and both Clare and Bellhammer became news. They appeared, separately and together, in photographs and feature articles in the magazines and the journals and even on the women's page of the national press.

'Mrs. Clare Eagleton, beautiful wife of Hugh Eagleton the horticulturist, who manages to run their lovely home Bellhammer and also her own career as partner to Daniel Forest the designer whose last show made head-lines back in the spring. In an interview with Alice Hall, Mrs. Eagleton said that she thought the secret of two careers lay in planning ahead and minutely-detailed organisation.'

'Clare Eagleton, pictured above on the terrace at Bell-hammer, the Eagletons' Spanish-style ultra-modern house, says that she finds no difficulty in being Daniel Forest's partner, wife to attractive husband, Hugh—he grows those lovely Eagleton freesias—and mother to Annabel, Piers, David and Baby. "It's a full life but a very satisfying one," Clare told us. We add that it is also a highly successful one.'

'Bellhammer the Hugh Eagletons' home which Giles Roache designed. 1) The panelled hall and old Spanish wrought-iron screen doors. 2) The drawing-room. 3) The kitchen—note ventilation shafts. 4) A glimpse of an upper corridor with stained glass windows. 5) Mrs. Hugh Eagleton with Annabel, their eldest daughter, in the loggia. The rose, left, is the famous "Clare Eagleton" a flame-coloured climber.'

'The kitchen of Bellhammer, home of Clare Eagleton, wife of the horticulturist, incorporates every possible labour-saving device.'

It did and the amalgamation of Clare, Giles Roache and Thompson the builder had produced an interior economy worthy of Roache's excellent façade. Every use had been made of electricity. There were no boilers and only one wood-burning grate and that a concession to tradition rather than a necessity. The children's wing was separated from the rest of the house by a sound-proof door, and the walls of the indoor nursery and outdoor playroom—it had its own small lawn and flower-beds—had a four-foot high 'scribbling' surround so that there was no restriction on any of the children's potential artistic talents. The lower floors were all of pine, with some particularly lovely rugs which Roache had picked up in Florence. Upstairs, fitted carpets of a beige-lilac shade covered corridors and bedrooms. There were four bathrooms.

On this particular April evening Clare, dressed except for her coat, gave herself a final critical survey in the long three-fold mirror in her dressing-room. There was no admiration for her own reflection, for admiration, at that moment, might have blinded her to some minute fault, and tonight she could give herself no quarter. Swiftly, coldly, she inspected each feature of the figure that looked back at her, as though she regarded a stranger. She considered her dark hair. 'Moulded' rather than 'set', the barely perceptible wave swept the whole into a shape which made of hair and features one entity, an effect of such simplicity that to the untutored it would have appeared 'natural'. She smiled slightly at that, for it had taken M. Jacques her hairdresser two or three hours to achieve. Her eyes lowered to take in her forehead and she picked up the magnifying make-up glass and peered into it. Naturally curved, slightly darkened eyebrows were winged across a matt brow. There was eye-shadow on the eye-lids; mascara emphasised already long dark lashes. Close-grained skin glowed beneath the powder. Coré's new lipstick was dew-soft on her wide, firm mouth. She nodded, satisfied, and put the hand-glass down. Neck, arms, hands . . . she held her hands palm downward and threw a quick glance at the smooth backs, the long fingers and rounded, beautifully coloured nails. The diamond Hugh had given her last year was on the fourth finger of her right hand; Daniel's bracelet, the one he gave her after their first really successful show three years ago, clasped her wrist.

The dress itself . . . admiration then, but, even so, not yet for herself, but for Daniel Forest. Her mind flicked back a couple of months to the day when they'd first heard that Jules Coré was coming over to the Exhibition of French Designers. And Coré *was* Paris. He was the Champs Elysées and the Place Vendôme and the reflection of Notre Dame in the Seine and the Ile de la Cité and Versailles. French politics might totter, Ministers come and go, the national economy rock, but while Coré was there to dictate what the women of Paris and London and New York should wear, France was France still. And Coré was coming to London, not on a 'private' visit to stay as he often did at the Dorchester, but publicly to attend the Exhibition and to be entertained by his country's Ambassador at the French Embassy. All fashionable London and Paris would be there. Royalty would be there. Italy and Ireland and New York would be there. Everyone who knew what 'clothes' were would be there—if they could secure one of the nine-by-six deckle-edged cards with the gilt lettering sent out by the Minister Plenipotentiary to the Court of S. James. Daniel Forest had received one of these cards which included Clare Eagleton and her husband Hugh, and immediately on its reception he had set about the design for Clare's dress. This was to be not only the dress Clare wore, but Daniel Forest's 'next step', the triumph which would set the seal on what had been the most spectacular spring show of his career. It had not only to express every facet of Clare's personality, to fit it like a glove, but it had to bear his own indelible imprint for all of that glittering, fashionable throng to see and recognise.

Perhaps one of Forest's greatest assets was his ability to 'pick up', and express in line and form and material, the personality of the woman he was designing for. 'Trends' as such barely influenced him. 'Lines' as a popular 'must' of the moment he disregarded, and yet his clothes always bore some indefinable mark of the particular style of the year, not branded on to the design but subtly suggested, a whisper of a thing, a Master's concession to those who were still exercised by the insignificant business of time and change.

For a week he chose, re-chose, inspected, touched and rejected materials: his hand moving over brocade, silks, satins, Irish linens. Flame? Green? Lilac? Gold? He was tensed, irritable and the office staff and the sewing-room girls reflected his nervous strain in quarrels and fits of jealousy and threats to leave. He decided on green, a lovely green-gold brocade, and set about the design: but after five days work, more tensed than ever, he threw up the whole abortive idea and Clare, who had been through it all a hundred times before, packed him off to his cottage near Penshurst with orders not to return for four days. He was back in two, all tension gone, bounding about the place on his small feet like a child, calling for a particular very heavy satin to be brought to him. Miss Felice—her real name was Nora Phoebe Higson and she was the most brilliant craftswoman in the business—brought it to his studio and, unrolling half a dozen yards, slung it over the stand, while he nodded and smiled and occasionally darted forward to pick up a fold between his thumb and first finger, turning it this way and that as the light fell then letting it slide back, watching every movement as it rippled into line again. That morning the word went round the workrooms and fitting rooms, the washrooms and the lavatories—'O.K. Stand easy. He's got it.'

The scene slipped from Clare's mind again and she concentrated on her reflection. It was as though, she thought, there were no dividing line between the dress and herself. They were one whole. How had he done it? She didn't know, never would know, as no one on earth will ever know the working mechanics of the creative faculty. The whole thing was as simple as the morning, or the ripple of light on a stream. He had merely taken a length of satin of the colour of rich cream standing in the rose-gold rays of a sunset (so that one was aware of a touch of colour without a trace of its defined presence), and he had woven it of light and shadow and formed it into 'herself'. And, because of his genius, 'herself' in this very year, was hall-marked with the present age, almost, she thought, hall-marked with something beyond this age, something which reached out into some less muddled, less cluttered and 'bitty' way of life. As with M. Jacques' work on her hair, the thing looked 'too easy'— the melody of a Chopin Nocturne, a sketch by da Vinci: something which had broken free of effort with all its toil and pain. That's what it *looked* like, and yet it had been created by effort and toil and pain, not only his but her own—and Nora Higson's and John Mercer the cutter's and a room full of sewing-girls as well.

With only the play of light and shade of the beautiful material, he had somehow contrived a sense of colour, or rather more a feeling that added colour would have spelt vulgarity, the gilding of a lily. And the coat—she reached behind her and took it from the hanger and slipped her arms into the wide sleeves. Here colour was a full chord, a triumph, the waving of a banner. For this he had used the same heavy satin as he had for the dress, but in that exquisite shade of soft gold-flame which marks the base of the bud of a tea-rose, a *living* colour. With a moulded 'romantic' collar it fell from her shoulders in sweeping cloak-like folds, the armholes masked within the folds themselves, the whole having all the movement and fluidity of flowing water, or of candlelight reflected in copper when someone moves across an old room. Dress and coat, too, were a unity, two parts of one whole. And the whole was beauty.

Clare drew a deep, slow breath and only then did thought escape her rigid, critical control. She closed her lids and opened them, not on to the reflection of Daniel Forest's creation but on to herself, Clare Eagleton; on to flesh and blood and expression; on to the woman that she was. And she knew that never in her life had she looked so near beauty: knew, too, with a shadowing of intuition, that she would never, possibly, look so beautiful again. 'This' she thought, half-ironically, half amused, 'is my finest hour.' It was an hour that was the culmination of twelve years of planning and striving and bearing with and believing in Daniel Forest. Twelve years of nursing him, encouraging him, defending him and coming between him and all the irritations of modern existence; ever since that day, when, meeting him again after four years of war and her own marriage to Hugh Eagleton, he had asked her to go back to him.

They'd been glad enough of the extra money then, she and Hugh, for Hugh wasn't finding it easy to put Eagletons back on the map again, but her old strong intuition that Forest was a genius in his own world had been proved right.

She moved slowly across to the window, conscious of the swaying of the material about her as she went. Directly below her, beyond the courtyard that Roache had built at the back of the house, the lawns, looking as though oiled, so deep and shining was each separate blade of grass, swept down to the beechwood where the light played about slim silver-grey trunks and turned the sap-filled branches to maroon lace against the sky-line. And just visible beyond the wood were the chimney-stacks of The Nythe.

They'd come a long way since those days at The Nythe— her mind flashed on to the inconveniences of the old house and darted off again—and tonight was the crown of, not only Forest's, but her own success; for without her, and she knew it, Daniel Forest would not have stood where he did. How many geniuses, she wondered, were unheard of because they lacked the very backing she had given Daniel, the 'cushioning' which took the shocks and left genius free to function? She had 'made' Daniel Forest, and tonight they entered on equal terms that world for which she had striven and toiled and sweated and which, up to this spring, had always eluded them. Tonight they went to meet fame, no longer an ephemeral hope, but there, tangible, solid. And Bellhammer was there ready to consolidate the new step, because she herself, convinced of its coming, had prepared it as the perfect background.

She had the odd fancy that she was driving a white and gold chariot thundering down a sunlit road, then with a half-smile at the nonsense, she picked up the evening bag and, with a final flick of a glance at swirling flame as she passed the long glasses, went through her bedroom and hurried down the corridor to the nursery wing.

The nurse, who had the Baby on her knee, gasped when she saw her.

"Mrs. Eagleton! Oh, isn't it beautiful. So beautiful."

"Yes, Nannie," Clare answered coolly, "it's very beautiful. Mr. Forest is very pleased with it."

"The colour of the coat!" the nurse exclaimed. "I've never seen . . . " She shook her head. "It must be wonderful to wear such lovely clothes," she ended.

"It's exciting," Clare answered and added, "we're just off. Is everything all right?"

"Oh, yes, Mrs. Eagleton."

"Baby's spots?"

"They're not quite gone. They're better though."

"You gave her the magnesia?"

"Oh yes, she's had three doses now."

"Good. I'll . . . "

The door burst open and David came rushing in. He pulled up short when he saw his mother, stared at her for a moment, then came hurtling towards her, his grubby child's hands held out.

"David! *David!*" The nurse, with a sweeping movement of her free arm scooped him up before he reached Clare. "You know you mustn't touch Mummy. How often have I told you."

"Won't touch. Won't touch. Want to see," David cried, his heels drumming on the girl's strong thigh. "Put me down. Nanny. Put me down."

"I think I'd go if I were you, Mrs. Eagleton," the girl said, "I'm terrified he'll get near you."

"Quiet, David!" Clare said sharply. "And stop kicking Nanny at once or you won't be able to come and see us off. That's better. Put him down, Nanny."

"Want to kiss you goodbye," David pleaded, his big eyes filling with tears.

Clare looked down at him. "I can't kiss you, darling, because I'm going to London and I've got a special dress on."

"Why have you?"

He was hopping from one foot to the other but the nurse still had him pinned by the shoulder.

"I *want* to see you go. I *want* to see you go," he insisted, his face reddening with a terrible anxiety.

"Don't you worry, Mrs. Eagleton," said the nurse. "I'll pop the Baby in and bring him down. He'll calm off. David!" She gave his shoulder a little shake.

"I'll have to go," Clare answered. "Can you manage, Nanny?"

The nurse nodded and Clare hurried out and the sound-proof door swung to behind her.

She went down the stairs. The hall-doors were open, and through the wrought-iron screen she caught a glimpse of the river, deep blue in the evening light. The hall was filled with the scent of freesias massed in crystal bowls. She heard Hugh's voice and turned across the hall, pressing a bell which summoned Felton the housemaid from the kitchen.

Felton controlled the expression which involuntarily came into her eyes when she saw Clare standing there, backed by the wrought-iron screen and the flowers. She controlled it, because she had been brought up by strict Puritanical parents to whom all material beauty was suspect. But the conflict between envy and fear tightened her mouth and gave her a queer 'lost' sensation in her heart.

"Oh Felton," Clare said, "I promised Cook should see the dress before I went. Call her, will you? And don't forget to leave some Ovaltine in a flask as well as the whisky. And sandwiches—the chicken would be best. Not more than a couple as we possibly shan't need anything. Tell Cook to come at once, please. I heard the car go round some time ago."

She watched Felton walk away and thought, 'Even her buttocks disapprove of me in Daniel's dress.'

She wondered, her mind flicking quickly on to the question, what it must be like to be Felton squeezed into her little grey cell, crying her 'No! No!' to all the thrust of colour in the world. Such an excellent servant. Content to be 'an excellent servant'? Obviously, or she'd have tried something else long ago. Strange, the way it went. Clare Eagleton going off in a Daniel Forest dress to the French Embassy with a husband who was as successful in his own line as she in her's. Four children, all healthy, attractive. A perfect home. She herself—yes, beautiful. Tonight anyway. Successful. Known. Envied. 'But I've worked for it,' she insisted. 'I've used my brains. The Feltons of this world . . . ' The train of thought snapped as Cook, with Mrs. Phipps the daily, came through into the hall.

Chapter II

PIERS was in the playroom reading when he heard Johnson take the car round, and, in a panic that he'd be too late to see them go, he dropped his book and ran across the grass instead of going round to the front of the house by the path. This was forbidden, but fear that he might miss them was greater than the fear of punishment, and he ran fast—his thin legs stretching out and back like a young deer's. The car was there and Johnson was coming along the path on his way back to the garage, his shirt-sleeves rolled above his arms.

"You get off that lawn, you young villain," Johnson frowned at him. "Always telling you," he muttered.

The breath was rasping in Piers' throat and the blood hammering in his ears. It exhilarated him.

"Aren't you taking them, Johnson?" he asked, the words tearing up on the rasping breath.

"No, thank God, I'm not." Johnson answered. "Hanging about till no one cares what time. Your Dad's driving."

Piers looked away from Johnson's hairy arms to his own smooth brown skin. He tried to imagine his arms covered with hair, but the thought nauseated him. He wondered what Johnson did when he went home to his cottage not far from The Nythe. Passing by one Sunday morning he had seen him, stripped to the waist, his braces hanging down over his trousers, shaving himself in the scullery. Then Mrs. Johnson, with her hair in curling pins, had come out and tipped a pail of water on to the garden.

Johnson walked on, and Piers looked up and saw Annabel coming round from the loggia. She had seen him, he was sure of that, but she walked slowly, reading a book as she came, though he knew she was only pretending. He watched her reach the curved shallow steps and sit down on the top one. She put up her hand and brushed a strand of her long fair hair away from her face. 'She's trying to be grown-up.' he thought and he strolled over and leaned against the wing of the car.

"Have you been down to The Nythe?" he asked, but she kept her eyes on the book and didn't answer.

After another minute had gone by she looked up and said, "What?"

"The Baby's got spots," he said. "It might be measles, then I wouldn't be able to go to boarding-school."

"Don't be silly," she answered scornfully. "It's her teeth. You keep thinking something will happen to stop you going. You're frightened."

"I'm not frightened. I want to go. I want to go awfully. My blazer came today," he added, but even as he spoke he felt sick with the fear which groped for him whenever he thought about the school.

There were ten more days. Yesterday there had been eleven. Tomorrow there would be nine. One by one the remaining days would come up and drop away, and when the last of them had come and gone . . . but his thought could not face that last day, for beyond it was darkness ripped through here and there by terrifying things he had heard or read about school life—the cane, the strap, the torments of the other boys for anyone they disliked; for a coward. He *was* a coward. He was afraid of spiders, and moths and maybugs made him panic when they buzzed insanely about the light in summertime. He was afraid of being hurt, of having his flesh cut and torn, letting the bood through. He was afraid of being alone in darkness. As long

as there were a little light . . . Staying down at The Nythe, he
waited till he knew Bill was asleep, and then he crept out of
bed and tucked a fold of the curtain back so that a chink
showed along the division where the curtains met. When he
got back to bed he kept his eyes fixed on that feather of light
in the darkness. But at school . . .

"Did you like going?" he asked Annabel, but she still
kept her head down.

"Of course I liked it," she replied at last. Then she looked
up and said, "I'm longing to go back this term, it's always
the best. I'm going to take my new racquet and I've
had to have more summer frocks because I'd grown out
of my old ones. But it's a fearful bore because I've got
to take my G.C.E. and I shall be absolutely livid if The
Hammer makes us stay in and swot when the weather's
decent."

She thought of the school train at Charing Cross. She saw
herself walking down the platform with her father. He stood
outside the compartment with his hat off, taller than anyone
there, shaking hands with Miss Patterson and people he
knew. He stayed there till the train pulled out and she went
on waving till they rounded the bend.

"Why do you call her The Hammer?" she heard Piers say.
"It's a silly name."

"You always call the Head *something*," she answered.
"Everyone does." She brought her wrist up and looked at
her watch. Her father and mother had given it to her for
her birthday three weeks ago, and it still delighted her. She
had to control the desire to make that movement with her
wrist every few moments. It made her feel adult. If only she
didn't have to get back into school uniform again—a jibber
and those repulsive hats! She played with the idea of running
away and going on the stage. She saw herself in front of the
footlights bowing to the hushed House. Annabel Eagleton
in . . .

"Here comes Dad," Piers broke in to her bright imaginings. "What's the time, Anna?"

She looked at her watch again.

"Half past."

"Will they be going soon?"

"I suppose. Mother said half past."

"Do you wish you were going, too?"

"It's only for *designers*," she answered shortly, but she saw herself sailing down the stairs, holding her skirt up as her mother did, and hurrying out to the car, leaving a waft of scent behind her on the air. She ached to be finished with childhood.

"Dad isn't a designer," said Piers as his father came through the screen doors and down the steps.

Annabel looked up and saw him, and an empty place in her heart contracted in a sweet, inexplicable pain. He was wearing full evening dress, and the long coat made him look slimmer than ever. His shoulders . . the pain twisted in her heart again, but she didn't know why; only, suddenly, she thought, 'One day he'll die' and the thought blotted out the lovely evening.

"Hello, you two," he said, as he opened the car door and put something into the dash-board pocket. "Come to see the circus go off?"

Annabel stood up and came towards him but he fended her off. "Don't get near me for Pete's sake," he said. "This god-forsaken black picks up everything. Haven't left any hairs on my collar, have I?"

He turned and swung his shoulders downward a little so that she could see, and she lightly flicked nothing away with her hand.

"Now it's all right."

"Good girl!" He smiled down at her. "What should I do without you?"

She thought her heart swelled to breaking point, but she

only said, "I'm up to your shoulder. Past, nearly. I'm five foot three. Is mother ready?"

He flicked a glance at his watch. "Any minute now."

"Does it look nice? The dress, I mean."

"Don't know. Haven't seen it. She was barricaded into her dressing-room when I came down." Again he smiled at her, shaking his head. "Take a braver man than I am to ask how it was going."

"I expect it's wonderful."

"I expect so."

She thought she detected 'something' behind his tone, but she didn't know what it was. She fancied that she groped towards him with her hands outstretched.

"Will you have champagne?"

"I fear we shall."

"Don't you like it?"

"It's all right, I suppose. On these occasions."

"Will they have glasses like ours, where it goes right down the stem?"

"Shouldn't be surprised."

"One day you'll take me, won't you? To a big dance or something in London? You will, won't you?"

He looked down at her but she couldn't interpret the expression in his eyes.

"When the time comes for that, it won't be me who'll be taking you," he answered, and flicked his lighter and lighted a cigarette.

Piers watched them and heard what they said, yet he thought it was as though he were separated from them by plate glass, quite alone in a world apart. He would have liked to smash through the glass and have gone to them so that he could have joined in the talk, but he couldn't do it. 'Perhaps,' he thought, 'he'll say something to me, soon,' but at that moment the nurse came out on to the steps with David.

"Oh, hello Nanny. Thought it was your bedtime, young David," his father said.

"We promised to let him see you go," the girl answered.

"Yes," David agreed and he gave two or three little jumps. "To see you go. To see you go," he repeated. He stopped jumping and said, "The Baby's got spots." He peered up to his father's face far above him. "Do you know where they are? They're on her—*bot*. Nanny put milk on them and she squeaked."

"David!" The nurse admonished, but his father laughed. "That'll learn her!"

David laughed, too, screwing up his nose conscious of success, though unsure of its origin.

Piers saw that the shadows were growing longer, reaching out across the garden, taking the emerald from the shining grass. Far down beyond the lawns, in the Wild Garden there was a breaking wave of gold where the daffodils were. The swan waddled awkwardly back to the river, stepped down and sailed off upstream looking magnificently self-satisfied. He wondered how many cygnets there would be this year, and realised, with a twist of grief, that by the time he came home at the end of July they'd be quite big.

"Can I go to Piers?" David asked the nurse and he looked across at Piers, pleading in his eyes.

Warmth opened in Piers' heart then, and he held out his hand and said, "Come on, then."

"I think you'd better . . . " the nurse began and at that moment Felton opened the wrought-iron doors and his mother was there, standing on the top of the steps. She stood quite still, and, watching her, he thought he was drowning in a loveliness that he couldn't explain, but recognised. He felt that the moment—the white house in the evening light, the shadowed and gold grass and the blue river, the others standing on the path and his mother on the top step dressed in those shining clothes—was pressing on

26

him with an intolerable pain which yet filled him with joy. And he knew, with something old and wise and detached in himself, that he would never forget one detail of any of it. That it would always live on in some hidden part of his being, live on in the aching of his love for her.

"Mummy!" he heard Annabel exclaim. "Isn't it marvellous! Oh, isn't Daniel wizard! You look like a painting." He saw, too, that his father threw his cigarette away and stood looking up at his mother, his lips closely set together.

"It is lovely, isn't it?" He heard her cool voice answering Annabel, and he watched as she picked up a fold of the dress and came on down to the drive while his father swung round and opened the car door.

He moved back praying desperately that she would say something to him, something for him alone, that only he understood; something that would show Annabel that he was a person—someone who counted. His mother glanced towards him, but the glance swung round to his father again and she said, "I don't think we'd better wait for Irma. I said I'd be at Belgrave Square by eight, and . . . " But even as she spoke a small car came up the drive and stopped with a jerk a couple of yards from the Jaguar and in another second Irma Lovat was out of it, walking towards them.

"I got held up," she began and stopped as Clare moved back from the car and she saw her. The slanting rays of the sun were all about her, turning the coat into a burning copper and giving a pearl-like lustre to the dress beneath. "Clare!" Irma exclaimed. "Oh, but—" She stopped and said, "I knew it would be lovely, but . . . " She shook her head. "One didn't think mere clothes could ever look like that. It's all so—so untouched, as though it had just 'happened'. I don't think I knew . . . "

"It is beautiful, isn't it?" Clare broke in, and Piers knew that she was in a hurry. "Daniel was nearly satisfied, I think. Irma," she went on, "do forgive us but we must start. I told Daniel we'd be there at eight, and then we've got to have dinner and be at the Embassy by ten."

"You're not going to *eat* in it!" Irma said. "It's sacrilegious. Suppose you . . . "

"Don't say it," Clare laughed. "Soup or a piece of salmon! I feel I ought to take an overall. Sweet of you to come up, Irma."

"I wouldn't have missed it. Aren't you terrified even to *drive* her, Hugh?"

Piers saw his father look down at Irma, his eyes crinkling into a smile. "I wondered if I ought to have taken out an *insurance*," he said. "We'd better move, I think." His hand was on the open door as he waited for his wife to get into the car. There was a new white cover on the seat draped down over the floor so that she would not hurt the dress. She turned and gave a slight wave towards the house. "Bye, David. *Straight* to bed. Night, Irma."

She glanced up at Nanny and Cook and smiled. The nurse lifted David so that he could see into the car and Annabel ran to the driving-window.

" 'Bye, Daddy. Have a wonderful time. You look like a prince and princess."

'Perhaps' Piers thought, 'she'll look out of my side as they go by,' but the car started to move while she was still waving to David and Annabel, and then, almost as they were past, she turned towards him and waved. 'It was for me, for myself.' he thought. 'She waved to me last.' He had the fancy that it was he who was sitting beside her in the car and that she was very proud of him because he had done something wonderful. "My courageous son," she said to him. "I always knew that you were lion-hearted."

"Now I must get back, too," he heard Irma say, and he looked up and saw her standing beside Annabel. She was dressed in a pleated skirt and jumper, but now that the tall figure in the beautiful colour had gone the front of the house looked un-alive, empty. He heard David yelling as the nurse carried him up to bed.

"How's the rowing coming along, Piers?" Irma said. He wished she hadn't asked him, it was so difficult to reply.

"I can do the right oar," he began and Annabel chipped in with, "He always forgets his left oar and all he does is go round and round in circles or crash into the bank."

"I don't," he said and he hated Annabel. "It was only . . ."

"I used to do exactly the same when I learned to row," Irma said. "Even now I always pull harder on the right."

"Do you?" Piers replied and he felt comforted, although he knew that she was only inventing it because she felt sorry for him. He thought she was kind but somewhat silly to think she had tricked him. He wondered if she liked writing books; he'd tried to read one of them but he didn't understand the language. She'd invited him to her cottage one day last year. There were scones and éclairs for tea, and afterwards they'd sat by a big fire, with blazing lumps of wood and she'd put chestnuts down to roast. While they were roasting she read him some poems, because she said that Simon, her son in Africa, always liked her to read poems to him in the firelight when he was eleven. He enjoyed the sound of her voice reading, and when he left she gave him the book to keep and he'd learned one of the poems by heart. He hadn't even told Annabel, because he knew she would think he was foolish. He thought of the poem then:

'Had I the heavens embroidered cloths,
Enwrought with golden and silver light,
The blue and the dim and the dark cloths
Of night and the light and the half-light,
I would spread the cloths under your feet;

But I, being poor, have only my dreams;
I have spread my dreams under your feet,
Tread softly because you tread on my dreams.'

He repeated the last line over to himself a second time.
"Tread softly, because you tread on my dreams." He
thought of his mother sitting in the car, the flame-coloured
coat all about her.

They saw Irma off, and when she'd gone Annabel said,
"Let's go down to The Nythe. The kittens were born
yesterday."

"Come on the river, Anna," he pleaded, "I'm not allowed
to go alone. It's awfully important," he went on, "because I
want to show Mother how I can row before I go to school.
She's going to be home one day next week. She said so."

"I don't suppose she will," Annabel answered. "She
never is when she says she's going to."

"She did say she was. She said it was because I was going
to school. It's a special thing. *Please* Anna."

"I might tomorrow."

"Promise?"

"I don't promise little boys."

"If I come to The Nythe now will you promise?"

"Let me see. No, I don't think I'll *promise*, but I might.
Depends how I feel." She looked at her watch. "It's quarter
to seven. We've got just half an hour and a bit before supper.
Come on baby, we'll run all the way down. I'll race you."

They sped off across the shadowed fields.

Chapter III

Hugh slipped out of the last of the lanes on to the main road and settled down in the driving-seat.

"We'll just do it," he said to Clare.

"I only hope Daniel isn't in a 'state'," she remarked.

"From what I know of Daniel, if there were two 'states' he might be in, I should imagine it's possible he'd be in both," he answered dryly.

"It isn't all that easy. He's been working at terrific pressure since last October," Clare said.

"I suppose so," he muttered, and, even as he spoke, the burden of his own anxieties of the last few months came back and sat squarely on his shoulders. Rising wages and the general inflationary tendencies were crippling him. Ten years ago, he'd put all he had into the business expecting, as everyone had been expecting, a lessening of taxation and a relaxing of restrictions. Instead they'd got the Bank Squeeze and bureaucracy gone mad. He'd doubled his office staff, and still couldn't keep pace with all the form-filling. There was no freedom, no fluidity. What was the *matter* with this generation, he wondered? Two wars and nuclear fission to pay for? Partly. But there was no content anywhere. The men, for the most part, worked grudgingly, without interest in the work itself, anxious only for their pay packets and perpetually on the look-out for any incursion against their 'rights'. They'd got to live, of course they'd got to live, and he was the last man to want to see any lowering of standards, and yet the discontent and lack of interest or whatever it was went on. Trouble with the packers, trouble with the lorry-drivers, the labourers, the boiler-men . . . the thing was endless. There was a perpetual coming and going on the road, in the fields and even among the women in the greenhouses. The cry went round that there was more money to be got on building, or some Government job—which at best only lasted a few months—and they were gone. And like as not, according to Harrison, turned up again when the 'new job' petered out or wasn't the Eldorado they thought it was. And yet the men who really mattered, men like Hans Calenfals the rose specialist, or Beucher on the carnations and half a dozen others, had been with them for the best part of thirty years. But those men were artists, men who loved the work, beside being of an older generation. And now Calenfals was dead and he'd got to find someone to take his place. And that was, possibly, the least of his troubles.

It would be all right, of course it would be all right. It was the everlasting pressure, the never a moment's 'let-up', the feeling that you were 'going it' alone. Sometimes you wondered what it was all for? To keep up Bellhammer and educate the children? For what? So that they in turn could live in another Bellhammer and educate *their* children? So that they could be blown off the earth by a bomb? What *was* this jinx on his shoulder tonight of all nights?

Here he was a 'successful' man, well-dressed, big car, driving a beautiful and well-known wife to an Embassy reception, an occurrence which, if anyone had proposed it twelve years ago, he'd have grasped with alacrity. Jealousy? Of Clare's success? The working of the mind was a curious business, but this thing didn't appear to answer that. Of Forest then? *Could* he be jealous of that nervy little man? Hardly. Yet it was, so to speak, in Forest's train that he was even now heading for the Embassy. 'Oh, stuff!' he thought to himself. 'I don't grudge the chap his dish. God forbid!' He caught sight of the folds of the coat about Clare's long legs, and in his mind's eye he saw her again as she came through the screen doors on to the steps, but even as the picture formed it flicked away again, to be replaced by a mental snapshot of her dressed in slacks and an old shirt, a streak of distemper on her face as she tackled one of the walls at The Nythe soon after he'd first taken her there. 'Good grief,' he thought, 'don't tell me that I'm wanting those uncomfortable, burdensome days back.' He thought of his bathroom at Bellhammer and compared it with the one enormous chipped-enamel bath of his childhood at The Nythe—the large brass tap that dripped cold water; the waste pipe which, little by little filtered even the hottest bath away. What *was* all this? Middle-aged nostalgia for some totally imaginary conditions of the past? Let those conditions come back and see how he liked it! Yet there was something about those days at The Nythe which wasn't in their lives now . . . a careless quality. Of youth? Obviously of youth, with all the striving and achievement yet to come. They'd worked together, laughed together, talked out their high dreams for the future together. Now the dreams were dreams no longer but realities. Was that the way of it, always?

"Poor Irma," Clare said, breaking into his thought.

"Poor?"

"I hurried her off a bit."

"She's not small-minded. She knew you had to get on."

"Oh, yes. One felt a bit—opulent. All this glory and Irma . . . "

"Shouldn't worry on that score. I think her view of clothes is that they're something to cover her nakedness with. Conventional necessities."

"Darling, what nonsense you talk! There isn't a woman living who doesn't yearn for lovely things to wear. Even Felton does, only she has to pretend she doesn't and stick to bloomers. Irma isn't any different because she writes books."

She laughed, a little teasing laugh with no malice in it. "She has such a gallant defender."

"Don't talk rot," he answered shortly, and he wondered if what she said was true. Did Irma secretly long for the kind of clothes Clare wore? If she did . . . She always looked pretty good, anyway. Tough though if, in her heart, she dreamed of the silks and satins. Be rather nice to give her boxes full—real luxury stuff, masses of tissue paper. Yet he couldn't really 'see' her in those kind of things. When he thought of her, it was dressed in something with the sleeves rolled up and her hair ruffled because she'd been out in the wind without a hat. She'd told him once, he remembered with a half-smile, that she didn't even possess a hat. He thought of Clare's cupboard in her dressing-room—rows of hats! But then she had to wear the things, it was part of her job.

"About the children," Clare was saying. "Luckily they both go from Charing Cross on Thursday. I was wondering if you'd be able to go up with them. You took Annabel last term, and I've got a wretched day—two American buyers who are only over for a matter of hours and I must be there to see them."

"Oh lord, Clare," he grumbled. "I can't possibly. I'm flying to Amsterdam on Monday and I shan't get in to London till . . . " He broke off and said, "What time do the trains go?"

"Annabel at twenty-three minutes past two and Piers at fifty minutes past. It's all right. It struck me that you might be free, but as you aren't I'll arrange for Johnson to put them on the Victoria train, and I'll get Miss Hawkins to meet them and take them over to Charing Cross."

"Wouldn't Patty go up with them?"

"She can't. I phoned her yesterday. They're taking Bill back by road—he starts on Thursday, too. Miss Hawkins will do it. I can get a typist to fill in for me while she's gone if I need someone."

"If I could manage to get an earlier plane . . . " Hugh began. And then, "What about Irma? She might go if she's free."

"*Irma?*"

"Someone they know. I don't . . . "

"They know Miss Hawkins. She's been down two or three times. In fact she met Annabel a couple of terms ago when I couldn't manage it. After all, it is only a question of getting them across London and putting them in charge of the school people. I'm going to take the Wednesday off so that I can spend it with them. Or maybe the Tuesday would be easier. I'll have to see which I can fix. You know, I think Piers is quite looking forward to going now he's got used to the idea. Nanny said he was enthralled when his blazer came this morning."

"I hope he'll settle down."

"Why shouldn't he? It's just what he needs. He wants to be 'brought out', get a bit of the rough and tumble, lose some of his shyness. He'll be all right when he's out on the cricket field with the other boys."

"I suppose so."

"Darling, of *course* he will."

"Don't know."

"I do. He'll be bursting with Jones Minor and Smith Major and what they did in the swimming-baths when he comes home in July."

He wondered if Clare were right. There was something about Piers which made him feel uncomfortable, a hidden and secret . . . *what* was it? Sadness? Grief? Nonsense! What would Piers have either to be sad about or grieve over? But Irma had once said to him, "He troubles me, Hugh. There's something—" but even Irma hadn't defined what the 'something' was. There seemed no end to the pressure of things.

"How Annabel loves that watch!" Clare was saying.

35

"She can't keep her eyes off it. She'll hate not being able to wear it at school."

He smiled slightly, taking the left hand stream of traffic as they came up Knightsbridge.

"She's growing up."

"Not yet."

"It's a process we can't stop."

"It's a process I should do my best to stop in my own daughter. I hate to see children of fourteen behaving as though they were thirty."

"Perhaps it isn't possible to stay a child in this world of nuclear fission and space-travel."

"You're not advocating nail-varnish and lipstick for Annabel, are you?"

"I was thinking more of her mind."

"You don't have a 'mind' at fourteen."

"Then what the deuce are we paying a hundred and twenty pounds a term for?"

"Don't be ridiculous. She's got to go to school and Westheath isn't any more expensive than others of its kind."

"Three sixty a year seems quite a bit of money if they're only teaching her to play hockey and over-develop her thighs. She's got a mind all right. Possibly a more developed one than either you or I had at that age."

"You talk as though she were seventeen or eighteen. She's only a child, Hugh."

"I wonder," Hugh said as he pulled the car up in front of Daniel Forest's house.

The drawing-room had been decorated since he had seen it last. It was now done in tones of grey, walls and carpet and all, with—rather effective, he thought—some singularly beautiful Florentine red curtains. There was one great bowl of sweet-peas of the same shade on a black table. Did the chap always match the flowers with the curtains so precisely? Expensive—and a bit too arty for words.

The door opened and Daniel, hurrying in, came straight over to him, taking no notice whatsoever of Clare.

"My dear Hugh . . . " He held out his hand. "Such ages . . . "

"Hello, Daniel. How are you?"

A weak smile touched Daniel's lips.

"Faint but pursuing," he answered with his barely perceptible lisp. "You look frightfully well. I suppose you are, aren't you? The tanned man of the lilies who toil not neither do they spin. How I would love to toil not nor spin!" He still continued to stare straight at Hugh. "But I'm afraid you've come up on a false trip. I tried to phone and stop you. I shall have to ring the Embassy and make some excuse, although that's high treason or something fearful, isn't it? Oh God. I believe one escapes insult to the French Republic if one can produce a doctor's certificate, doesn't one? I can. I shall. It's no good, Clare," he went on. "I know perfectly well what you are going to utter, but it is *no good*. I simply cannot look at you because if I do, I shall be sick. I realised two hours ago that the thing is a *failure*. Don't contradict me. I *know* it. I should have continued with the green brocade. It came to me while I was lying down with a couple of cachets. My head! The worst migraine I've ever had in my life. Why I imagined the satin would be anything but banal, even vulgar, I can't think. I got up from my bed and tore down to look at the sketches. Abortive. Impossible. No one must ever see it. You must promise me that you will never never mention it or this tragic, dreadful night of supreme humiliation again. You have failed me. You have all failed me. Why didn't you . . . "

"Daniel!" Clare cut in. "*Will* you stop this hysterical nonsense at once and offer us a drink like a civilised being. Go and pour them out, Hugh. Over there on the cabinet.

37

You'd better make Daniel's a brandy, a strong one. I'll have
a Martini. Now Daniel . . . " She walked towards him, but
he lowered his head on to the crook of his arm and stood
there, his shoulders hunched. "Daniel! Stop behaving like a
moron at once. Look at me. Or rather look at your work *on*
me. We went through all this with the de Vaudré designs
and I won't have it again. Daniel!"

'Queer,' thought Hugh, pouring out the drinks. 'Very
queer. All over a *dress*, something to cover the naked flesh.
We've come a long way from the Garden of Eden. I suppose,' he explained to himself, 'the thing's an art, on the
same plane as painting or poetry, and all artists and poets are
a bit dotty or they wouldn't be artists and poets. Even old
Mark—' He thought of Mark roaring about The Nythe, his
beard threshing, if something he was painting didn't go
right. Though, in fairness, Mark and his virility would have
made short shrift of Daniel Forest with his just too perfect
evening suit. But one wondered how Clare bore with it all.
She did. And appeared to be not unduly exercised over it
either.

"What did I *tell* you?" he heard her say as he carried the
drinks across the room and he saw that Daniel's head was up
and that he had a shamefaced, yet somehow ingenuous
smile on his face, which gave him a childlike, almost appeal-
ing appearance. "You are the most awful fool," Clare said.
"Now apologise for that pretty little scene. I'm ashamed of
you."

"Oh, but I *do* apologise. I do." He stepped forward and
touched the collar of the coat with his long, thin hand, and
then darted round to Clare's back, nodding his head. "I
believe . . . Yes . . . Yes . . . Take the coat off Clare. Here, give
it to me." The flame satin was a banner across his arm.
"Now—back a bit. Further. *Further*. Yes. Yes, it's all right.
Turn. Yes. Steady. *Yes*." He breathed deeply. "It's all
right. Dear grief, it's all right. Clare you don't *know* what

I've been through. I thought . . . In my mind, my memory, it looked *impossible*, one of those *agonising* mistakes one makes. Even the sketches . . . But, my dear, *why*? That is all I ask— why? Why does a thing *change* so damnably? Not in reality but in one's mind. Clare, *why*? So ashamed, darling Clare. Biting the dust. Mouthfuls of dust. And sackcloth and ashes and . . . Oh, Hugh! How good you are. Thank you. And how defamed I am. 'Oh what a rogue and peasant slave . . .' Have you seen the dress, Hugh? It's lovely, don't you think? And she's wearing it superbly. My dears, you'll just have to forgive me and we'll go in. Drink your Martini, Clare. There's no one coming, just ourselves, thank God. Potten has created me a new consommé for the occasion. It's taken him a month to get it right, and it really *is* superb. Clever Potten . . ."

"Did you say 'Potten'?" Hugh asked, looking down at Daniel, and he thought, 'This isn't happening. It's fictional. The Mad-Hatter's tea-party over again.'

"My chef," Daniel answered. "A genius, isn't he, Clare? Don't be put off by his Happy Family name Hugh—I really do know someone whose dentist's name is Fillingham— what that boy does with an egg is sheer poetry. Come along. You look wonderful, Clare. Wonderful . . ."

'Potten' thought Hugh, knew what he was at with the consommé, for all his ludicrous name, and the salmon was perfect—Irish, a little conceit of Daniel's towards his dimly-Irish ancestry. Yet, poses and all, you couldn't help liking Daniel, and once he'd got his jitters over he always talked interestingly enough on any subject that came up. In spite of that and the over-gracious manners, Hugh himself felt out of it, the odd man who didn't speak the language, as though, he thought wryly, Clare and Daniel were the married couple and he the guest. 'Perhaps I'm getting too old for the glitter,' he thought, and immediately contradicted himself with, 'Forty-five isn't old.' It was simply, he supposed, that the 'pretty lights' which had once burned so brightly looked a bit garish now, though the word stuck in his throat when they drove to the Embassy and went in. Banks of roses and lilies, sweeping beautiful gowns, and the scent of the flowers mingling with the perfume of the women's scent; colour, shining lovely heads; the deep blue ray from a sapphire, the white glint of diamonds clasping a smooth throat . . . the word 'garish' was an insult, a boy's rude jibe. So much of beauty. Too much? Too studied a beauty? No simplicity left? There it was again. What was the matter with him? Why think now of Annabel saying, "You'll take me one day, won't you?" And the sudden pain in the heart at the thought of her standing on the threshold of this world? Annabel, all the children, were all right. Hadn't they given them 'everything'—home, clothes, education, the best of food . . . ? He looked at Clare just in front of him as they moved slowly forward. She turned and smiled at him, her eyes brilliant.

This is achievement, thought Clare. This the moment. There was a little house in The Boltons where a thirteen-year-old girl lived next door to a student artist called Daniel Forest. There was the pinching and scraping for The Slade and Daniel starting in one room in Baker Street. There was the beginning of the climb, only to be thrown back to the ground by the war. There was marriage to Hugh, the children, and then Daniel again and the climb starting for the second time. Now they were there, way up above the crowd, above the failures and those who'd dropped by the wayside. Way up above Mark and Patty and the old Nythe days. Hugh on one side of her, Daniel on the other. The home and the career, throwing the lie to the faint-hearted who said a woman couldn't do both. She had done both. She had walked the tight-rope between the two things and kept her balance. Hugh—how distinguished he looked—loved her. The children loved her. Daniel, yes, Daniel loved her, 'after his fashion'. Bellhammer was there in the background . . .

"Mr. Daniel Forest. Mr. and Mrs. Hugh Eagleton." Their names went ringing across the room and they walked forward to meet France.

Chapter IV

ANNABEL and Piers were breathless when they reached The Nythe. They raced into the house by the back door and through the scullery to the kitchen, where Patty was rolling out pastry on the marble slab that had once been the top of a wash-stand. Piers dropped back, but Annabel flung herself on a chair, her legs stuck straight out, her hand on her chest.

"We ran," she gasped. "All the way. I'm bursting. Can we see the kittens?"

Patty regarded her from her bright, dark eyes, her floured hands resting on the rolling pin.

"They're in the barn," she said. "You look as though you might burst. Have they gone?"

Annabel nodded. "Just now. You didn't come up to see the dress."

"I didn't have a minute. I'll see it later. Was it lovely?"

"Irma said it was, and Mummy said it was Daniel's best thing. The coat was all coppery. No, not that. I don't know. Shining. They're going to have champagne and salmon and caviare. I think, caviare. How many kittens were there?"

"Six."

"My! That's a lot, isn't it?"

"They do sometimes."

"*Can* we go and see them?"

"Don't touch them or Melinda might desert them. The boys and Karen are out there somewhere." She cut six shapes with a pastry cutter and looked up again. "All ready for school next week, Piers?"

"Yes, thank you," he answered and the fear clutched at him as it always did.

"I was sorry I couldn't take you up on Thursday," Patty went on. "But we're driving Bill down this time as we have to see some people in Southampton."

"*Were* you going to take us?" Annabel asked. "Daddy does sometimes when Mother can't."

They didn't know that Clare had phoned because neither she nor Hugh could take them, Patty thought, and wished that she hadn't said anything about it.

"It was just in case they couldn't manage it," she said.

"I don't suppose it was," Annabel answered and her expression became cold, adult. "Oh, well," she added, "I expect Johnson will take us, though I could easily look after Piers. I know where you get a taxi from at Victoria."

Piers looked down at the brick floor. He saw his own foot with one of the laces of his shoe undone. He'd thought of his mother sitting beside him in the taxi, and that she'd be there to say who he was to the Master. He wouldn't know what to do or where to go. He might get on the wrong train. He thought that there was something pressing on his shoulders, a weight forcing him downwards. He felt the tears beating up into his throat, but he bit the inside of his cheek hard and they didn't come into his eyes. He suddenly hated everyone and everything. He hated Annabel and Patty and his father. He nearly hated his mother.

Annabel stood up and said, "Are you coming to see the kittens, Piers?"

"Yes," he answered and moved towards the door his face turned away.

"Would you like to stay and have supper?" he heard Patty ask Annabel. "You can if you like. There's enough."

"I don't know," Annabel answered slowly. "It's our wholemeal bread and carrots night. What have you got?"

"Steak pie. It's in the oven now. It's a big one because none of us had much lunch. I was making some tarts with the bits left over. You can stay if you like. I'll phone through to them."

"Shall we, Piers? We're not supposed to have pastry."

Piers' mind was torn, thinking first one thing, then the other. He wanted to stay and yet he didn't want to. He wished it were just to be Patty alone. Mark was too big.

"Oh, he never knows what he wants to do," Annabel said. "If you phoned they'd let us, I expect. I'd love some steak pie. I'm starving. Have you really got enough?"

"Yes. Plenty. I'll tell them someone will see you up the lane."

"You are a pet," said Annabel. "Come on Piers."

"Don't go near the studio, Annabel," Patty called after them. "Mark's not painting but he's wrestling with Income Tax and he's inclined to be ferocious."

"Help!" Annabel called back, and they went across the yard to the barn.

Adrian's bicycle was upside-down just inside the open doors where the western light fell. His head was bent, and his short sleeves were rolled above his already tanned arms. His fingers were black with grease. He looked up when he heard their footsteps, and smiled at them from his mother's dark eyes. "Hello, you two!" He brushed his fair hair from his forehead with the back of his hand. "Come to see the kittens? Bill and Karen are in there somewhere. Just follow the din," he added, as the sound of raised voices came from the monochrome cavity of the barn.

"We're staying to supper," Annabel told him and Piers thought, 'She's being grown-up again. Her legs suddenly look like a lady's, not a girl's.'

"Splendid," said Adrian. "Hope Mum won't be long with it, either. I'm what they call 'clemmed'."

Annabel laughed as though he had said something very

44

amusing. She went on laughing. She put up her hand and brushed her hair back from her face as she had done on the terrace. She looked at her watch.

"Did you have a puncture?" she asked Adrian.

"New inner tube. The old one was patched like a gypsy's coat. *What* I'd give for a car," he added.

"Couldn't you get one like Johnson's? He only paid forty pounds for it. He told me."

"Forty pounds! I'm not the Aga Khan, girl. I doubt whether the old man's got that much, let alone me." He grinned. "You're at The Nythe, now. Not Bellhammer." He bent over the bicycle again. "Never mind! I'm going to dig potatoes or wash up in a Lyonses in the long vac., then I shall be able to buy a Bentley. Perhaps."

"Would you like a Bentley?"

Adrian's head was right down as he bent double over the machine.

"Would I like the moon and the stars?"

"Perhaps you will, one day."

"Aye. When I'm too tottery to drive it."

"We'd better go and find Bill and Karen," Annabel said, and they walked on into the gloom towards the sound of the quarrelling.

Bill was flat on his back on a heap of old straw and Karen was bending over him, hitting him with a book.

"I hate and loathe you, you beast, you snake, you tadpole," she was yelling. "I hope you die a fearful death. I'd like you to be all strawberry jam on the road so that I could scoop you up with a shovel. I hope . . . "

"Shut up, Karen, you swine," Bill shouted as he tried to twist away from the descending book. "If you don't stop I'll . . . " He threw his arms over his head and lashed out with his legs. "Blast you, you moron . . . "

" . . . all your teeth ache at once," Karen continued her interrupted sentence. "May you rot in small pieces and your toes drop off one by . . . Oh, hello!" she ended as she looked up and saw them. "Mum said you might come."

Bill heaved himself up from the straw and peered at them from a scarlet face. Straw was sticking to his hair. He bent forward and whisked the book away from Karen.

"You can have it," she said indifferently. "Whew! I'm hot. Do you want to see the kittens?"

Crunch, the spaniel, came padding towards them. His mouth was open, his tongue lolled out and he was breathing hard. His legs and the underside of his coat were wet and thickly matted.

"Crunch, you villain," said Bill. "Look out! He's been in the sewage again. Gosh, he stinks! Get out, you old smell-pot, you. Buzz off."

The dog didn't move. He raised his head a little, and opened his mouth wider so that he appeared to be laughing. He looked supremely happy, slightly self-satisfied and wholly zany. From him came a stench. Bill held his nose with one hand and aimed the book at him with the other. "Ged oud, you cedspool," he said with difficulty. "You are the bost disgusding adimal. Don'd you cub near be." He waved his free arm before his face. "You smell worse thad Adriad's hair-oil." He released his nose and said, "I must be ill. I can't breathe through my mouth. I expect it's thrombosis."

The dog, still panting and smiling, looked at him with his soft, wise eyes, then he turned and plodded back up the barn again, his head down.

"I'm not going to bath the old stinker," Bill said. "I had to do it last time. Hey, Piers, when do you go to school?"

"Next Thursday."

"God help you," Bill said fervently. "They'll probably roast you alive, I expect. Mistake you for a sardine. Poor old Piers, burnt to a cinder. Let's go and see the kits. They look like rats anyway."

"Are you going to keep them all?" Annabel asked.

Bring Back the Singing

"What *six*? Don't be potty," Bill answered, "If six cats had six wives . . . Hah! Hah! We'd have thirty-six cats next year, only we shouldn't because two are Toms. We'd have twenty-four, though. There's mental arithmetic for you. Can you imagine the old man with twenty-four cats running round the studio? He'd go crackers. And in two years time we'd have . . . six fours are twenty-four, remember four, Karen. Two to carry. Six twos are twelve, thirteen, fourteen . . . a hundred and forty-four dear little kitty-cats!" He rolled over and laughed, his arms spread wide on the straw. "A hundred and forty-four! Oh, Jehoshaphat!"

"Shut up, you ape," shouted Karen, and Annabel said, "Are you going to give them away?"

"No one wants any. Dad's going to drown them tonight. We might keep one, he said, so that Melinda won't pine."

"Down to Davy Jones go the kits," said Bill.

"How wretched!" Annabel cried. "I wish we could have one," but Piers turned away in horror. He thought he knew what it would feel like to go down and down till the cold, dark water closed over your head, and then . . . But imagination snapped in a wave of terror.

"Let's go and see them," said Karen, and they climbed the stairs to the hay-loft.

A filter of gold-green light came through the dirty window, throwing a misty beam on to where the mother-cat lay on an old rug. The kittens, smooth, sleek, crowded round her, nuzzling for the milk. One raised its flat, heavy head and peered at nothing with its sightless eyes, then it burrowed back into the others again. The mother gave a slight mew of pain, and went on purring as she stared up at them.

"Clever Melinda!" said Karen gently. "All your babies. There *are* two ginger, Bill. That means it was the Johnsons' Mustard. Dad said it was. Oh, Melinda! *What* a husband to choose. That awful Mustard. Darling you should have had

47

the Manor Persian and we might have made a bit out of you."

Melinda went on looking at them, and then she turned away and stared straight ahead, still purring. In the fading light, she might have been a tiger in a jungle, Piers thought. If only she had been they wouldn't kill the kittens. He fancied that he came back into the barn in the dead of night, climbed the stairs, picked them up on the old rug and took them away somewhere deep into the woods where they would live, not die. He saw himself pressing into the darkness, bearing the precious burden of them.

"Bell," came Adrian's voice from below and they went down the stairs again and back across the yard to supper.

Mark sat at the head of the table. He was leaning forward, his hands clasped, his elbows resting on the arms of the carving-chair, while Patty served the food from the side-board.

"I can never understand," he remarked in his booming voice, "why anyone finds it difficult to accept the machinations of the devil in this age. They have only to try to fill in an Income Tax form to know that lunacy and chaos are loose on the world. Last year, it took the Inspector of Taxes six weeks of intensive correspondence to discover why I found it necessary to pay three pounds each for sable brushes, when Woolworths have a fine selection at sixpence the piece. The filthy spider of this imbecile beaurocracy binds us in its web like flies, and, when the last hair-like strand is tied and we are helpless, it sucks the blood from our bodies to sustain its own repulsive life." He banged the table with his fist. "*And we can't see it*. We think we're getting on fine. Progressing. Marching to the Promised Land. And the Promised Land we're marching to is total inanition. There is only one life and that life is *creative*. It is movement and conflict and striving and . . . "

"Will you have carrots, Mark?" came Patty's voice from the sideboard.

"What?" He glared across at her.

"Carrots," she said again.

"*Carrots!*" he repeated. "Good God, *Carrots*. Yes, I'll have carrots," he added helplessly and he looked down the table to Annabel and said, "What are you two doing here at this time of night? Thought you had to be shut in your gilded cage by seven."

"We came to see the kittens and got asked to supper," Annabel answered.

Karen, who was helping Patty serve the meal, put Mark's plate before him and he picked up his fork and speared a piece of meat and put it in his mouth.

"Has your mother gone off to that nonsensical parade?" he asked, and Patty, carrying her own plate to her place opposite him, said, "Mark!" in a warning tone.

"Mark, *what*?" he glared at her. "A lot of vulgar dressed-up baboons of women running around with their emasculated, lisping inamoratas! Well, what else is it, then?" he flung at her.

"That's only your *opinion* of it," Patty said. "There's more gravy in the jug, Adrian."

"What else can I have *but* my opinion of it, you silly woman?" Mark roared. "It wouldn't be any good to me if I had *your* opinion, for the simple reason that you don't even possess an opinion. You are merely a tape-recording of every women's magazine thrust on a long-suffering world. You wouldn't even recognise an opinion if you saw one glaring at you." He dropped a piece of pie from his fork, scooped it up again and talked as he ate it. "You *advocate* all this peacock exhibitionism, I take it? You applaud. You cry 'Oh isn't it beautiful!' with the rest of your sheep-like sex." Again he banged the table with his fist. "*It is not beautiful*," he emphasised. "There is no true beauty in the whole of the fashion world start to finish. It is a racket. A commercial proposition run by exceedingly clever men and cunning women like my cousin Clare. It has only one criterion, one standard, one aim, one burning passion—money. Forest and Coré and the rest of them sit hatching up their wretched plots in their so-called studios, just like any mediæval Jewish usurer hatched his plots to trap fools. And what happens? After weeks of falsely-stimulated excitement, they bring out what? The 'sack'! A piece of stuff with two holes cut in it for the arms to go through and a third for the sheep-like head, the kind of garment primitive woman hacked out of a skin to cover her nakedness. And they 'launch' this piece of effrontery on the world and call it a 'creation'. And the morons of women fall for it in their thousands. They rush to pay a hundred guineas for the most insane idea ever generated by civilised man, and they all hobble about in the atrocity grinning like pleased apes." He waved his fork. "And the poor fools don't even see that the thing's nothing but a financial trick to thieve their money and line the pockets of a lot of fat, hard-headed business men in London and New York."

"I expect it was the same in Babylon and Thebes," said Patty calmly. "Women always have dressed up and they always will. Why shouldn't they? Look at butterflies."

"Look at butterflies!" Mark scorned. "Butterflies are the creation of the Almighty. And so are woodpeckers and humming-birds and splendid striped tigers and S. Joseph lilies and speedwells. But, beautiful as they are, the Almighty doesn't cash in on them. He does not foist them on us for *gain*. The butterfly is unaware of its own beauty. It is without vanity. It is content to be what it is and it doesn't prink and preen into mirrors and drop saliva from its self-titillated jaws, nor strive to hide its loveliness with a *sack*."

"More pie, Bill?" Patty said. "Adrian?"

Bill passed his plate and she went to the sideboard to serve him.

"We can't go about naked," she said as she cut the pie. "Nudists are just comical. Everything's a racket today."

"It is our sin and forever our shame that we accept it," Mark mourned. "We don't even care any more. We have created the god of mammon and we bow down before it. We kiss the feet of its chief priests and temple harlots, Coré and Forest and my cousin Clare and all their scented, erotic brood."

"Mark!" warned Patty again. "Not in front of the children. Be quiet."

"Children aren't fools," said Mark, staring down at his plate. "They are very, very wise. They see the truth." He suddenly raised his head and smiled from his brilliant blue eyes. "Don't they, Annabel?"

"I—I don't know," she answered.

She hadn't understood half of what he'd said. One phrase only had flicked into her mind like an arrow and lodged there—'Cunning women like my cousin Clare.' Was her mother cunning? She remembered that her father had once called a woman in the village 'cunning'. The woman was old, with a lined face and wispy white hair. She walked with her head down so that you never saw her eyes. The door of her tumble-down cottage was bolted, and dirty lace curtains were drawn tightly across the rain-and-dust-pocked windows. Cunning . . .

"Creamed rice or rhubarb, Annabel?" Patty asked her.

"Creamed rice, please," she answered and Karen passed her the plate.

The children washed the dishes, while Mark and Patty drank their coffee by the wood fire in the inglenook of the L-shaped dining-room where, sixty-odd years ago, William

Eagleton had jotted down his expenses in a penny notebook by the light of an oil lamp.

Adrian was at the sink and the others dried and put the clean things away.

"The forks and spoons go through to the dining-room," Karen said to Annabel. "Sideboard drawer. And you have to put them straight or you catch it from Mum."

Annabel gathered up the forks in one hand and the spoons in the other and went into the dining-room. She opened the sideboard drawer, and one by one laid the spoons in line with those already there. Round the corner of the 'L' she heard Mark and Patty talking; his deep, rumbling voice and her lighter tones replying. She thought how odd it would be to have Mark, with his bearded face, for a father and to live, not at Bellhammer but at The Nythe again. It was strange to remember that once they had lived there, but it seemed different now that Mark and Patty had it.

Suddenly she became aware not only of the sound of their voices but of what they said, and she stood quite still, the forks clutched in her left hand.

"You are not to say such things in front of Annabel and Piers," Patty said. "I've told you before."

"What did I say?" Mark rumbled. "I didn't say anything. Did I?"

"Oh, Mark!" Patty's tone was half-sad, half-despairing. "You called her 'my cunning cousin Clare', and then went on to tear up high fashion into little bits. You know very well you did."

"Oh, *that*," Mark said. "It was all true. Why shouldn't I tell the truth?"

"You can't tell the truth to children."

"Hah!" Mark gave a queer, sharp laugh. "Children are the one set of beings left in this false, imbecile world you can tell the truth to. No one else recognises the truth, anyway. They've all been educated out of it. If you could see into those children's minds, you'd have a shock, my good girl. Because you'd discover that their opinion of their idiot mother coincides with mine, only they wouldn't be able to express it. You think you'd find a lot of sentimental mother-adulation. You wouldn't. No woman can do what Clare does and get away with it. You can fool some of the people some of the time . . . If she wanted to live the best part of her life with Forest, why the devil didn't she go to the man altogether and let Hugh marry someone like that strapping nurse who does everything for the children she condescended to bear? What do those poor little half-starved brats mean to her? I'll tell you—they mean a further inflation of her own ego, something to add to herself as she adds another bit of jewellery or the latest suit. What's she ever *given* them for God's sake? She doesn't care about them."

"Lower your voice," Patty said urgently. "Why must you be so uncharitable to Clare?"

"Because I despise these half-women . . . " Mark began, but the rest of the sentence was lost to Annabel as Bill came in from the kitchen and said, "Haven't you put those in yet, Tortoise? We've finished." He stared at her. "What's up? Here, give 'em to me." He opened another drawer, laid the forks in it and pushed it to again. He touched his temple with his forefinger. "Rice pudding in the head-piece." He went out of the door which led to the hall chanting, "Poor old Annabel, rice pudding brains and a funny smell. Hey!" his voice drifted back through the open door. "Someone's taken my air-gun. Karen. *Karen* . . . "

'She doesn't care about them . . . Something to add to herself as she adds a bit of jewellery.' It wasn't true. Mark was a liar. A beast. She hated him. And Patty and all of them. She would never never come here again. Her mother *did* care for them. She *did*. She was going to have a day off next week to be with them before they went to school. She had promised it. She would take them into Westmill in the car.

She might even take them to London . . . Her mind was racing like a mill-stream urged on by a hidden wheel that was turning and turning in her head, hurrying away from something dark and shapeless which pursued her far, down beyond the things that were familiar, loved. She felt that she had to find someone, someone who knew about it all, someone who . . .

"Hello, I thought you'd gone out with Bill," Karen said, as she came into the room and saw her there.

Annabel looked back at her. She fancied that Karen had changed since they'd had supper, had become someone she didn't know, a stranger. She felt that she was looking at her through the wrong end of a telescope, that she had become small and far away.

"Would you like to come up and see my new dress?" Karen asked her. "Mum bought it for me when we went to London last week. It's a summer one, so I shan't be able to wear it now, but it'll be here when I come home. We went to the Academy after we'd done the shopping and saw Dad's picture. It was fun to hear people saying things about it when they didn't know who we were. We were in hysterics."

"Where's Piers?" Annabel said, and she felt that she must make sure he was somewhere close.

"He went out with Adrian to finish the bike," Karen answered. "Adrian said he'd come with us when we take you back."

Annabel wanted to go then, not wait at The Nythe another moment, but she couldn't bring herself to say so, and she followed Karen across the room. Patty smiled as they passed.

"I'm going to show Anna my dress," Karen said to her.

"Yes, do," Patty answered and she spooned up some sugar from her coffee-cup and ate it.

Mark lowered the paper from his face and regarded them.

"Little peacocks!" he said, And then, "Come here a moment, Annabel." He laughed, his red lips parting in his beard. "Don't look so scared, child. I'm not going to eat you. Come on."

She went towards him, trembling, her eyes on his face, and he put his hand on her arm and turned her slightly, peering up at her.

"I shall paint you next holidays, young Annabel," he said. "You always did have good bones, now they're showing through your puppy-fat." He gave her a little push away from him. "You needn't tell that little podgy lump beside you," he said, "but you're going to be beautiful in a couple of years' time, my girl. Don't get a swelled head now," he called after her. "It's nothing to do with you. You didn't make yourself."

"Gosh, you are lucky being fair," Karen said. "Dark people always look dirty."

There was balm in Annabel's heart, as they went upstairs, dispelling the pursuing fear. Mark had said she would be beautiful.

"I love dark people," she said to Karen.

They were sitting on Karen's bed talking when they heard the bell ringing faintly through the closed door.

"Come into prayers." said Karen. "It won't take long, then we'll walk back across the fields with you. We can as Adrian's coming, too."

The sound of the bell was clanging up the stairs and along the passage.

"Oh yez, oh yez, oh yez," came Bill's voice. "Come and save your dirty souls you sinners. On your knees before you get thrust down into the burning fires of hell. Come you—"

"Bill, shut up," said Karen, opening the door. "We're coming."

"—Lilies of Judah," Bill continued with his chant. "You sons and daughters of Ephraim, because if you don't say your night prayers the Lord will smite you through his servant, Mark Sheridan, R.A., and the smite will possibly be upon the hinder parts. *In saecula saeculorum* Amen. Hey," he ended suddenly, "that's my pen-knife, Karen. You pinched it in the barn. Hand over."

"I haven't done with it, yet. I'll give it to you tomorrow. Promise."

"Women!" snorted Bill and clanged the bell again. "Come you . . ."

"Bill," came Patty's voice up the stairs. "Bill. Be quiet. You'll wake Roddy."

"I'm saving his soul," he called back from the head of the staircase. "When he's an old, old man and about to die he'll thank me. Why should he . . ." His voice faded as he reached ground level and Karen said, "We'd better go down."

The chapel, which Mark had made when he rented The Nythe from Hugh, was part of the original building, believed to date back to the fifteenth century. Long before William Eagleton's day, when The Nythe was a farmhouse, it had been used for storing grain and animal fodder, and William himself had fitted it up as a carpenter's shop where he cut the frames for the first glasshouses he had constructed, and it had remained a species of work-shop and junk-room right up to the time of Mark's tenancy. It was a stone-built room of lovely proportions, and Mark himself had cleared out the accumulation of the years and fitted it up as the small family chapel it now was. In doing it he had discovered, with excitement, the traces of a shadowed cross, barely discernible, on the east wall, which had upheld his first intuition that the room had actually been the fifteenth century chapel of the original building.

He and Patty and Bill were already kneeling there when Karen and Annabel went in, and almost immediately Adrian and Piers entered. Annabel had forgotten that if they stayed to supper they'd probably go into the chapel, but she didn't mind particularly, because there was something old and quiet about the room, and tonight there were crystal bowls of daffodils on wrought-iron stands each side of the altar. Backed by the grey stone walls they looked lovely. It was odd, she thought, how everyone appeared to become different and yet remain the same in the chapel. Adrian's sleeves were rolled up, Bill's hair was ruffled and Mark was still huge and bearded, yet, suddenly, he had become gentle, not frightening any more, and even his voice when he said, "In the name of the Father . . . " was gentle, as though he, too, were someone small and unimportant. She remembered again, with a glow of pleasure, that he had said she would be beautiful.

"The first glorious mystery, the Resurrection," Mark began. "Our Father who art in heaven . . . " The room was divided up into sounds: Mark's leading voice and the little murmur of the others following him.

Piers, kneeling beside Adrian, was half asleep. Sometimes he heard the murmur of sound and sometimes it almost faded away. Dimly he remembered Melinda lying on the rug with the kittens, a tiger in a jungle. He knew that there was something he had to do for them but he couldn't remember what it was. His mother had waved to him last. He saw her lifted hand as the car slid away. He thought he would like to stay kneeling in the dimly-lighted chapel always, for here he was safe and the things which were too big and confusing for him were all somewhere outside.

"House of gold. Ark of the Covenant. Gate of Heaven. Morning Star . . . " Mark's voice became suddenly loud in his ears and faded again as his eyes closed, but the words went on repeating in his drowsy mind. 'Gate of heaven. Morning Star. Morning Star . . . ' 'Tread softly because you tread on my dreams.' There was something beautiful just there in front of him, but he couldn't quite reach it because

he was so tired. So tired . . His head dropped on to the back
of the chair in front of him and the little stinging pain in his
chin roused him from the comforting darkness. He remembered that they'd still got to walk home, yet.

"O Lord support us all the day long," came Mark's voice.
"Till the shadows lengthen and the evening comes and the
busy world is hushed and the fever of life is over and our
work is done. Then in thy mercy grant us a safe lodging
and a holy rest in peace at the last . . . "

As they got up and went out through the arched door
again, the words 'a safe lodging' remained in his mind. He
liked them.

There was no moon, and once away from the house and
over the first stile Adrian put the torch out. Karen and Bill
and Piers had dropped back, but Annabel walked beside
him. He towered over her, his head slightly bent as he trod.
The curving sky above them was bright with stars.

"Is it Thursday you go back?" he asked her.

"Yes. You don't go till the twenty-eighth, do you?"

"Twenty-seventh."

"Is it nice at Oxford?"

"Aye. Pretty good."

He thought of his room in S. Edmund Hall, and of the
river on a May evening with the willows and laburnums
dipping into the water, and of the High crowded with
traffic on a Saturday morning. He thought of bicycles and the
Newman Bookshop and laughter and tankards of beer. He
thought, and stopped thinking of Anglo-Saxon manus-
cripts. Instead he remembered Laxman's sister with her red,
red hair and queer raspy voice.

"Dad said he might let me go when I've finished at school.
It seems ages to wait, though," Annabel said.

"Oh, I don't know. You're fourteen now, aren't you?"

"It's so *young*," she answered.

They'd reached the second stile and he looked back peering along the path by the wood.

"I suppose those kids are coming along. Little ruffians," he said. "Here they are," he added, as their three forms left the darkness of the trees. He held out his hand to help her over the stile. She hadn't thought he'd do that—usually she vaulted it in a flying leap—and nervously she laid her own hand in his and stepped on to the rather high step. She was above him, then, looking down into his face as he leaned against the cross-bar. She moved her head slightly and her hair swung forward over her shoulder. He smiled at her.

"You look rather nice up there. I like this stuff." He put out his hand and touched her swinging hair. "Don't you go hacking it off."

She thought she must die with some wholly new, delicious, yet half-sad loveliness which seemed to be coming to meet her over the quiet fields. It caught the breath in her throat, and she wanted to press both her hands against her heart hard. She felt bewildered with some half-understood knowledge deep in her blood which trembled on the brink of discovery. She saw his bright eyes and the square, lean set of his shoulders beneath his jacket, and she felt old, as the night was old, and full of pain.

For a moment they stayed quite still, two figures carved into time, then he moved and looked away from her down to the ground and he kicked the side of his shoe, once, against the step. When he raised his head again, he said, quietly, "Over you go."

She stepped over the stile and jumped to the ground and he followed her. Silently they walked on to Bellhammer under the stars.

Chapter V

IT WAS nearly ten when Clare woke the next morning, and, after one swift glance at her watch, even while she lay with closed eyes, her mind leapt into action.

The reception last night had been an unqualified success, of that there was no doubt. She relived that heightened moment of excitement when, with Daniel and Hugh, she had passed into the Embassy in company with famous international names—passed in, she emphasised, on equal terms, themselves among the known, the recognised. France had been charming. She had curtsied to Royalty. Jules Coré himself had not only spoken to Daniel but, later, had sought her out, and, expressing his desolation that he was only in London for so brief a time, had begged her to visit his 'little house' when she was next in Paris. He would be honoured, enchanted . . . He had introduced her to the young and lovely Lady Maltravers who had come up with a cry of 'Jules! *Dear* Jules!' while he was speaking to her—and Ursula Maltravers was the most talked-of woman in three continents.

Success. Clare drew in a deep breath of the distilled essence of it, giving her mind and body up to the indulgence of retrospective delight and well-being. She reached out her arm and pressed the bell for Felton while the mental review continued.

'The concrete results?' she asked herself. They might not appear immediately, but that they would appear she was convinced. Once a certain curve of a wave had been reached, there was no stopping the inevitable break and run in to the shore. The sheer weight of the water brought it to the crest and flung it upward and forward in a triumph of power. That was true, but the position would have to be consolidated, for in that sphere, as in every other sphere, you couldn't stand still, you either went on or you dropped back. There could be no dropping back.

Felton came in with orange-juice, toast and coffee on a tray.

"Good-morning, Felton. You didn't wake me?"

Felton's small mouth was tight.

"The master gave orders you were to sleep on."

Clare frowned slightly. "It's made me very late. Has my husband gone?"

"Yes, Madam. He left some time ago."

"Thank you." Clare picked up the glass and drank the orange-juice. "Send Cook up, will you, Felton. I can talk to her while I have my breakfast. I shall be phoning London in a minute and I'll let you know what I'm doing when I've spoken to Miss Hawkins. Bring the papers directly they come, please."

Felton went out without another word, and Clare made a schoolgirl moue at the closed door. There were times when Felton's puritanical disapproval became absurd and yet . . . She glanced at the perfectly-laid tray and shrugged her shoulders. Nothing, she decided, would be gained by cutting off the nose to spite the face.

She poured out coffee, buttered a piece of toast, then picked up the telephone receiver on the bedside table. Two minutes later, Miss Hawkins was informing her that Mr. Forest had neither telephoned nor arrived yet, that they had a luncheon appointment at the Savoy at one thirty and that the press reports were most exciting.

"I'd better come up on the twelve eighteen," Clare told her. "Don't send the car, I'll pick up a cab at the station.

And if Mr. Forest isn't there by half past twelve, phone him at Belgrave Square and remind him of the appointment. It's quite possible," she added, "that he's forgotten all about it. I had myself."

"It's a pity you couldn't have stayed down today," came Miss Hawkins thin, prim little voice into her ear. "You must be tired after last night."

Clare picked up her cup with her right hand and sipped the coffee. "I haven't had time to find out, yet," she answered. "It would have simplified matters if the Savoy could have been postponed, but we can't afford to snub America yet! Have you heard from Vaudré's?"

"No, there's nothing from them. Mr. Gonsheim's written and there's a reply from Haley's. The rest is all routine. Everyone's very excited and longing to know how it went."

"I'll be in about ten to one," Clare told her and put the receiver down as Cook knocked and came in. "Oh, Cook, good," she greeted her. "I've just been on to London so that now I can arrange things. I hoped I needn't go up today, but I'm afraid I shall have to. That means I shan't be in for lunch but I'll try to get either the five or six train down. In time for dinner, anyway. Something simple, I suggest. Grilled steak, do you think? Oh, yes, and you'll remember to complain to Collins about the kidneys, won't you? He can be very tiresome sometimes. Soup first, of course, and then I think the Brie. Now about the children . . . "

One by one the arrangements for the day were dealt with, and finally she picked up her notebook from the table and looked at the notes she had made yesterday.

"I think that's all. Wholemeal flour from Horsham. Honey. Phone Harrods. We've been into all that. Oh, yes. An iced cake for Wednesday, please. The children go on Thursday. Not rich, because of the travelling. Quells . . . that's Nanny's department. I think that's all for you, Cook."

"Will there be anyone for the week-end, Madam?"

"Not that I know of."

"Miss Annabel said something about The Nythe children."

"Her own idea, obviously. I'll see her when I come down. It would only be for tea, anyway. Bread and honey and cake. Nothing spectacular. Perhaps you'd better tell Annabel to come up when you go down. I'll go along to the nursery and see Nanny after I've bathed."

"The children are both out, Madam."

"Oh? Where?"

"They went off in the car with Mr. Eagleton quite a bit ago now. I think Felton said they were going to Northmill with him."

"He didn't tell me."

"You were asleep, Madam."

"Yes, of course. All right. Take my tray, will you, Cook."

"Did you enjoy it last night, Madam?"

"Yes. It was most successful, Most successful."

"The dress and the coat were wonderful. I said to Mrs. Phipps, there couldn't have been anything better there."

"I wouldn't go as far as that," Clare answered. "It was pretty competitive. We'll know more about it when I've been to London. I do wish they'd send the papers earlier. Can *nothing* be done?"

"We get ours one of the first, Madam. I'll let you have them the moment they bring them."

"Yes, do. And Cook, a cup of China tea before I go at twelve, please."

The door closed and she lay back on the pillows again, wishing that she hadn't to go to London and despising the weakness even before it had become concrete. She wondered why Hugh had told them not to wake her. The obvious reason was that she was tired, but it was unusual for him to give such an order unless she had asked him to. She thought, with a suspicion of uneasiness, of their drive back from the reception. She herself had been still on the crest of the wave.

63

He? He'd talked a little, answered her questions, asked some of his own, yawned once or twice as he drove. They'd reached Bellhammer and he'd had a last whisky-and soda and she, instead of the Ovaltine she'd ordered, had had one, too, because she wanted to hold on to the night a little longer, could hardly bear to let it slip back into the accumulation of the things that were past. She felt vitally young again, the stream of her blood running fast in her veins. The only possible end to the wonderful day was love. She desired love, needed the final excitement of Hugh's love-making to throw a bridge between the triumphant night and the morning which must inevitably follow. And he? Was it that he had misunderstood? *Hugh*? He had certainly had the extra effort of driving back from London, but . . . A deliberate, and kind, refusal? Why? For what reason? It was such an astonishing reversal of the normal course, for she had sometimes refused him, but never he, her. Of course love was no longer the urgent demand it had once been between them. It was quieter now, less tempestuous, less agonised. For all that—the thought broke as she remembered his kind goodnight kiss on her forehead, the way he had taken her arms from round his neck and kissed her hands gently, first one, then the other, and laid them back on the sheet with a little pat and a 'Sleep well. You must be exhausted. I'm glad it all went so splendidly.' Consideration for her? She frowned. What else? He may even have thought it was she who was being generous and denied himself for her sake. Obviously it was that. And that the reason, too, for his telling them not to wake her. What other reason could there be? She brushed speculation aside. 'I'm becoming one of those women who fritter their imaginations away on a tangle of emotional nonsense,' she thought. 'I'll begin to suspect him of unfaithfulness in a minute!' She picked up the receiver again and called the Plantation at Northmill and asked for him. 'Who,' she teased herself lightly while she waited for him, 'would he be likely to be unfaithful *with*? Miss Brewster, the arty trousered young woman who brought and arranged the house flowers? His little blonde secretary? Irma Lovat?' She smiled slightly as she heard him say, "That you, Clare? Had a good sleep?"

"Too good. I'm wretchedly late," she answered.

"You didn't need to be early, did you?"

"Not particularly. I find I've got a lunch appointment at the Savoy that I'd forgotten in yesterday's excitement. Ethel McCleary, the American fashion writer. I daren't stall. I'm going up on the twelve eighteen and I'll be down, I expect, on the five. You've got the children up there, haven't you?"

"Yes. They were hanging about so I brought them up. They reminded me that I'd promised to one day, and the time's getting short. You didn't want them, did you?"

"Oh no. I didn't know whether they were with you or if you'd dropped them at The Nythe or somewhere. I'll see them this evening."

"Do you want me to meet the train?"

"No. I'll take my car and leave it at the station."

"Right." She heard the range of his voice alter. "Put them down, Roberts. I shan't be a minute. And I shall need the Hamilton file, too," then, speaking into the receiver, he said, "See you tonight, then. Bye."

She gave another glance at her watch. 'Ten minutes,' she told herself and consciously relaxed her muscles, but behind her closed lids, her mind continued with its incessant, inevitable dialogue; presenting queries, suggestions, speculations and offering her, at every moment, the inescapable balance of choice. This thing or that thing. This way or that way. To act. Not to act. To move. To remain inert.

'Soon,' she thought, 'I shall get in touch with Giles Roache about the swimming-pool. I rejected the plans he submitted before, but now we could afford to consider the second idea he sketched. If he got on to it soon, it might be finished by autumn when Coré will be over again.' She left the swimming-pool, completed and flood-lit, and planned the dinner-party for him. An evening when the hills were blue and shadowed and the dahlias were out. Coré and Daniel and Ursula Maltravers . . . Frances Leyton? Maybe. Intelligent but a little heavy. Possibly Julian Reeve and his wife. Julian Reeve was a man to keep in touch with. It would be a scoop for Daniel to design the star's clothes for his next play; and he himself was always amusing. Keep the whole thing small, intimate. Daniel would let her borrow Potten for the evening, if Potten himself could be bribed or enticed in some way. His famous consommé? No, perhaps not. Oysters—the season would be just beginning. And then Coq Au Vin. Or what about that marvellous thing he did with veal? Daniel might not want to give that away though, even to her. Then zabaglione and some second-crop strawberries in wine. Pears should be delicious then, and the peaches not over. Candlelight of course.

Hugh put the receiver down and sat limp in his chair, his head lowered, as he recalled only too sharply the way in which he had taken Clare's arms from round his neck and kissed her forehead as she lay in bed in the early hours of the morning. The movement had been involuntary, a sudden realisation that to make love to her was impossible. Why? He didn't know then and he didn't know now. The jinx that had been on his shoulder all the evening was still there queering everything as he undressed, yet never had Clare looked more beautiful and never had she so obviously invited him to love her. And he, unforgivably, had refused . . . he who had once ached for her need of him, had been made foolish with a humble pleasure if ever she had expressed that need. He frowned and raised his hand to his face and drew his fingers across his chin. Had she realised, or had she taken it for granted that his consideration was purely for her? Her manner on the telephone had been normal enough, but that didn't say much, for she was experienced in hiding all traces of her feeling. Whether she'd realised or not didn't answer the question of why he'd acted as he had. Nothing in their lives had altered, and yet, suddenly, she had become someone strange to him, wholly remote, someone he was quite incapable of getting near. When he thought of her, his mind and body were cold, untouched. He closed his eyes.

Piers stood beside Brodie, the waterman, among a thousand roses unfolding from tight buds into perfect flowers. All down the great glass-house with its whitewashed windows the roses marched in long, lovely, symetrical rows of deep crimson—roses, roses, roses, for as far as you could see, wherever you looked. Their dark leaves shone as though polished, the scent of them drenched the air. If he stood on the step by the door he could look down on them and they became an army of crimson men, but when he stood beside Brodie as he sprinkled them from the hose, he could only see a forest of leaves, for the flowers, then, were above his head.

"Can I hold the hose, Brodie?" he asked.

"Ye canna. And you know it's no use you pestering. You may stand beside me but you don't so much as lay your finger to ma hose. If one o' they took a wee drappie too much water Ah'd have ma cards in ma hands before I'd have time to say ma own name."

"I'd like to be a waterman," Piers said. "I'd like to live in one of the glass-houses, and then I'd only ever have roses all round me."

"Eeh! And after forty-eight hours ye wouldn't know if it was roses or cabbages, you looked at."

"Don't *you* know, then?"

"Ah do not. When you've been watering thirty years the

things mean no more to you than little wee daisies. Ah'd rather have the heather on the moors."

"But heather doesn't smell like roses, Brodie."

"After thirty years watering ye don't smell so much as a whiff of them. Move now. Out of ma way."

'I wouldn't ever not smell them,' Piers thought, and he imagined a little house built in the middle of the glasshouse. No one would be able to see it because the windows of the glass-houses were whitewashed to protect the roses from the light. He would have a chimney in his house and a fire, and when he went to bed he could watch the embers glowing, and in the morning, when he woke and looked out, he would see nothing but roses. And he'd never have to go to School.

The door at the far end opened, and he saw Annabel standing framed against the outer light. He couldn't see her face, only her shape, and the sun shining on the side of her hair. He pretended he hadn't seen her, but she shut the door and came down the steps and along to where he stood beside Brodie. He didn't want her there, and he wished she'd go away.

"Children all over," muttered Brodie, and Annabel said, "Are you coming home? Miss Brewster's going down with the house flowers and she says we can go with her if we like. Dad won't be ready for ages."

"I'll go if you come on the river," he answered. "You did promise."

"I didn't. I said I might if I felt like it."

"Well, do you feel like it? Oh, come on, Anna."

"You're so stupid," she answered. "You'll never row."

"I will," he said, speaking urgently, yet quietly, for he didn't want Brodie to hear. "I nearly can now. I expect I'll do it this time."

It had become more necessary than ever to him to be able to manage the boat before the day his mother was to spend

68

with them. He saw himself stepping down into it and giving it a shove away from the bank with the oar. He stood balancing nonchalantly as he swung out into the stream, and then he sat down, slipped the oars into the rowlocks and pulled hard on the left to straighten. He looked up and smiled at his mother as she stood admiringly on the bank before he went off downtide, rowing with long, steady strokes. When he came back and moored the boat again, she said, "Piers! I'd no idea you could manage the boat like that. You're better than Adrian."

"Oh, all right," Anna said. "But not for long. Half an hour by my watch."

'I've got to do it in half an hour,' he thought. 'I've *got* to,' and he felt as though someone were chasing him.

"Come on, then," Annabel urged, "or Miss Brewster won't wait."

"Good-bye, Mr. Brodie," Piers said. "I'm going to school," he added.

"Aye," Brodie answered, pulling the hose up a few feet.

"I'll see you when I come back," Piers said, and he took one last look at the forest of green leaves in the green light.

"Aye," Brodie muttered again and he went on with the watering, up and down the long rows of scarlet and flame and cerise and white, house after house, day after day, year after year, training the jet of water on to the thickly-manured soil, his bald head bent, the bibbed rubber apron tied round his stocky frame, dreaming always of the highland heather he had last seen thirty-two years ago.

Piers and Annabel shut the door and walked down the avenue of glass-houses stretching away on either side of them. Through clear patches where the whitewash had thinned, they caught glimpses of scarlet and gold, of a man's bent head where a budder was at work, or, through a momentarily opened door, a vast silent sea of white carnations.

As they passed the packing sheds, Annabel said, "Let's go as far as The Nythe with Miss Brewster and then walk up through the fields."

She longed to follow the exact path they had taken last night; to climb over the stile again and relive, even more sharply than she relived now, the moment when she had looked down at Adrian. She drew in a swift, short breath as the memory became vivid, and the bitter-sweet pain was diffused in her heart again till it became almost unbearable. If they went by way of The Nythe and the fields, she might see him, not to speak to—that suddenly became agonisingly impossible—but in the distance, walking across the yard, perhaps.

"Oh, Anna!" wailed Piers. "It's so far. There'll hardly be any time for the river if we do."

"We can go this afternoon."

"You know you won't."

"Yes, I will. I promise I will."

"It might rain or you'll say you've got a headache or something."

"No I won't. Cut my throat. Look, there's Miss Brewster. She's waiting."

They ran to the little grey Ford van and climbed in. The seats were warm where the sun had been on them. The scent of the roses packed in the back came filtering through and mixed with the hot smell of the engine.

"Will you drop us at The Nythe, please, Miss Brewster," Annabel said. "We're going to walk up across the fields."

"My! You're energetic, aren't you?"

"We thought we would," Annabel answered.

She did not see the cool green of the new beech-leaves, the misty patches of bluebells at the wood's edge, nor the wild cherry-trees thrusting up their blossom-heavy boughs as they drove along the lanes. She had no being in the world where they were, but lived in another dimension, another time; in a world of starlit glory and in an hour that had passed.

A few hundred yards before they came to The Nythe they saw Karen coming towards them on her bicycle.

"Oh, please, Miss Brewster," Annabel said urgently. "Could we stop a minute? I must speak to Karen. It's awfully important."

"But you wanted to stop at The Nythe, anyway," Miss Brewster began, and Annabel broke in, with, "Yes, I know, but . . . I must see her." She put her head out of the window and called her. "Karen! Karen!"

Karen jumped off her bicycle as the van pulled up.

"Oh, hello!" she said. "I was just going to the village. Have you been up to Northmill? You might have called for me."

"We went with Dad," Annabel answered. "I didn't think you'd be up."

"I've been up hours," Karen answered. "Dad and Adrian and Bill went to London on the eight train. They're having a stag party, just the three of them. They're going to stuff themselves at Simpsons and then prowl. I must go," she added. "Mum's waiting for the baking powder."

He wasn't even here. He was in London. He was 'stuffing himself'—cruel, horrid phrase—at Simpsons. That strange lovely thing had meant nothing to him at all. Annabel's world receded. It became thin, like smoke drifting, losing all reality. She fancied she stood with outstretched arms yearning towards it, unable to grasp it or call it back.

"I must go," Karen said again. "See you tomorrow."

She jumped on her bicycle and went pedalling up the hill, her head down.

"You might as well get out here, mightn't you?" Miss Brewster said. "You can cut across the meadow."

"I think p'raps I don't want to walk," Annabel answered from the centre of a void that was all grief. "Let's go on to the house, shall we, Piers?"

They put Clare's call through to Hugh's private office at Northmill at four o'clock. Although he had intended to go over to the Westmill Plantation at three, he'd been kept at Northmill with Roberts and the accounts.

"Hugh!" came Clare's voice. "Oh, there you are! I tried to get you at Westmill but they said you hadn't been there yet. Listen! I shan't be able to get down after all. I can't be explicit over the phone but something very exciting's happened and I simply must stay up tonight. We've been asked to submit some designs for a Royal Tour. Daniel's in a fever as you can imagine. It's the first time we've been Commanded. Isn't it marvellous?"

"Splendid," Hugh answered, and the jinx which had slept while his mind was occupied with Roberts and anxiety woke up and sat on his shoulder again.

"I'll be down tomorrow," he heard Clare say. "I'll have to have a word with Cook after dinner, and I'll let you know which train, then. You'll be in, won't you?"

"Don't know," he answered. "I might go across to Byford later. Not sure. I shan't be through here for some time."

"Get someone to let them know at the house that I shan't be down, will you?" Clare asked.

"Yes, all right. I'll ring them now," he answered and he heard the click of the line being cut. He called 'Hello' twice, but evidently Clare wasn't remaking the connection so he put the receiver back.

For five minutes he continued with the work he was doing, then he laid his pen down.

Forest's partner . . . But good grief she'd been Forest's partner for twelve years, and if she hadn't been Forest's partner they wouldn't be living in Bellhammer. Neither, possibly, would the Northmill Plantation be in existence. And if they hadn't been living in Bellhammer? Then they'd have been living at The Nythe and Eagletons would probably have been half the size it was. Half the anxiety. Half the work. Half the . . . What a blind fool he was being. Yes, but he'd have had time to 'stand and stare' a bit. Time to sit quietly sometimes without the constant pressure of things on him. Time to think. To read. Was all this the onset of age, he wondered again? They'd planned all they'd achieved, he and Clare. Planned success. Planned the perfect home. Planned everything and accomplished damned nearly all they'd planned. From the first, Clare had said, 'I could never be content if I didn't have something to do "in my own right". I must fulfil myself as a person.' And when she'd met Forest again and the question of her going back to him had come up, she'd said, 'This is what I've been waiting for. Daniel will get to the top. I know he will. He's got genius, and with both of us making money we'll be able to have so much that we can't afford otherwise. I had enough pinching and scraping to last me a lifetime when I was a child. One day we'll get out of The Nythe and have a lovely house, and the children shall go to good schools and wear the right clothes. You'll make Eagletons famous and I'll make Daniel famous.' And that's how it had been. How it was. The lovely house, the good schools, the right clothes, the success. All there. And something inside him twisted as a corkscrew.

He shook his head and lifted his shoulders slightly as though the movement would free him from constriction, then he picked up the receiver and asked to be put on to Bellhammer.

"I'd like dinner at seven," he said to the cook after he'd told her Clare wouldn't be down. "Annabel and Piers could have their meal with me as I shall be eating earlier. That can be managed, I suppose?"

"Oh yes, sir."

73

"Right. I'll be back by half past six or so."

He rang off, but immediately made another call through to Miss Brewster in her office by the packing sheds.

"Will you have a dozen Lady Sylvia and a dozen Ophelia packed for me to take when I go, please? I shan't be leaving till six so they'd better be brought over here."

"Transport packing, Mr. Eagleton?" Miss Brewster asked smartly.

He hesitated for a second and then said, "No. Hand delivery."

"I'll bring them across at five," Miss Brewster said in her slightly affected tones.

"Thank you," he answered and picked up his pen again and worked for another ten minutes.

The sudden heat still held and he had his sherry in the loggia. Annabel, her long hair brushed, came out there to him.

"You're looking awfully clean," he said, smiling at her, and he thought of Clare saying, 'She's only a child.'

"Nanny made me change. We're having supper with you," she answered.

"A penance?"

"What is a penance?" she asked him.

"Well, I suppose it's doing something you dislike—find hard's better, perhaps—to make up for something shady you've done. The books call it the law of compensation, I believe."

"I haven't done anything shady, have I?"

She thought of standing on the stile looking down at Adrian, but now the memory was all grief, the lovely thing spoiled. She was desolate.

"I hope you haven't. I'm afraid I was teasing you. I expect, if the truth's known, I wanted you to contradict me and say you wanted to have supper with me?"

74

"Oh, I see," she answered and the desolation gathered in her heart till she wondered if it would be possible not to tell him. Yet to tell him was unthinkable. She longed for comfort.

"Why didn't Mother come back?" she asked him.

"Something important kept her. She'll be down to-morrow."

"Do you think she will?"

"Yes, of course," he answered, and Piers came up the steps and sat down on one of the upright chairs.

"Was it something to do with the reception?" Annabel asked.

"Was what something to do with the reception?"

"Why she didn't come home."

"Indirectly, possibly. I really don't know much about it. She'll tell us tomorrow, I expect."

"Did you see Jules Coré? What's he like?"

"Just like all his pictures. Short, rather fat, going bald."

"What's 'cunning' mean? Really. I sort of know what it does. Once you said that Miss Rigsby was cunning."

"She's dotty rather than cunning. It means crafty. Sly. Underhand, I suppose. Why?"

"I just wondered. Is Daniel very rich?"

"If he's not, he soon will be."

"All designers are, aren't they?"

"The top men are. You're full of questions tonight."

Piers was sitting on his hands, gently rocking to and fro.

"Well, did you see Brodie this morning?" Hugh asked him, and he wondered, as he wondered so often, where the boy had got his queer, shy, almost surly temperament from.

Piers nodded.

"Say good-bye to him?" he questioned.

"Miss Brewster said Brodie's as old as Methuselah," Annabel broke in. "How old *is* he, really?"

"Sixty-something, I believe."

"It's awfully old to work," Annabel said soberly and her father smiled slightly.

"I can row," Piers announced suddenly and his dark eyes were bright.

"Two strokes," Annabel scorned.

"Yes, but I did it," he said urgently. "I didn't go round I went straight." He held up his hands and looked at the palms. "I've got corns," he added.

"You only went a couple of inches and then you put your oar in the reeds," said Annabel, and she ached for the starlit darkness of the previous night to return.

"Yes, but I went straight first," he insisted.

He had. For that one brief moment, the oars had ceased to become malevolent, intractable, cruel masters who did what they liked with him. Suddenly, with all the surprise of sunshine breaking through a cloudy sky, they had obeyed him, swung backwards in unison and dipped into the stream behind him, cleaving through it. He had felt the blades pressing against the water and the pressure had run up his arms to his shoulders till he recognised, with a surging in his heart, that at last he'd done it. Now he knew. Achievement was no longer a great, blind shape he strove towards, but was something *experienced*. Even the fact that his mother wasn't coming home didn't matter, because now the dream was so near fulfilment that postponement was insignificant. More, it gave him—if he could persuade Anna—another chance in the morning to repeat the perfect, the enthralling, thing. And after tomorrow there was Sunday and Monday, and on Tuesday, when she was to spend the day with them, the long-desired moment would come. His heart was no longer sick with the fear of failure. He, too, had accomplished, and even the horror of school had receded from the forefront of his mind. He saw his mother standing on the bank smiling. 'I am so proud of you, Piers,' she said. 'So proud of you.'

76

"I'll do the lighter for you," Annabel said, as her father took a cigarette from the box, but before the flint ignited, Felton came through to say dinner was ready and, wishing they could have had supper up in the day-nursery as usual, because he was always nervous when they had it in the dining-room, Piers followed them into the house.

As he went, he suddenly remembered Mark's voice saying, 'Gate of heaven. Morning Star.' And afterwards, 'A safe lodging.' He repeated the phrase to himself, wiping his finger over a chair-back as he passed into the hall—'A safe lodging.' He thought of the house he'd imagined in the middle of the roses.

Chapter VI

HUGH leaned his shoulder against the flint wall watching Irma arrange the roses. He noticed that she had lovely hands. She stood back from the table regarding the arrangement, then changed the position of one of the flowers. "What a pity it is that one can't have beautiful things without money," she said.

"Oh, come," he rebuked.

"Too sweeping? Perhaps. And yet . . . " She indicated the flowers. "The Dorchester. The Savoy. Moyses Stevens. A film-star's bedroom . . . who else could afford them?"

"You'll tell me I'm an evil capitalist for growing them in a minute."

"No, I didn't mean that," she said quite seriously. "I sound ungrateful."

"Decidedly," He smiled.

"I can't remember the last time I had roses given me. I don't think I want to remember. There! Nice?"

"Nearly as good as my Miss Brewster."

"I'd like to think so. She's brilliant."

"She has to be."

"Arrogant?"

"Just businesslike. The old game of getting twice the value for half the money."

"It's not like you to sound the bitter note."

"Indigestion I expect. I'm not going to offer to carry that for you."

"I'll take it. You bring the tray."

He picked up the tray and followed her into the sitting-room. "Oh, nice," he said, indicating the fire with a movement of his head.

"It gets cold in here still in the evenings. That's the excuse I make anyway. See to the drinks, will you?"

"Whisky for you?"

"Weak. And ginger-ale, not soda. There! Don't they look lovely there?"

"Wonderful."

"You *must* like them."

"Why the emphasis?"

"Wonderful!" she repeated. "You only reserve that for the rarest occasions. The usual remark is 'very nice'."

"Is it?"

He kept his head down, pouring the drinks.

"Didn't you know?"

"Don't think so. One just says something. 'Very nice' sounds like my maiden aunt."

"It sounds much more like Hugh Eagleton."

"Then he must sound like my maiden aunt." He gave her her glass and sat down, stretching into the chair, relaxed.

Peace, he thought. The one place where the strain dropped away. Odd how it had come about. They'd known her—what?—eight years? Known her casually. Irma Lovat who wrote books. If they gave a 'local' party they invited her. On one occasion, two perhaps, they'd been there to dinner. Clare saw her from time to time. And then, one night last autumn, he'd come down from London with her and had been mildly surprised how pleasant the journey had been. He'd given her a lift home from the station and carried her case into the house for her. The next day—he smiled slightly to himself because the thing was so banal—he'd found her gloves in the car and had taken them in on his way home from Westmill. She'd given him a sherry and, because Clare wasn't coming down that night, he'd stayed on for a bit, talking to her. Strange the way people changed for you when you came to know them. In all the eight years he'd never really noticed that her eyes disclosed her mood long before she'd uttered a word. They were sad eyes, yet sometimes they lit with sheer gay laughter. Yet, until recently, he couldn't have said with any certainty whether she possessed eyes or not. And he hadn't even noticed the shape of her hands till this very evening. He'd taken to calling in as he passed from time to time, and once she'd had Piers down there to tea. Clare had teased him mildly about her. He wondered then, what she appeared like to Clare, if she so much as impinged on Clare's mind at all. She must do to a certain extent or Clare wouldn't have insisted that Irma, in company with all women, liked beautiful clothes. Or was that merely a superficial generalisation?

"*Do* you like beautiful clothes?" he asked her suddenly.

She looked up, startled, from her own train of thought.

"Do I what?"

"I was thinking of the reception last night," he half-lied. "In retrospect, it seemed rather a *lot* of clothes. Too many and too shining. An overdose of strawberries and cream."

"Of course I like beautiful clothes," she answered. "Who doesn't? But I'd hate to have to dress up always. After a week I'd be back in my old things, I expect. Did you enjoy it?"

"The reception? Not really. Well . . . Oh, it was all right, I suppose. Shouldn't want to do it often."

"I thought Clare looked wonderful."

He remembered that Clare had put her arms round his neck when he said good-night to her, and that he had kissed her forehead and said, 'Sleep well.' Why was it that nothing was ever what it appeared to be, as though everyone lived a surface-life that was one thing and a second altogether secret and hidden life that was quite definitely another, a life that one would be ashamed or embarrassed to reveal to anyone else. We had to keep up the fiction that we were this, that or the other, when all the time we were something different. He wondered how many people at the Embassy last night really wanted to be there, in their hearts. Or how many, if they were honest, would have preferred bed and a book. Not Forest, of course, and not Clare, for their living depended on it.

"Are you ambitious?" he asked Irma.

She didn't answer for a moment and then she said, "No, but I don't usually admit it."

"You must be to a certain extent," he said. "What about writing?"

"I loathe writing."

"Oh, come."

"But I do. I'd never write another word if I needn't."

"Then why do you?"

"I've got to eat."

"Yes. But you're successful."

She shrugged her shoulders. "Only moderately. I had to be, to a certain extent anyway, when the boys were small. Pistol at my head."

"But if you really hated it, why did you do it? Why not something else?"

She thought before she answered, looking back over the years, searching for motive.

"I was young," she answered, eventually, "and I'd often played with the thought of writing. Like everyone else— nearly everyone else—I pictured myself tossing off master-pieces with one hand and running the home with the other." She smiled slightly. "How credulous we are when we're young. But the main reason was, that it was the only thing I could think of to do and keep the boys with me. I suppose I had a certain natural gift for it, but the main reason was that. Of course, later when they were old enough they went away to school. Then I used to write madly all term time so that I could have the holidays with them."

"But now they've both gone abroad," he said. "I mean . . ."

"Yes," she agreed, "but I never expected, never wanted, them to stay with me always." She stopped and then said, "We didn't have much money, but the thing we did have can never be taken from us. Neither from them nor from me. It just is so. If I had any ambition I suppose it was that."

"What?"

"Just that we'd be together," she said rather helplessly. "Have as normal a home as I could give them under the circumstances."

"But wasn't it difficult to write books with two small boys around?"

"It was nearly impossible. Not quite, luckily. Everyone thought I was a fool to try and I often agreed with them, but I felt I had to be with them myself. It seemed more important than new carpets. But people have always seemed more important to me than things. Things are all right, but they can't talk and laugh and give you affection. And you can't understand them or shape them by the way you treat them. They're not *living*."

"But money isn't to be despised," he said. "Financial insecurity can damage children, too."

"I wonder sometimes if that isn't over-stressed," she considered. "A lot depends on the parents' *attitude* to money, or the lack of it, I suppose. We were awfully poor as children but I don't remember ever being made morbid because of it. We had an old boat and an older donkey, and . . ." the sentence trailed away.

He looked across at her. "I wonder why we clutter ourselves up with your 'things' so much."

So many 'things', he thought. Suits you wore once a year.

China you used possibly less than once a year. Cars, television sets, radios. Mountains of 'things' ever increasing, being added to. It wasn't for food that you worked and slaved and exhausted yourself, but for 'things'; more and more 'things'. For another garage to put yet another car in, because it was madness to use the big car for pottering round to the Plantations. But you had to keep the big car, too, because Hugh and Clare Eagleton couldn't be seen in London in a small one. Even in your own exalted state you still played the game of 'keeping up with the Joneses'.

He remembered, then, that five years ago Mark's brother, Philip, a not inconsiderable actor, had suddenly thrown up his Knightsbridge flat and all that went with it to become a Carthusian monk. Clare had insisted that she 'knew' Philip, and that in six months time he'd be back frequenting his old haunts, a Martini in one hand and a cigarette in the other, instructing the chef at Manielli's that there was one tear-drop too much garlic in the salad.

Philip had come to The Nythe the week-end before he left, and they'd gone down on the Sunday night to see him. He didn't appear to be changed in any way. He was still the same gay, slightly whimsical chap that he always had been; still waved his white hands about as he talked; still held the floor. 'Playing to the unseen audience;' Clare had said and added, 'He's got to have an audience, if it's only the house cat or the canary. He's the total exhibitionist.'

And then, just before supper, he'd found himself outside the house with him, and Philip had suddenly drawn a deep breath and sent the newly-lighted cigarette curving out into the dusk and he'd brushed his fingers one against the other, as though ridding them of some slight stain. There was something about the gesture that had broken the ice of pretence and polite non-interference which had characterised their meeting with him, and he'd muttered a, 'What's it all for?' to him. 'Why are you doing it?' Philip only laughed and repeated the very words Clare herself had used previously. 'An act, old boy. Didn't you know?'

'Don't be a fool' he'd snapped.

Philip had stopped in his stride—they were walking up and down on the path outside The Nythe, the darkening fields all spread before them—and he'd said 'I couldn't see the wood for the trees. I suddenly realised that I was completely shackled, not even by circumstances, but by *things*. By my flat and my servant and my pretty bits of furniture and my car and my delicious meals and my vintage wine and my perfect little parties. By my suits and my books and my cigarettes. I was spending the minutes and the seconds and the hours and the years of my life on myself. Not even that, but on the self that I had *decided I must be*. On the vast accumulation of "things" which that self demanded, thought it must have, to keep up the fiction of itself.'

'But' he'd said, irritated at all the "talk", 'You'd made a go of it. Were successful. I can't understand you. You didn't live much differently from any of the rest of us. What's life for, in heaven's name?'

He had been bending over a wall, his elbows on the still warm stone and Philip standing beside him, had sent him down a swift half-smiling grimace. 'I lived for myself and worked for myself, Myself and none beside. Just as if Jesus had never lived, as if He had never died,' he'd quoted.

Bill had come out of the house then, calling them to supper, and as they strolled back Philip had said, 'It's true, you know. We've built up a Frankenstein, haven't we, a monstrous god of a thing we're chained to? We serve him night and day in his temple. We burn the incense of our cigarettes to him, and pour out our libations of gin and French at his feet. Because we're his slaves, we're lashed to work for him from the moment we fight our way into the eight thirty to the moment we fight our way back on the six ten. We pinch and scrape to pay him our tithes which he miraculously changes into drugs and mental wards, showering his care on us from the moment of our A.I.D. conception to our last six feet of state-controlled ground. We offer him our bodies rotten with cancer and thrombosis from our anxieties, and our minds made imbecile with our fears. Scientists bring him the first fruits of their harvest, the bacteria which will destroy thousands and the contaminated mushroom of the hydrogen bomb. Our children shut out the sun and the scent of the hayfields to follow goggle-eyed the working out of the sadism in which he delights. He is the god of this world. The god of "things"—things that decay as you touch them.'

They reached the shadow of the house and the thought had struck him, 'Clare's right. This is sheer exhibitionism. Philip Sheridan declaiming a passage from Philip Sheridan. And I'm the audience.' But just as they reached the door, almost as though he'd read Hugh's own thought, Philip said, 'Exhibitionism old boy. You ask my cousin Clare.' And then he'd shrugged his shoulders as though shrugging off a weight, and added, 'I sold my car yesterday. It was the last thing to go. Now I'm free, bar—' he'd swept a look down his person to his shoes—'this lot.'

'Monk or no, you'll still have to eat,' he'd said coldly.

'The food will be coarse.'

'And sleep.'

'On a hard bed.'

'Someone will have to clothe you, house you.'

'I shall work for my board and keep in the fields. Get corns on my lily-white hands. And the Habit, so I believe, lasts one a lifetime.'

'The great escape,' he'd thrown at him, feeling as though it were essential to beat him down, override him, subdue some damned intangible elation in him.

'Correct,' came Philip's voice.

'Escape into what, for Pete's sake?' he'd lashed, as the

beam of light from the opening door licked up the shadowed path and threw a brilliant artificial emerald on to the rose leaves climbing the house wall. 'You can't jump into a vacuum. Escape into *what*?'

'Into,' Philip said as he bent his tall head beneath the lintel and went into the house, 'I hope into, what someone once called "His glorious peace".'

He shifted his position in Irma's chair and thought, 'But he didn't come back. Was he still an exhibitionist? Still, at heart, Philip Sheridan the actor? Did he, waking up at five on a raw winter morning, ever regret the "things" he had left—those very "things" which, ten minutes ago, he himself had felt were a great weight on his shoulders. He would never know, for silence had swallowed Philip Sheridan, and Mark merely shrugged off any enquiries about him, with a brief, 'Of course he's all right.'

He looked across at Irma, and remembered that the sidetrack which had led to his remembering Philip had started from his asking Irma if she liked beautiful clothes. Queer, the way the mind scudded off on its hidden ways, delving down into memory . .

"Yes, but what else can we do?" he said to Irma. "We can't all suddenly go native, or return to mediæval conditions, can we?"

"Sometimes I wouldn't mind," she answered. "I've often thought how *quiet* it must have been. No engines splitting your ear drums. No jets shrieking overhead. No trains, no motor scythes, no tractors, even the country is one almighty noise now."

"No baths or indoor sanitation. The ubiquitous reek of oil lamps and guttering candles, the Plague, and me taking half a day to get up to Northmill on a horse," he scorned. "Pretty thought," And he added, "We couldn't stop the wheels even if we wanted to. I'd better get back."

"Another drink?"

"Will you?"

"No. I don't want one. You, though."

He got up and filled his glass and stood with it in his hand, one foot on the stone hearth. The scent of the roses was being drawn out by the fire. It drifted about the room, fading and returning again, as the air currents altered.

"And still life is life," he answered, and so quiet was the night that he heard the Westmill church clock strike ten. The tractors had ceased work. The night flying planes had not begun. There was no sound of a train going down the line across the marshes the other side of the river. "We still bear children and suffer and die. And love. *Is* this love?" he asked her, without altering his tone, his head still inclined as he looked down at the fire.

She didn't answer for a minute, and then she said, "No. No, it's not love. Not that kind of love."

"Are there 'kinds' of love?"

"As if you didn't know. I'm older than you are."

"Oh God, *ages*. A handful of years. And all the millions before and behind us. What's that got to do with it?"

"There's friendship," she said, but he moved his hand slightly in a disregarding gesture, pushing friendship away.

"Between a man and a woman?"

"Why not?"

He shook his head.

"But there is, Hugh."

"No," he said firmly. "Sorry to contradict, but you're wrong. Between two men, yes. Between two women—possibly. But not between a man and a woman."

"There's love in friendship."

"Affection. Devotion if you like. Not love."

"Perhaps devotion's a better thing, in the end."

"I didn't make love to Clare last night," he said and his voice came suddenly clear.

Irma moved her hands slightly. "Why do you tell me? It's nothing to do with me. I don't want to know."

"Because I was thinking of you," he said.

"No. No Hugh. No."

"Yes. Clare wanted me to make love to her."

"You can't tell me. You *can't*. I don't want to know."

"We came back from the Embassy and she wanted my love. I had none to give her. Suddenly. Like that."

"It's a phase. A passing thing. You're tired. Want a holiday."

"Glucose and vitamin B injections," he said wearily, and added, "No. It isn't a phase. It's a sort of peak, the slow climax of years. I'm Forest's partner's husband. As if I didn't know."

"That's rubbish. Self-pity, You're Hugh Eagleton."

"And who is he?"

She lifted her hand towards the roses.

"Isn't it something to be the biggest Grower in the country?"

"And have failed yourself?"

"But *why*, Hugh?"

"And your children."

"You—" she began, but the sentence died, still-born. She thought of Piers squatting on his heels by the fire, tossing a chestnut from one hand to the other to cool it, his too-pinched little face lighted by the flames. She thought of Bellhammer in the evening sun, and of the group of them standing on the terrace as she pulled the car up. She thought of Clare, dazzlingly beautiful in the Forest dress and coat. But why was it all troubling him now, *now*, recently? Whatever one's private judgment, one had always thought of them as successful, their lives running on wheels oiled not only by financial security but by achievement. She would have said that 'they'd got what they wanted'. It wasn't what she would have wanted, but that was beside the point.

"Even you," Hugh said dully. "You can't deny it."

Was it, she wondered, 'the slow climax of the years'? His loneliness ate into her heart. So easy to comfort him. *So easy.* And then, what? 'If only I were young,' she thought, 'I could pretend to myself that this was something real and true, an irresistible passion. I could pretend to myself that he did love me. But I'm not young, and I don't even believe in 'irresistible passions' any longer. They flame up into a torment of desire and then they die again, leaving a little black patch on the grass. And even in the midst of it, you scream for the thing to be over, to be free of it, to get back to serenity; reason. I couldn't go through it all again.' And yet the pull was there, deep in the heart—to be loved, desired, needed. To be filled with the old spring-like vitality . . . She felt the slow turn of her being to the beckoning warmth. For a second or two it spread from her heart into her veins on a wave of nostalgia, crying 'You could live again. Feel the sunshine. Have you forgotten what it is to be loved? To be a woman held dear?'

'Fool,' she scorned herself. 'Will you never learn?' You couldn't enter into these things *alone.* You thought you could, but you couldn't. You thought, 'This is my own affair, personal to me and to him.' But it wasn't. Like a stone thrown in a pond, the circles went on widening, touching other lives as they went, gathering them in. Affecting them. Again her mind swung involuntarily to Piers and she remembered the white patch round his mouth last night when Annabel goaded him for putting the boat in the reeds. Piers' life, and Annabel's.

But Hugh . . . solitary, needing comfort so desperately. Couldn't Clare *see?* Was she totally blinded by her spectacular success with Forest? But why had the situation ever developed? Hugh wasn't a weakling, neither was he incapable of earning enough money to keep his family. How little one knew of people. You met them at a certain point in their lives, and all that had gone before was a closed book to you. *They* knew what had brought them to that point, you, never. And neither they nor you could ever explain themselves. Never make themselves clear.

But he was wrong, there *was* another kind of love. It went unrecognised, scorned if anything, because it was unspectacular. There was no excitement, no thrill, and nearly always there was anguish in it. But it was love just the same. It was what everyone wanted, at heart . . . Not to be desired or flattered or held in high esteem, but *loved*.

"What *was* all that about?" Hugh asked her, but he still stood with his forehead on the back of his hand, his head bent.

"Thinking . . . "

He lifted his head then and said roughly. "I'm tired of reason. The moment you think, use your brain, all beauty goes. I don't want your thoughts. I want you. Why not? Oh, I know, because I'm married. Because, just occasionally my wife remembers that I'm her husband and that there are certain marital obligations, which habit dictates." He swung away and said, "Oh, damnation."

"I was thinking of the children, as it happens," she said.

"I suppose so. Even they might be better off. You can't tell. Sometimes I feel I'm withering up inside." He lowered his head on to his hand again. "You'll tell me that's self pity, too, I suppose."

"Hugh, don't . . . " She got up and stood beside him. "You make me so—so *hard*."

"I don't mean to. I thought you cared. You don't. That's all."

"That's not true. I do care."

"As you would for the dog. I thought—" He didn't finish the sentence, but lifted his right arm and put it round her shoulders. "It's been like heaven here. Peace. Now you won't let me come any more."

"I do care," she said again, and his arm round her was security.

'I'd forgotten that,' she said to herself. '*Security*. A man's sheer physical presence, physical strength. Someone to take the weight. An end to battling on one's own. Let all responsibility slide. Oh Clare you fool, you *fool*.' She thought, 'To have all this and let it go. What I'd have given for it. What I'd give for it now.'

Again the warmth opened in her heart and spread over her body. So easy. Life so short. So pitifully short. She would make a *home* for him. A place of return. And suddenly, not Clare's face, but Piers, looking up at her with his troubled eyes. She wanted to force his face out of her vision, but it wouldn't go. His eyes pleaded with her. But for what? For *what*?

"It's got to be this way," she said to Hugh. "I do care. But it's got to be this way. Secretly, in myself, knowing that you and I . . . How could I meet Piers?"

"You won't have to meet Piers. He goes to school on Thursday," he said shortly and he knew that all the talk and argument was killing the thing stone dead. You didn't argue over love. You rushed towards it without thought, swept up into the swift stream of it, blinded and willing. Neither people nor circumstances stopped you. How he needed her. And he could have her, now, this moment; sweep all this argument and morality aside. He'd only to swing her round to him and lift up her face and kiss all the nonsense away. As if he didn't know that. Hadn't he felt resistance go down in her?

And he made no move.

'Because I'm a weak fool,' he told himself a quarter of an hour later as he drove back to Bellhammer. 'Because I'm no man but a worm.'

The fields were white with moonlight. Bellhammer was a ship, sailing on the thin mist coming up from the river.

There was a dreamlike quality about it, an other-worldly purity.

'I couldn't meet Piers,' she'd said. 'How could I?'

She couldn't because she was that much ill-used almost forgotten word 'good'. Because she was strong and true. And dear, God, how dear.

Now, at this moment, and most strangely, dearer than ever. Why, heaven alone knew, but it was so.

Upstairs, as he opened the door with his key and went into the house, Piers turned in his sleep and flung his arm across his eyes.

Chapter VII

CLARE did not come down the following day. She telephoned through to Hugh at Northmill at noon, telling him that owing to trouble with Vaudré she was obliged to fly to Paris on the afternoon plane.

"Isn't it wretched!" she said. "It's upset my arrangements all round. But it's absolutely essential that I go myself. I had looked forward to a slack week-end, but with the Tour designs to get out, we just can't afford a mistake."

"But, good grief, Clare," Hugh answered shortly, "this is the children's last week-end before school starts. They've counted on your being down."

"Darling, don't snap!" came her voice out of the earpiece, in the tone she might have used to Annabel. "I know it's their last week-end and I wanted to come down. I didn't arrange this purposely. It's one of those unforseen things that could happen to anyone. And it's far better that I go over today so that I can have Tuesday at home with them. In fact, with luck, I shall try and take Tuesday and Wednesday. Not sure yet, but that's what I have in mind. And Hugh?"

"Yes."

The word came out in abrupt exasperation and Clare said, "Darling, *why* this attitude? It's so unlike you. Don't you realise that this is something I can't help? It's business, not pleasure."

How say anything, anything at all over a telephone, he asked himself. And say what, anyway? This kind of thing was nothing new. It had been going on more or less for years. And for years he'd accepted it, taken it as a matter of course, been, if anything, as zealous as Clare herself that she should make a success of her work. He frowned as the thoughts ripped at lightning speed across his mind. Was it, basically, nothing but jealousy, because Clare had got to the top? What nonsense! He was at the top himself. Irma? Then he ought to be damnably pleased that Clare wasn't coming home. Dear heaven, how muddled one's emotions were. Nothing straight, clear-cut.

"There isn't anything wrong is there?" came Clare's voice. "Everything's all right, isn't it?"

"Yes, everything's all right," he lied. "You said you'd be home that's all."

"You quite frightened me," Clare said half-teasingly. "Listen darling, I shall be down either Monday night or early Tuesday morning. When do you leave for Holland?"

"I shall have to go up on Monday, as I've got people to see in the evening. About five I should say. I shall have dinner in town."

"Then it doesn't look as though I shall see you."

"Shouldn't think so. I can't leave *much* later than five. What about Thursday?"

"The children? I've got all that fixed. Johnson is going to put them on the train and Miss Hawkins will meet them at Victoria. If I possibly can, I shall slip along to Charing Cross in time to see them before they leave. If not, Hawkins will cope. Their trunks will go on Monday, so there's only a question of hand luggage and Nanny's got all that side under control. You won't be back in time to get to Charing Cross will you?"

"I doubt it. I shall if I can."

"Well, it can't be helped. Hawkins will be all right, and the school people are used to dealing with new additions. Annabel's an old hand anyway and it's only a question of

Piers. I got on to Patty earlier and suggested that Karen and Bill came up to a final-burst tea tomorrow, but Patty thought it might be better if Annabel and Piers went down to The Nythe. They've got some child or other staying, a friend of Karen's I think she said, so I said they could. I've told Nanny. And Cook knows what I want done about food. I don't think there's anything else."

Nothing else, he repeated in his mind. Everything under control. Nothing neglected. Trunks, trains, tea-parties, even the food they would eat while she was in Paris. Nothing left out. Not a single thing unaccounted for. 'But then,' came Irma's voice in his mind, 'people have always seemed more important to me than things.' And out of the dusky summer twilight, Philip said, 'I was shackled by things. Things. Things. Things.' And a pretty mess we'd be in if she hadn't made all the arrangements, attended to the 'things' he told himself. I'd look fine if it had been left to me. Children's luggage. Tickets. Johnson and Miss Hawkins. Fix meals for the week-end. And Clare works as hard, or harder than I do!

Wonderful, wonderful Clare Eagleton. Forest's partner. Wife and mother. And never a hair turned; never an 'i' undotted or a 't' uncrossed. Dear heaven, what more did he want of her? He thought of Irma, lying back in the easy chair, her hands at peace. Not doing anything. Not even talking very much.

"If I don't get down in time to see you on Monday, I'll definitely be home again on Friday," Clare said. "I've got Giles Roache coming over on Saturday with plans for the pool. Be nice if we could get it done while the children are away. Something to interest them in the long holiday. I told Giles the afternoon would be best. You haven't anything fixed, have you?"

He thought, 'When I was a kid at The Nythe, I swam in the river. Battled against the tide and felt like a hero the first day I got across to the Westmill shore. We made a raft out of empty oil drums and old planks fixed together with an agonising contraption of wire. The planks were rough and splintered at the edges, but the raft floated.'

"I don't think so," he answered Clare. "You know what you want, anyway," he added.

"Yes, but I like you there," Clare said. "Moral support."

"Moral, my foot," he answered.

"And we'll have a quiet week-end," Clare went on. "I could do with it."

"I suppose you could."

He heard her small laugh. "You said that as though I were someone calling to deliver a tract." Her tone changed. "You are all right aren't you? Not ill, or anything? You sound as though . . . "

"Of course I'm all right," he broke in. "Got a good bit on at the moment, with the accountants due and having to get across to Holland and a couple of meetings and one thing and another."

"We both need a holiday," Clare answered. "We'll have one, too, in late August or early September. We'll work some definite dates out at the week-end and Hawkins can deal with the Travel people. I'd better go or I shall be late," she added.

"All right."

"Seen Irma?" she asked suddenly.

He was startled and her name escaped him before he realised. "Irma?" he echoed. "Why?"

"I only wondered. We do see her sometimes. Struck me she might like to have lunch on Sunday. The children are quite fond of her."

"I shouldn't think so," he answered quickly.

"Darling, you don't know. Why not ask her?" She laughed again, very lightly, hardly a laugh at all. "Don't tell me *you* don't want her," she said. "I thought you were her gallant defender. The very *parfait* gentle knight."

"Don't talk rot," he said shortly.

"All right darling. Just as you like."

Was there some faint tinge of relief in her tone?

"Till Friday, then," he heard her say. "Hope the Amsterdam trip goes well."

"Hope so," he agreed. And added, "And Paris."

"It's got to," she answered. "Bye, darling."

He put the receiver back and raised both hands to his face, covering his eyes.

"I don't know," he muttered. "I just don't know. I don't understand one damnation thing."

"Not that one, you moron," Bill shouted. "The *left*. Oh Jehoshaphat, don't you know your right from your left, you repulsive little worm? Now, pull on it. *Pull*. Harder. Look out, you're swinging round again. You'll have us in the reeds in a minute. Go on. *Harder*. Watch your right. Oh, mercy me! That's better. Now together. *Back*, in. *One*, out. Harder on the left. It's an oar not a teaspoon. In . . . In . . . Go on, you're all right. Together. Pull. Now you'll get the current to help you along. Left. Left. Don't weaken. You've kept straight for at least five yards. *Harder*. Not too hard, oaf. Here comes old Percy Pontefract, out for his constitutional. Don't look so scared, he won't come for us."

The swan came level with the boat, passed it as though unaware of its existence and sailed on upstream, intent on its own proud concerns. A crowd of starlings rose suddenly from the reeds and wheeled out over the river and were away, high in the blue. The oars wobbled into the stream, jerked out, wobbled unevenly backward again. But the boat kept moving.

'I'm doing it,' Piers exulted. 'I'm rowing, We're right away from the bank. I'm really doing it this time.'

The muscles of his arms and shoulders strained under the effort. His palms were stinging with bitter pain and the

97

breath was tearing up from his lungs. But he'd done it. He was rowing. It didn't matter that she hadn't come home at all this week-end. It was a good thing. Because Bill had taken him out in The Nythe boat and now he was really rowing. Not like he did with Annabel, but really. Now he'd be able to show her. Now she would stand on the bank and *really* be surprised. No pretence any more. The real thing. The power and the glory. 'Piers! You didn't *tell* me . . .'

"Look out, soppy," Bill shouted. "You've gone off again. On your left. Keep out of there for Pete's sake, it's the Pontefracts' house and the old girl'll let fly if you disturb her. Here, we'd better swop over and I'll run her back. Must be teatime. All right, let her go. I've got her. *Steady.* Keep to the middle, you clot."

Splendid in his triumph, unaware of blistered palms and aching shoulders, Piers walked up beside Bill to The Nythe. There was tonight and all day tomorrow. And then at last it would be Tuesday.

He matched his thin aching legs to Bill's longer stride. His eyes were shining.

Sunday tea at The Nythe during the school holiday was a meal. Brown loaves and white loaves. Butter in blue dishes. Honey and jam in sturdy two-pound pots. Buns. A cartwheel of a cake on a pastry-board because there wasn't a plate big enough to take it. A basin of whipped cream. Biscuits.

Annabel came in with Karen and Jane Fenning. There had been a pitched battle with Nanny about coming to The Nythe, but the battle was lost before it began. All the way down across the fields she hated Nanny. The hatred had burned and seethed in her heart, and by the time she and Piers reached the house she felt sick and was having to force back tears. She thought if she saw Adrian she would die. She hoped, with every effort of her mind, that he would be

out. She could bear anything as long as she didn't have to
see him.

Adrian was out. Karen mentioned it casually as she introduced Jane. "Adrian said he'd come and pick you up in the
car, but he had to go over to Tony's."

He wasn't there. The tears in her heart changed from
tears of hatred against Nanny to grief. He wasn't even there.
She needn't have bothered. He'd gone out. The night she
had stood above him on the stile trembled into her mind.

"Shall we go to the barn or do you want to walk?" Karen
asked, and answered herself with, "Let's go to the barn.
Walking's such a bore. Go and get your photographs, Jane,
Anna would love them," she pleaded. "She's got a colour
camera, the beast," she explained to Annabel. "You have to
put the films in a pre-viewer and they're all sort of three-
dimensional. Terribly grand. Bring the Irish ones, Jane,"
she called after her. "She's just come back from Killarney.
Her grandmother lives there," she rattled on to Annabel.
"I'd love to go to Ireland, Dad says we might, next year."

They spent the hour till teatime looking at the films and
talking, but all the time, even when she was seeing the lakes
of Killarney or the Connemara mountains rock-carved into
a sunset sky; all the time she was saying, 'Isn't it magnificent'
or 'Is that you, Jane?' the night she walked home with
Adrian was still there, a picture behind all the other pictures;
more vibrant, more alive, more darkly real.

Mark poured out the tea and Patty cut the bread. It was
always that way at The Nythe, for, while Mark could carve
the finest sliver from a piece of wood, he couldn't cut a
straight slice from a loaf.

Patty buttered a piece of bread for Roddy, perched up on
his chair on two cushions. She spread honey on the bread
and cut it into fingers and passed him his plate. He looked
down at it and then raised his head.

"You've cut it in *dolly* pieces," he accused her disgustedly.

"Oh, darling. Sorry. I wasn't thinking."

"I don't have dolly pieces *now*," he rebuked.

"No, I know. I'd forgotten."

The accusation was burning in his eyes, lifted to Patty's face, the awful accusation of public indignity and hurt pride.

"Darling, I did say I'm sorry. You have to forgive people when they say they're sorry. I always forgive you when you do. I'll cut mine in dolly pieces too."

Roddy sighed. "Yes, but it's still dolly pieces," he said with unalterable logic.

Patty met his eyes, blue-lit with the accusation and there passed between them a glance of understanding beyond all apparent disloyalty, or momentary hurt. It was an understanding which acknowledged the enormity of public humiliation, pleaded for forgiveness and was taken back into the warmth of the love which existed between them.

The accusation left Roddy's eyes. "You didn't mean it, did you?" he said magnanimously. "You only forgot. Poor old Mum."

"Bill," said Patty, "do look after Piers and don't hog all the jam yourself. Where did you two get to?" she asked.

"River," Bill answered, swallowing a vast mouthful of bread and jam. "Piers rowed."

"Rowed!" scorned Annabel. "He can't row properly."

"Oh, terribly House and Garden," Bill mocked. "But you're wrong for once, chum. You didn't teach him right. He needed a Master on the job." He took another bite from his bread and jam. "He got it. He *can* row now, better'n Adrian, and Adrian's number four in the college boat's best friend. So put that in your gold watch and chain, old girl."

"Did you really, Piers?" Patty asked. "I am glad."

"Did he really?" echoed Bill. "This place! No one believes anything a chap says. Course he did. Navigated past old

Percy Pontefract like the Queen Mary passing Nantucket. You did, didn't you Piers?"

Piers felt the hot colour flush into his face as they all looked at him. Their concentrated gaze came at him like so many small sharp probes, seeking to enter the secret place in himself, the place which was forever hot and tremblingly vulnerable, the place from which tears so quickly came, the place which dreaded publicity and to be discovered.

Dumbly, fighting to overcome, he nodded. Bill leaned across the table towards him. "Lost your tongue, duckie? Tell 'em, you clot," he hissed, and Patty said, "Bill, don't use that repulsive word," while Piers, triumph dissolved as though it had never been, wrestled to find the hated phrase.

"I . . ." he began, but rescue came with the door opening and Adrian coming through into the dining-room with a "Hello, everyone. Any tea, Mum? Don't move. There's room here. Shove up a bit, Bill."

'I can't bear it,' Annabel thought, 'I really can't. Suppose I'm sick,' and she prayed desperately that she mightn't be. She clasped her hands tightly together in her lap. He hadn't even noticed that she was there. He'd just thrown down a "Hello, everyone," had brought up a chair next to Bill and was buttering a slice of bread. 'Stuffing himself . . . ' 'Don't let me remember those awful words,' she thought desperately. 'I can't bear to remember them.' She hated The Nythe. Beneath her lowered lids she saw that Mark passed Adrian his tea. He put the cup and saucer down carefully on the small space on the table.

"Fix up about the motor scythe?" Mark asked him.

He nodded, looking at Mark over the rim of the cup in his hand. "They'll let us have it in about ten days. You can keep it for a week."

Mark refilled his own large breakfast cup. "Just in time for you to give me some help before you go up."

"Miserere me."

"Toughen up your girlish muscles."

"Oh, come, come."

"When I was your age . . ."

"I know. You lifted a shire horse with one hand and a ten ton truck with the other."

"Whipper-snapper," grunted Mark, smiling, and added, "I didn't hear the car stop."

"Correct. It's in the lane near Bellhammer. Someone had used all the petrol."

"Haven't I told you . . . " Mark roared.

"You have," Adrian broke in calmly. "And I didn't. I'll walk up with a spare can after tea."

"The Fennings are coming at seven to pick Jane up," said Patty. "They'd give you a lift."

"It's all right. I'll walk up with Piers and Annabel when they go." He looked across at Annabel. "Or are you staying to supper?"

"No," Annabel answered, and she thought that suddenly everything had burst out singing. "No, we're not staying to supper. We've got to be home by half past six."

"Right. I'll come along with you," he said.

Mark banged the table with his fist. "I will not have this open defiance," he stormed. "I allow you to use my car on the condition that you treat it with care and respect. When I went to take it into Westmill last Thursday, there wasn't so much as a spoonful of oil and not much more of water. Now it's *petrol*." Again his fist came down on the table. "I will not endure it, I tell you . . . "

Annabel was aware of the crash of his fist and the thunder of his voice, but it was all vague and far away. And above and beyond and all round the clatter, enveloping it and eventually blotting it out altogether, she heard only the splendour of the singing.

Bill squatted on his heels in a patch of sunlight outside the chapel, watching Mr. and Mrs. Robinson and Sid undulate through the newly-cleaned tank and glide downwards to the imitation sea-bed he had constructed on the bottom, their mouths opening and shutting, their gorgeously-striped Oriental bodies swaying with ballet-like grace.

Eschewing all text-book instructions he took outrageous liberties with the fish, who, in spite of prophecies of disaster, throve on his curious treatment. Mark had suggested that it would be fitting to name them after the great Chinese dynasties, but Bill had stuck to his own choice. 'They're naturalised, now,' he had told Mark. ' And when in Rome, they must do as the Romans do and be called as the Romans are called.'

"I'm afraid Mr. Robinson's a greedy old hog," he said to Piers, who stood leaning against the wall above him. "He's got a nasty, smug, paunchy look in his eye. I wonder if they get giddy going round and round the tank," he went on. "P'raps they don't know they're doing it. They might think they're in the sea, I suppose, and each time they go down to the rocks, they probably think they're different ones. What a fearful 'have'. Poor old Robinsons."

Piers, looking into the tank from above, saw three oddly-shaped multi-coloured fish, distorted out of all reason by the rays of the sun on the water. The water itself appeared bright emerald with floating, shape-changing rocks and trails of seaweed which reached out their wispy fingers to catch at nothing. There was a nightmare quality about the distortion which was frightening. He thought how terrible it would be to be shut in the tank and not be able to get out, ever.

Roddy came round the corner of the chapel wall. In one hand he clasped a drooping little bunch of daisies, dandelions and grass. In the other he held the handle of a large pottery jug with a broken lip, dragging it along the ground as he came. He reached them breathing hard, steadied the jug, stood upright and said, "These are my Jesus-flowers. Put me some water in, Bill."

Bill lifted his head from contemplating the fish. "Don't be dotty," he answered. "You can't put 'em in that great thing. Did Mum say?"

Roddy nodded, his eyes anxious. "Yes, she *did*," he insisted. "She said you'd lift me up to put them." He jumped from one foot to the other a few times in agitation. "Please, Bill. She did say."

"Oh, *all* right," Bill answered. He stood up. "Wait a minute and I'll get a smaller vase. Don't you go near the Robinsons or I won't lift you."

"Sid's on the bottom," Roddy said, squatting down and peering into the tank. "Why does his ears move?"

"They're his gills, fathead," Bill answered. "That's what he breathes with."

Roddy's clown-like back in his baggy jeans was bent over as he watched. His hands were planted on his spread knees like an old man.

"Well I never did," he remarked and Bill went off to find a vase.

A minute or two later he returned with one and Roddy picked up his flowers and stuffed them into it.

"There!" he said on a satisfied sigh and he scrambled up from his knees. "Now come and lift me to put them, Bill."

"Oh lor'," Bill muttered. "Come on, then."

Bill took the vase and Roddy trotted beside him through the arched chapel door. Piers followed them some paces behind, but remained standing just inside the doorway itself. The chapel was west-lit with the setting sun. Long rays reached obliquely from the windows to the red carpet before the altar, and lay there in pools of scarlet light. They played on the bowl of forsythia on the wrought-iron stand, deepening its yellow to gold.

Piers watched Roddy march up beside Bill to the rails and wobble to one knee. He saw him climb the three shallow steps, lifting up his legs sideways to negotiate them, and Bill handed him the flowers and lifted him up so that he could put them on the altar.

He saw him reach out his hand and place the vase, and when it was in position Bill put him down and he stood on tip-toe trying vainly to see the effect. After a moment he marched back down the steps, turned again at the rail and a second time wobbled to one knee, then he came trotting between the chairs towards the door and went out into the sunlight. As Piers followed Bill outside, he saw him racing off across the courtyard, his small red-sandalled feet flying.

"I'm going to take the Robinsons in," Bill said. "They'll get the asthma," and he bent down to lift the tank.

"Why do you have to go on one knee?" Piers asked him.

"Why do I *what*?" Bill said and he looked up at him, his forehead creased in enquiry, then, comprehension dawning, he jerked his head towards the chapel and said, "Oh, that. Because God's there, you silly dolt." He lifted the tank and added, "Shan't be a tick."

Piers stood where he was for a moment, then, with a glance to make sure there was no one about, he went back and stood inside the chapel door again.

It was very quiet. He remembered kneeling there half-asleep hearing Mark say, 'A safe lodging'. He wondered what God was like. Felton had once told him that He saw everything you did that was bad and wrote it down in a book so that He could punish you for it. He hated the thought of God watching all he did. He wondered if he saw him in the lavatory, and was immediately embarrassed and afraid in case God would write it down and punish him for being rude. It was all very confusing, he considered, because when he'd asked his mother about the book she'd laughed and said, 'Felton really does talk nonsense. I'll have to speak to her about it.' 'What does God do, then?' he'd asked her, but she'd only said, 'Oh, Piers, do stop bothering your head about such things, there's a good boy,' and then there'd been a telephone call for her and she'd had to go. And yet, he argued with himself, Bill didn't seem to mind God, neither did Roddy for he'd gone right up to the altar and put his flowers on it—*and* they were half-dead dandelions anyway. Perhaps God liked flowers. He must do, he supposed, for there were always some in the chapel. He hoped He wouldn't punish Roddy for putting dead ones up, though.

Carefully, holding on to a chair-back, he, too, went down on one knee and rose to a standing position again. The action pleased him and he did it a second time. He was too engrossed to hear Mark's approaching footsteps, but when his figure blocked out the light, as he came in at the door, he turned swiftly, terrified at being caught in the chapel. But Mark didn't appear to be angry.

"Hello," Mark said. "I thought you were with Bill. Where is he?"

Piers looked up to the great bearded face far above him and his heart began to race.

"Don't look so scared," Mark said. "There's nothing to be frightened about. No one minds you coming in here. In fact they like it." He put out his hand and laid it on Piers' shoulder as he made a move to slip past him. "Don't run away. Come and sit down a minute and I'll show you my sketches."

Longing to escape, yet too much in awe of Mark to disobey, Piers edged on to the chair next to that overflowing with Mark's great bulk.

"Think they look all right?" Mark asked him, moving his knee a little to bring the block within Piers' range. "I'm doing them to send to my brother Philip. Give him an idea of what we've done with the chapel. Like them?"

"Yes." The word was barely audible and Mark shot a

look at the boy's thin fingers gripping one another between his bony knees.

'The poor little devil's a neurotic at the age of ten—a twisted bundle of fear,' he thought. He felt fury rising in his heart against Clare; a terrible anger. Couldn't either she or that fool Hugh see the boy's need? No, they couldn't, because they didn't recognise the need themselves. All they recognised was that they'd given him a modern house, expensive shoes and a television in the children's playroom. And what could *he* do about it—great, blundering fool that he was, who couldn't even keep his temper for two minutes together. Dear God, he went on thinking, the pity of a world turned away from your Beauty, shut in its claustrophobic little cage of a civilisation, unaware of the glory beyond the meagre seventy years of scratching for a living. Nothing to strive for but a bigger and better motor-car or a new coat of paint in the dining-room. Nothing to lift the heart to but a well-paid job, a cocktail-cabinet and a larger washing-machine than the neighbours. And the children—this boy here—longing for security, for certainty, for love. They stood with groping hands crying out their heart's need and were given a wrist-watch or another set of trains. Hundreds of them, thousands, conceived in indifference and borne in discontent. Even the animals did better, the birds, the tigers. Dumb creation accused man to high heaven.

Piers shifted his position and he glanced down and saw the boy's left palm reddened with blisters. He picked up his wrist and looked at the sore places.

"Rowing? You'd better get those done up before you go home. Be painful if they break. Patty'll do 'em for you."

Piers himself looked down at his palm. His fingers were curved slightly, for it hurt to straighten them. The reddened flesh nauseated him, but the nausea went down before the memory of triumph. 'I am so proud of you, Piers . . . '

Suddenly, his shoulders lifted up, his knees pressed together, he said quickly, "God doesn't write all the bad things you do in a book, does he?"

"God doesn't what?" Mark roared, in a voice that made Piers jump. 'Dear Lord,' Mark said within himself, 'is it possible that we have twisted your Love into a sadistic little weapon to terrify the hearts of children? How tell a child who knows nothing of you but meanness that you are the fulfilment of every man's dream of happiness? "Our hearts are restless till they find their rest in You." The hearts of the children. The hearts of us all. Why do you give me this job, Lord? Why me?' he groaned.

He took out his handkerchief and blew his nose, a trumpet of a sound which cut into the silence, then he said, and his voice wasn't loud, but gentle, "Someone's not told you the truth, young Piers. I'll tell you what God does do, though. He writes all the *good* things you do, not in a book but in His heart. Those are the things he remembers, even the smallest of them. The bad ones he forgets all about." He put his arm along the back of Piers' chair. "You remember that, young Piers. You remember that whatever you do, good or not so good, He loves you. He's the one Person who'll love you, through thick and thin, come wind come weather, rain or shine. And there'll never be a moment when He *won't* love you, from now to the end of time. You remember that, boy."

Piers didn't speak for a minute or so, and the oblique rays of light moved slowly on across the altar.

"Does He like flowers, then?" he asked at last.

"Of course He likes flowers. Dash it, He made them," Mark answered. "*And* He loves great splashes of colour—reds and blues and violet and orange and gold. And tall waving trees and little pink-frilled daisies and white, white lilies with ochre stamens that stain your fingers when you touch them. But he likes boys of ten best," he added. "He even likes damn-fool men of forty-five, too," he said, half to himself. "Though He alone knows why."

Piers sat as he was, hunched in the chair, looking straight ahead, then suddenly he stood up, and said, "I think I'll go now," and in another second the chair was empty and Mark was alone.

He leaned his head down on his hand, gripping the back of the chair in front of him. So wholly inadequate. So paltry. 'Angels and archangels and all the company of heaven'— and he'd gobbled over it like an idiot. The great redeeming Love that longed to share His own undying glory with men —and he'd muddled and botched it so that the boy had got up and bolted. "Dear God," he said into his hands, "You ought to have sent Patty in, not me. Really You ought. Or am I telling You how to run Your universe as usual?"

Adrian, carrying the can of petrol walked beside Annabel across the meadow path. Piers followed them two or three yards behind, slapping at the hedges with a stick he'd picked up as he went. Patty had bandaged his left hand where the skin had broken, so he could hold the stick without it hurting. The bandage looked important. He liked it.

Annabel's and Adrian's voices drifted back to him. Once they laughed and Annabel pushed her hair with her hand and he knew she was being grown up. He thought of the Robinsons in the tank and of Roddy putting the flowers up, and of Mark saying that God only put the good things down and forgot all the bad things. He remembered that he had really rowed properly, and that today had nearly gone and that there was now only one more day till Tuesday. He could hardly bear to wait. And then, as he hit at a bit of bramble, he remembered that on Thursday he would have to go to school, and the panic-fear rose in his mind again. He told himself that he would run away so that he needn't go, but even as he saw himself setting out from Bellhammer with a knapsack on his back, he knew that he'd never do it. He knew that the moment would come when, in the grey flannel suit and the cap with the badge on it, he'd be sitting in the train on the way to London; knew that the moment would come when the Charing Cross train would pull out, and he would be with strangers; far away from Bellhammer and the playroom; far from all the things he knew.

His feet dragged as he walked. He no longer slapped at the hedges with his stick. He thought it was as though he were quite alone, the only person in the world.

He looked up and saw that Annabel and Adrian had reached the stile. He watched Adrian put the petrol can down on the grass and then take hold of Annabel's hand and help her up as though she were a lady. When she had crossed over and was still on the far-side step, she suddenly turned round and put both her hands on the cross-bar and stood there looking down at Adrian on the ground. Her hair had fallen forward each side of her face and she was laughing. He thought she looked very silly stuck up there on the stile. He thought that when he got home he'd tell her how silly she looked.

After a little while she turned round and jumped down and Adrian stepped back, took a little run and vaulted the stile, jumping sideways, one hand on the bar, his long legs together as he swung them over. Then he bent down and hitched the can up, and he and Annabel walked on together. He could hear their laughter drifting back to him as he went along.

Chapter VIII

HUGH left for London and Holland at five on the Monday evening. He had been kept at Northmill later than he anticipated, and didn't get back to Bellhammer to pick up his case until half past four. Johnson was driving him up in the Jaguar and Felton had packed his things, but, even so, by the time he had changed he only had a few minutes in which to swallow a cup of tea.

Annabel came in while he was drinking it, standing in the hall.

"Hello," she said. "Aren't you going to have any proper tea?"

He shook his head. "Haven't time. I've got to be in London soon after six."

"Will you be?"

He glanced at his watch. "Don't know. I hope so."

He looked at her over the rim of the cup in his hands, his lids lowered slightly. She appeared oddly changed, someone, he thought with a stab of fear, that he didn't know. There was a quality about the change that alarmed him. Or was he being a fool? Suddenly he frowned. "What have you got on your ears?" he asked her shortly.

She lifted her shoulder slightly. "Earrings," she answered in a tone he had never heard her use before.

"Does mother know you wear earrings?"

"No." There was what could have been an insolently questioning note behind the single word.

"Where did you get them?"

"In Westmill." He saw the colour come into her face. "Why shouldn't I wear earrings? I'm not a baby."

"Neither are you old enough to wear earrings," he said sharply. "Especially cheap ones."

"They aren't cheap ones."

"My dear child . . ."

She swung away from him. "I'm tired of being treated like someone in the nursery. Heaps of people my age wear earrings."

"Not our kind of people."

How much did it matter he wondered as the clock ticked the minutes on. A child dressing up, stretching out her hands to a life she saw that was all excitement, or something else, some darker uglier thing? Oh God, one didn't know. The terrible responsibility of her swept over him. Suppose something happened to her . . . He looked at her again and saw, not as a father, but as a man, the budding attraction in the soft slightly pouting mouth, the fall of her corn-coloured hair, the pointed young breast beneath her jumper, and all his own weary knowledge of lust and desire, of high hopes and bitter disappointment swept over him. To fend it from her, keep her inviolate . . .

"I don't think Mother will approve," he said, and thought how inadequate it sounded.

Again she lifted her shoulders slightly. "Mother can't stop me growing up."

"No," he said. "But she can stop you from wearing cheap jewellery. You'd better take them off before she comes home," he added.

"Is she coming home?"

"Of course she is," he answered quickly. "Either tonight or tomorrow morning. She'll be calling to let you know which in five minutes or so."

"You don't know she's coming. She often says she will and then she doesn't."

"Only if something happens to prevent her," he said and felt sick at heart.

"She's not coming to meet us at Victoria on Thursday. Miss Hawkins is. Why can't I get a taxi and take Piers across? I know what you do."

"It's Piers' first time," he answered. "Better have someone with you I think. Mother will be at Charing Cross to see you before you go."

"Will you be?"

"I shall try to. It'll be a bit of a scramble. I might just make it. Where is Piers?" he asked.

"Watching television, I think. Do you want him?"

"I must say goodbye to him."

"I'll call up and tell him," she said, and she walked over to the house telephone while he poured himself another cup of tea.

"Nanny?" he heard her say. "Tell Piers to come will you? Daddy wants him. He's got to come at once."

As she put the receiver back, she suddenly looked a child again, pitifully young, defenceless.

Piers pushed open the sound-proof door and walked along the corridor. He was disgruntled at having to leave the film, which was showing wild life in Africa. He'd only said 'Why have I got to go?' to Nanny and she'd snapped at him as though he'd done something wrong. All the way down the stairs he was trying to remember if he had done something wrong. When he reached the hall he went forward with his head slightly down, still trying to recall what it might be.

"Hello, Piers."

His father's voice didn't sound as though he were angry, and he lifted his head and looked up at him, though he made no answer.

What was the matter with the boy, Hugh asked himself again. There was never anything 'fluid' or 'giving' in him.

Always on the defensive. An almost secretive way with him, a barrier you couldn't get past. My son . . . The son who, as the eldest, would follow him into Eagletons. The fourth generation. From the single home-made little greenhouse run up by his great-grandfather to the present-day vast concern—not a bad inheritance. And yet . . . He couldn't picture it. Couldn't 'see' him there. No personality. No charm. Why? His mind flashed to the day of Piers' birth and his own proud delight. Annabel he was besotted about, but . . . my son. He began to glimpse a hundred delicate threads of life he'd never considered before—old Hebraic rituals, the 'first-born'; the law of primogeniture, royal succession, the prince, son of the king. They were no longer archaic tribal tendencies, there was a deep mysterious force behind them, some inexplicable law which had its beginnings when the mastodons came out of the forests and scared the cavemen. The mastodons had died out, but the cavemen had lived on, because, even in a world yet unfitted for them, they had had a dream of future glory. He, too, had dreamed his dreams, groping out into a future when an adult Piers, the father-son relationship welded into partnership, would shape the Eagletons that Piers' own grandson would take over. Together they would plan that future, together steer the ship into the unknown. They would travel—Florence, Venice, little Yugoslav villages he'd always hankered after seeing. And farther afield to the Southern Cross islands—queer lonely places like Tristan da Cunha and the Easter Islands; to India and Japan.

He looked down at Piers in his grey flannel shorts and sweater, and his heart twisted at the memory of those bright dreams. And yet, he went on thinking, for the first six months of his life he'd appeared attractive and vital enough. Admit that his coming hadn't been at an exactly propitious moment, for his own financial burden at that time was heavy, and as Clare had just gone back to Daniel Forest, a baby was a distinct handicap to her. He remembered her initial anger with him, as though he alone were responsible for the child, and for the first months she had been resentful. Whether, later, she'd come to terms with the inevitable, or whether the new association with Forest had taken her mind off the resentment, didn't matter very much. She'd gone through the final phase with her usual expertise, everything organised in advance, running on oiled wheels—although in those days the 'oiled wheels' were those of The Nythe, not Bell-hammer, and within a few weeks she was back with Forest again. And then Irma's voice in his memory said 'I'm troubled about him, Hugh.' His mind slid to her as she sat in the chair backed by the roses he had taken her. 'There is another kind of love . . .'

He swallowed the last of his tea, put the cup down, fished in his pocket for his wallet and took a note and held it out to Piers.

"I'm off to Holland, in a few minutes," he said. "You'll be gone when I get back. Mother's seen to your school money, but this is a bit extra. Go on, take it." He smiled. "Never seen anyone of your age so slow in picking up a tip before." As he spoke, there was another picture at the back of his mind, the picture of a laughing boy who pounced on the money and stuffed it into his pocket, or made a grimace and asked with cheeky familiarity if that were all he could spare. He put his hand on Piers' shoulder, "Hope it all goes well at school," he said. "I'm sure it will. Be a bit strange at first, but you'll soon get into the swing of it."

Piers, jerked suddenly from watching a lioness suckling her cubs in the jungle, had for a moment forgotten both that his father was going to Holland and that such a thing as a school existed. Not only in the lives of the great silent-treading animals, but expressed on their proud kind faces, he recognised—though he couldn't have expressed the thought in words—something he had sought and never found amongst people. Only once, watching the lion turn his head and roar, he had remembered Mark. And the animals hadn't frightened him. The lioness playing with her cubs delighted him, and he'd imagined himself there with them, one of them, very safe in the guardian security of her lovely flanks, safe under the tall green trees. He looked up at Hugh and reality came flooding back. School. His father holding out the money. The trap closing.

"Well," he heard Hugh say. "Aren't you going to say thank you?"

"I suppose I've *got* to go?" The words were forced from him in a last minute panic.

Hugh pressed his shoulder. "You'll be all right, old boy. We all feel this way the first term. You'll wonder what you were ever bothered about after a couple of weeks."

"Shall I?"

"Of course you will. Come on, now."

"Don't I get a tip then?" Annabel asked Hugh, and she held out her hand.

He smiled at her, thankful to have the difficult moment arrested. He opened his wallet again and flicked a note at her. "No more cheap earrings."

She grinned as she took the money, and he saw with alarm, that she had varnished her nails. He felt he ought to do something about it, but it was already ten to five.

"You will come up to Speech Day, won't you?" she asked him. "You promised you would. It's miserable when you don't come."

"We'll come if we possibly can."

"You could, even if Mother doesn't, couldn't you?"

He smiled. "All those women by myself!"

"Other people's fathers do."

"Brave men!" He took a cigarette from the box and lighted it. "I'll be there I expect." He picked up his brief case. "I must get on."

He was intensely aware of Piers, standing on his left. He wanted, with all his being, to make some move towards him, to break through the barrier that appeared to surround the boy, and approach him with sheer natural affection. He couldn't do it. The impulse was there, but the action was impossible. The thought flashed across his mind that Piers was a 'thorn in his side', and immediately self-hatred followed the thought, and something that was almost a resentment against him, as though it were the child himself who was preventing him from becoming loving.

"Goodbye, then," said Annabel, and she held up her face to be kissed. He bent his head and touched her soft skin with his lips.

"Bye, Piers."

Piers looked up at him, his eyes still troubled, accusing. 'After all,' he told himself, 'the boy's got to go to school sometime or other.'

"Goodbye."

He put his hand on Piers' head. "I'll expect to hear great things of you." He laughed, and the laugh, he thought, had a false sound to it. "Wish I were just going off to school, you lucky chap. While I'm swotting at a desk all summer you'll be out playing cricket or swimming. Don't suppose we'll recognise you when you come back ... great shoulders on you and muscles like a prize fighter. Enjoy yourself, son."

'Talking to myself,' he thought. 'That's what I'm doing, talking to myself.'

"We'll come and see you off," Annabel said, and she opened Giles Roache's wrought-iron door.

He picked up his hat, put it on and followed them down the steps to where Johnson was standing by the open car door. He got in, Johnson snapped the door shut and went smartly round to the driving-seat and started the engine.

He put the window down and called a last 'Goodbye' as the car moved. He looked back as they reached the end of the drive, and saw them still standing outside Bellhammer, cool and lovely in the evening light.

"You've got earrings on," Piers said to Annabel.

"I know I have. Why shouldn't I?"

"Nanny'll make you take them off."

"She won't see them. I only put them on for fun." She looked at herself in the mirror, turning her head from side to side. "Do you like me in them?"

"They're awfully grown-up."

"I like being grown-up. Don't you want to be?"

He couldn't think if he did or not. His imagination couldn't picture any state other than that which he knew. "I'd like to smoke a pipe," he said.

"What a queer thing to want to do. You'd only be sick."

"Will you take your earrings to school?" he asked her.

She looked at herself in the mirror again, and put up her hand to her left ear and touched the earring. "Yes, I shall. I shall stuff them in the toes of my bedroom slippers."

"You won't be able to wear them."

"I know. I can show them to the others, though. You won't say anything, will you? Promise."

"Promise," he repeated, and he felt pleased and important because she had shared a secret with him.

The bell rang for tea and she slipped the earrings from her ears and put them in her pocket.

"Did you really row yesterday, or was Bill making it up?" she asked him as they went upstairs.

"I really did," he answered, "I sort of feel I can now. I know how it goes in my arms."

"That's how I felt about tennis last year," she said. "You try and then suddenly you can do it. I expect you'll always be all right now."

He thought he had never known her so nice, almost as though he were not four years younger than she.

"I did like your earrings," he said, because it was the only remark he could think of to make her realise how nice he thought her.

She put her fingers to her lips. "Shh . . . "

He nodded. "I won't say."

"Did you see Adrian help me over the stile when we were coming home last night?" she asked him in a low voice as they went along the corridor.

"Why did he?" he asked. "Usually you take a running jump."

She stopped walking, half-turned and leaned back against the wall, her head raised a little. He looked up at her and he thought that her face seemed as though there was a light shining on it. It fascinated him and he felt that he must go on looking at her.

"I'm in love with him," she answered.

"*Are* you?" he asked and he felt that he was on the brink of something most mysterious.

"I shall marry him, I expect," she said and the light was still on her face.

"They won't let you, will they?"

"One day I shall, even if they don't let me."

The bell rang again and she moved away from the wall and walked on with her head down. "If you tell that, I'll never forgive you," she said. "Never. Promise on your heart you won't. Say, 'I promise on my heart'."

"I promise on my heart," he repeated as they reached the door and swung it open.

The day-nursery was full of sunlight. The table was laid for tea, and David and the Baby were already in their places.

"You're late," Nanny said, but there was no anger in her tone. The second post had come in ten minutes ago with a letter from Brian Carter, the merchant seaman she was going to marry. He had been in the Far East with the British India

Company for four years, but his term was now nearly over
and he would be in England within eight weeks or so. She
longed day and night for her own home, her own children.
When she lifted the Baby warm with sleep from her cot, she
played the game of pretending that she was her own child.
Sometimes she resented her because she wasn't her own.
When she'd first gone to Bellhammer, she'd welcomed the
fact that she would have sole charge of the nursery without
interference, but it had turned out to be a pretty half-and-
half business, with Mrs. Eagleton directing everything by
telephone and, taking it by and large, she herself had been
more bossed around than at her last post, and that was
saying something. The conditions were good, of course, and
no pinching and scraping over money, but Felton was a
moody thing to get on with, though Cook and Mrs. Phipps
and young Ella, the nursery maid, were all right. The pay
was better than anything she'd had before, and she'd a nice
little nest egg tucked away for when Brian arrived. And it
hadn't been too bad during term-time when Annabel was
away and Piers out at day school, but it was hard going in
the holidays with the four of them to see to, and Annabel
had become such a little madam in the last year that there
was no holding her. They'd have trouble with her if they
weren't careful. She'd be sorry to leave the Baby, but there
was no doubt about it, you couldn't love another woman's
children as you could your own. What the Eagletons wanted
was an older woman, someone who'd given up hope of having her own children, and who'd be content with someone
else's . . . if there ever were such people. You heard of them,
read about them in books, but they always sounded a bit
too good to be true. There was something unnatural about
them to her way of thinking. But that kind had died out, if
they'd ever existed at all, and anyway Mrs. Eagleton wouldn't
employ anyone who was getting on. The latest methods or
nothing; and a dietitian into the bargain. She remembered

that Brian, answering one of her letters had said, 'A trained children's nurse you may be, my girl, but when it comes to my kids, you can lay off all that fancy stuff. If anyone had said 'carbohydrate' to my mother, she'd probably have thought they were talking about Dad's bicycle lamp, and she wouldn't have known a vitamin from a hyæna and we turned out all right.'

A memory of him came sharply before her . . . his shoulders, which, when you lay your head on them, were solid as rocks; his bright blue eyes, accustomed to looking over the sea; the sheer male strength of him. For a moment the longing for him was heavy as lead about her, a physical drag on her limbs. Eight more weeks . . .

"Whatever have you done with your nails?" she asked Annabel.

"My *nails*?" Annabel repeated, as though she didn't understand.

"You've been using your mother's varnish. At *your* age! You'll get that off the minute you've had your tea."

"I was going to, anyway," Annabel said casually. "And it isn't mother's, it's mine. I bought it in Westmill. Mother only has red, or gold sometimes for evenings. I know because I looked."

"You've no business in your mother's room. I've a good mind to tell her when she comes down."

"Oh, Nanny! You make such a fuss. A little bit of nail-varnish!" Annabel lifted her hand and surveyed her fingers. "I think it looks magnificent. Don't you think it does? Haven't I got nice long nails?"

"You're getting too vain for words lately. Everlasting looking at yourself in the mirror and combing your hair. Now it's nail-varnish."

"Didn't you ever use nail-varnish when you were my age? I bet you did."

"I didn't get the chance, my girl," Nanny said, and her

mind slipped rapidly to the big farmhouse kitchen on a winter's night. Lamp-light and an old fashioned range and eight of them sitting down to tea—five children younger than herself, from Frank aged nine to Susie just over a year. You didn't get much hope of nail-varnish by the time you'd helped clear the tea and wash up and got that lot ready for bed. And when you'd finished there was your homework. She smiled back over the years, picturing her father's expression if she'd turned up with varnished nails. 'Looks like they're dipped in blood,' he'd remarked of one of the summer visitors they'd had one year. 'I've seen Mother's the very spit of her's when she's been paunching a hare.' And he'd laughed and rubbed the back of his hand over his bald head as he always did when something amused him.

"Finish your tea for goodness sake," she said to Annabel, "and then go and take it off before your mother comes down or you'll get *me* into trouble."

"She hasn't even phoned yet," said Annabel. "She mightn't come tonight at all."

"If she doesn't come tonight, then she'll come in the morning."

"I wonder where she'll take us to. I wish we could have gone to 'My Fair Lady'. Adrian's been."

"You have to book up months ahead for that."

"Sometimes you can get tickets. Adrian's friend did."

"More lucky than righteous I should say."

"Perhaps we'll go to a film. 'The Bridge on the River Kwai' is on in Milford.'"

"Piers wouldn't like that."

"I must go on the river," Piers said urgently, "You see, I've got to show her how I can row."

"Suppose it's raining," said Annabel.

"Stop teasing," Nanny rebuked her sharply and she added, "You'd better have some more gentian on your blisters tonight, Piers. That plaster looks filthy."

Ella came up, cleared the tea and sent it down to the kitchen by the lift. She was sixteen, a queer, dark, slim little thing, shorter than Annabel. Three weeks ago, Mrs. Eagleton had given her a discarded party dress of Annabel's and her mother, who was a dressmaker, had altered it to fit her. Tonight she was going to wear it to the Church Hall Dance. She'd been in a dream all day, and at dinner-time she'd broken a glass and got a telling-off from Nanny. There was only the nursery to tidy now, and then she could go. She thought of the dress hanging behind the curtain of the corner cupboard in her bedroom, and she could have burst out laughing then and there, she was so excited.

"I'll play draughts with you, if you like," Annabel said to Piers. "Only you've got to play properly. We'd better stay in the house, because of Mother phoning," she added.

Piers didn't want to play draughts very much, but Annabel was still being nice and he knew that if he refused she might change and become difficult. His intention had been to slip away after tea and go down to what he called in his mind, his 'place'. This 'place' was beyond the Wild Garden where the daffodils were, on the fringe of the woods. There, between two tangled rose bushes, was a patch of short emerald grass. The rose bushes met overhead and formed a house. With the dim mystery of the wood behind him, and before him the sweep of the daffodils and the lawns rising to Bellhammer itself, he felt safe. When the tide was high he could just see the river. He had particularly wanted to go down there after tea, so that he could think about tomorrow and make his plans and savour in advance each moment of triumph. He didn't need anyone to tell him that he was a failure. The knowledge, an oppressing undercurrent was perpetually with him in the form of an ever-present inability. But tonight the pressure was cut through with a shaft of light. In a matter of hours now, the moment would come when he would untie the painter and push the boat out from the shore. The moment would come when she, standing on the bank, bending down a little with excitement, as he came pulling back to the landing stage, would say aloud the words that had been ringing in his head for days. 'Piers, you didn't *tell* me . . .'

He wanted to think it all out, picture it. He wanted to think that Annabel would be there and that he would walk back to the house with them both, the oars on his shoulder.

"Well, do you want to play or not?" Annabel asked. "You're so slow."

"Yes, I do want to, but . . . " he began.

"Well go and get the board then," said Annabel. And she looked down at her shining nails. She might, she thought, smuggle the nail-varnish back to school, too. She put her hand in her pocket and felt the earrings. Piers brought the draughts and the board, and they set the pieces out and began the game. They had been playing for ten minutes when the telephone rang in the corridor outside, and they heard Nanny's voice answering.

"That's Mother, I expect, to say when she's coming," said Annabel. "Do you bet she's coming tonight?"

"I don't know," he answered, and he thought that there was a warm, dark smile in his mind.

"Of course you don't know," Annabel scorned. "I said, 'Do you bet she is?' I bet you a shilling she isn't coming to-night, so that means you have to bet she is."

"Why do I have to?" he asked, but the smile was still there in his mind.

"Don't be so idiotic," said Annabel. "If I bet one thing, you have to bet the other."

"Well . . . " Piers began, but the door opened and Nanny, still with the receiver in her hand, said, "Annabel! It's your Mother. She wants to speak to you. Come quickly."

Piers watched Annabel cross the room and take the receiver from Nanny's hand. Then Nanny went back to bathing David and Annabel was there alone. She was silent for quite a long time, listening to the low croaky noise that was all he could hear of his mother's voice. Then he heard her say, "Do you mean you aren't coming then?"

Again the low croaking noise came and continued coming, and then Annabel said, "What kind of present?"

The sun beating through the window was warm on the left side of his face. He opened his fingers and looked down at the two draughts he had been holding. They felt warm and rather sticky and he lifted the top one from the bottom, so that they lay side by side on his palm. He looked out of the window and saw some smoke coming from The Nythe chimney, and he remembered Roddy walking to the altar to put his flowers up.

"He's here," he heard Annabel say, and she called his name. "Piers! It's Mother. You've got to come."

He hated talking on the telephone. He could never hear properly and it was difficult to think of what to say.

"Come on," said Annabel, and she covered the mouthpiece with her hand. "She's speaking from Paris," she said to him as he went across the room. "She can't get back after all. She's going to send us presents. Something's gone wrong."

"Do you mean . . . " he began, but Annabel thrust the receiver into his hand. "For goodness sake," she said. "Hold it tight to your ear, silly."

He could hear his mother talking, but he couldn't, at first, make out what she said, then, quite suddenly, he could hear her quite clearly.

"I've told Annabel," she said, "and she'll explain to you. I'm sending you both presents. Miss Hawkins is seeing to them and you'll get them on Wednesday. You'll be good, Piers, won't you? No fusses."

He didn't answer and she said, "Hello? Hello? Are you there, Piers?"

"Yes," he answered and he looked up at Annabel.

"Here, you'd better give it back to me," Annabel said. "They'll cut you off in a minute. Say Goodbye first."

"Goodbye," he said into the mouthpiece and he handed the receiver back to Annabel.

"It's me, Annabel," he heard her say. "He hates the telephone." She listened for a bit and then she said, "Yes. Yes. All right. No. He went just before tea." Then she said, "Do you want Nanny again? All right, I'll tell her. Yes, I know. Goodbye."

She put the receiver on the stand and walked past Piers into the room and over to the window and stood with her back to him.

"I knew she wouldn't come," she said. "I told you she wouldn't the other day."

It had all happened so quickly that he felt confused. "Isn't she even coming tomorrow then?" he asked, but the words sounded quite unbelievable.

"No," said Annabel and her voice was short and hard. "She's not coming tonight and she's not coming tomorrow and she's not coming on Wednesday. She's got some extra work to do and she'll have to stay in Paris."

"Then . . ." he began. "Then I won't . . ."

"Then you won't what?" said Annabel, but she didn't turn round. "I knew she wouldn't come," she said again. "I knew she wouldn't take us out. I told Karen she wouldn't. I don't care. I don't," she repeated. "I expect the film would have been silly, anyway, and we mightn't have had lunch out."

Piers looked down at the plaster round his hand. Where the edges had come unstuck the adhesive was grimed with dirt. He pulled at a loose piece of it and rolled it back with his finger. The skin underneath was white and crumpled looking. He had to keep rolling it to try and fend off the darkness that was creeping up from his heart and concentrating in a heavy drag behind his eyes. His throat ached. Beyond the darkness and the aching, breaking into it and then receding again, he kept seeing her standing on the river bank.

Chapter IX

MAY, June, July . . . Sunrises and sunsets. Rain. A few days of hot, bright weather, and rain again.

Clare was working harder than she had ever worked before, as she pushed Daniel Forest up the last few rungs of the ladder; coped with his temperament, coped with the additional staff they'd taken on, with the secrecy that surrounded the Tour designs, with reporters, with American buyers, with strained nerves and a thousand irritations. She flew to Florence, to Dublin, to Paris: and when she did manage to get down to Bellhammer for a week-end, she spent as long as possible in bed, surveyed the work on the swimming-pool, now nearing completion, made arrangements with Cook and Nanny about the household and the two younger children, wrote to Annabel and Piers and was off again early on the Monday morning.

"Three more weeks and the worst will be over," she said to Hugh when she was down at the end of June. "This pace is killing. But we've pulled it off, that's the main thing. Final fittings next week and, if all's well, only the finishing touches after that. And then, I hope, then Majorca. I feel I shall never get enough sun into me."

He made some superficial reply, because, so he told himself, to do anything else was quite pointless. Besides which, he didn't know if he wanted to be anything other than superficial. He felt almost indifferent about the whole situation, an indifference which seemed to be growing with each week, numbing his senses to anything concerning Clare.

Occasionally the indifference was shot through with anxiety; or sometimes with near-despair, but he had learned to grapple with those moments.

Up at Northmill, Jan Meinema, the rose specialist he'd engaged in Amsterdam, was taking over from the dead man, Calenfals. His English was poor, but he had brought an English-speaking nephew with him which facilitated matters to a certain extent, though there were some initial difficulties with the men. Whether the fellow would be up to Calenfals' standard remained to be seen. He was, too, contemplating plans for a canning factory to deal with the vast mushroom production. At the moment the entire crop was sold to other concerns, but it would not be without advantage, he decided, to start something of their own, cutting both transport and sales costs. There was a piece of land, just outside Westmill itself, which he had in mind, though he'd possibly be up against the Council over the erection of a factory. He'd already approached Giles Roache for some rough ideas, and had been groping his way into the world of latest-type machinery and production.

More 'things'? he'd asked himself, one night. Adding to the weight? Juggling with finance. Increasing responsibilities? It was as though you were caught up in a treadmill. You had to go on revolving for the simple reason that you couldn't stop the wheels; couldn't get off, even if you wanted to. And what else was there to do but throw himself into his work? There was Irma . . .

Driving over to see her one evening, he told himself that being with her was more pain than pleasure, yet even as he used the phrase, he knew that it wasn't true. He couldn't, now, picture his life without her; without her warmth and comfort and understanding. Friendship? So she insisted. Kept to her first resolve . . . 'It must be this way, Hugh'. And there was no argument, he knew that. If he wanted to see her at all—and God knew he had to see her—it must be on those terms. A dozen times he told himself that he'd cut it out, not go there again, and each time he made the decision he rescinded it. And, oddly enough, while he was there with her, he was content. It was only after he had left her, and was driving back to Bellhammer, that the conflict started again. Solution? There was no solution—unless he asked Clare for a divorce? The word made him wince. Bellhammer, the children, Annabel . . . the terrible tearing-down process. And Clare herself? How much would she care? Would she marry Forest? The very notion seemed absurd, and yet, three parts—more lately—of her life was given to Forest. She might even be glad of freedom. That was a lie and he knew it. If, latterly, her every energy had been given to her career, it was because of the accumulation of circumstances: the extra work that had come flooding in after Forest's initial success. But success had to be bolstered up, continued, as he knew only too well. There was no point at which you could call a halt, even if you wanted to. Clare might speak of a future slackening, but it wouldn't work out that way. The fact that Forest had made a vast majority of the Tour clothes was not, as she said, an end, but a fresh beginning. The prestige on that level would increase their commitments, force them to both retain a standard and exceed it. And that meant work and ever more work. It meant that more and more of Clare's time would be absorbed by designing; less and less would be spared for the home.

How much did he care, he wondered? Wasn't he just as well off as things were? Clare still managed to keep Bellhammer running perfectly . . . even if it were by a species of remote control. He himself was free to come and go as he pleased, with no obligation to consider the demands of a wife. When Clare did come down he could, so to speak, 'meet her on her own level' and always there was Irma's friendship. Wasn't that as much, more, than most people got out of life? Wasn't he, if anything, fortunate? What if

Clare had been as many women were, frustrated, nagging, bound to the little wheel of 'home-life'? At least he hadn't got that to contend with.

Drawing up in front of Irma's cottage, he thought, 'If only Irma would recognise the facts and get rid of her Puritanical streak, we could be so very happy. There's no point in all this resistance. Clare simply wouldn't care, and nothing need be *disturbed*, no one hurt.' It was the civilised, the only, answer to a problem of this kind. Yet, even in the space of the few steps it took him to reach the door, unlatch it and call Irma's name, there was some damned 'thing' which rose in his mind to make hay of all the 'reason', the civilised 'answers'.

It was her birthday and he had planned to take her out to dinner. As she came down the stairs he was startled at her near-beauty. The dress she was wearing brought out all her gentleness and charm; brought out, too, some other quality in her. Suddenly he could remind himself that she was an author.

He smiled up at her as she stood a little above him, her hand on the rail.

"You do look nice," he said.

"Not wonderful?"

He made a grimace. "Blow you, woman. You do though. Colour suits you."

"You think so?"

"No question. Just the right shade." He stood back from her, leaning one shoulder against the frame of the open study door. "Not sure I'm not a little scared of you."

"*Scared* of me! What rubbish."

"No. It's not rubbish." The line between his eyebrows deepened a little. "It's another aspect of you. Someone I haven't met before. Rather exciting."

"I'm me, just the same."

"Which you?"

She nodded her head in her own particular gesture. "Yes, all right, 'Within my earthly temple there's a crowd'."

"So you remarked before. 'One that's broken-hearted for his sins, and one who unrepentant sits and grins.' I can change from one to the other in the time it takes me to walk from the car to your door. I've seen me do it."

"You're not the only one. And yet, there is a someone who's constant somewhere in us, isn't there?"

He pushed himself away from the wall.

"All this philosophy! I don't care *how* many there are of you. And my 'constant' self, the only one I can count on with certainty, is telling all the rest it wants its dinner. Now I suppose you'll tell me 'my god is my belly'."

"How gross!"

"Gross, my foot. Aren't you hungry?"

"Starving. I didn't have any lunch. Saved up for this evening."

He took the coat from her arm and held it for her.

"Hope you're going to like the place," he said.

He had taken more trouble over the arrangements than he had any intention of letting her know. The hotel which he had decided on was unusual. It had been built originally as a private house from the ruins of a demolished Irish Abbey. The stones had been shipped across from Dublin and rebuilt in a clearing in a wood a quarter of a mile from the sea. On the death of the owner the house had been taken over by an Italian and his Austrian wife, and they had contrived to retain the simple beauty of the place and create an atmosphere far removed from the usual run of hotels. There was a freedom, a casual, almost Continental, air about it that was charming. When he had first suggested taking Irma there she had refused, and he'd only got his way by forcing the 'birthday' note and childishly promising to mention the arrangement to Clare.

"You don't, I suppose," he'd said drily, "want me to ring

up and ask if I *may* take you out to dinner do you? Clare's in Paris this week and I don't think I could get hold of her."

"You needn't be ridiculous," she told him. "You know quite well what I mean."

He'd wanted to ask her if he were supposed to acquaint Clare with every occasion on which he spent any time with her, but he let that go. If it pleased her to think Clare knew, it didn't matter to him one way or the other. Possibly, though she herself wouldn't have thought of it in that light, it was the better way. And if Clare teased him mildly about her, that was the better way, too. To be with her was worth all the little nonsensical restrictions she laid down.

So he was thinking as they drove through the suddenly calm and lovely July evening towards the coast—to be with her was worth all the restrictions. He was at peace with her. At home with her. The Plantations, the new canning factory, Clare and Bellhammer—they all seemed shadowy and far away. Driving with her in a warm silence through the summer evening alone held reality.

He'd done well to bring her here, he thought, as they sat in the courtyard, sipping dry Martinis before dinner. On all four sides, the stone walls rose high above them, roofed by a sky of deep cloudless blue. Arched doorways stood open, showing lighted rooms within. There were other people sitting at the widely-spaced tables, but one was not aware of them. Voices reaching them were indeterminate, a background of half-sound which seemed to emphasise their own intimacy.

"Is it Spain it reminds me of?" she asked him. "I can't place it."

He shied away from that, remembering his and Clare's holiday in Andalusia where they'd first planned to build Bellhammer.

"No, not Spain," he answered quickly and added, "I don't think it's like anything, quite. Certainly not like anything English that I've seen."

She looked up at the walls cutting into the sky. "There's peace here, not—" She didn't finish the sentence, but said "Perhaps the stones were from an Abbey originally, they still hold the impress of peace. How sad the monks would be."

"Sacrilege? I don't think I agree with that quite. Surely it's better to rebuild the stuff into *something*, rather than leave a lot of ruins lying about in decaying uselessness."

There, she thought, spoke the practical business-man, the man who'd used every stick and stone, every inch of lee-way to build up Eagletons. He didn't often emerge from the man she knew, but he was there, part of his make-up.

"Besides," he was saying, "the chap who built it only intended it, I imagine, for his own private occupation. I don't suppose he even considered the possibility of its becoming a hotel. I think it's fortunate, taking it by and large, that these people took it over. It doesn't need a great deal of imagination to realise the havoc that could have been made of it. A smart-alec country club with smooth young men and giggling debs and station-waiting-room food at Savoy prices. Or 'olde worlde' with terra-cotta dwarfs and a table-full of home-made pottery. At least these people haven't piled desecration on desecration. They've had the sense to leave it alone."

"I wasn't *criticising* it." she said on a little mild rebuke. "It's unique. Lovely."

"I did want you to like it," he said, and they went in to dinner.

They sat at a natural-oak table. There were a few genuine tapestries on the walls. The vaulted ceiling arched above them. The appointments were almost austere, yet the austerity was a relief, resting the eyes and relaxing the mind. The meal itself was not austere, far from it, but it was simple with a simplicity of genius. The Minestrone had taken days to prepare. The Mornay sauce on the small, sweet soles, was a work of art, delicate as a water-colour. The duck had been fattened on the adjacent farm: the tiny peas and little round potatoes grown in the kitchen garden. Flavours were kept true, deepened, never obscured. The stuffing—a concession to the English—left the duck a triumphant monarch. It was a handmaid, an auxiliary, knowing its place, having been shown its place by a Master. And the same Master had added, if you desired such frivolity, a riot of sweets, all set out on an enormous dinner-wagon—gateaux of spiralled creaminess, baba au rhum, an old-fashioned tipsy cake, little whole strawberries soaked in Sauterne; a salad of fruits—peaches from the south wall gathered when the sun was on them; small sweet green grapes from the hot-house vine, miniature garden strawberries, a few tender cubes of the heart of a cantaloupe melon; coffee ice-cream of the texture of velvet, topped with pistachio. These for the sweet of tooth, but for those of sterner stuff, cheeses: Brie, Austrian smoked-cheese, Port Salut, a Wensleydale that really had come from Yorkshire and a Stilton that must be approached with a silver knife.

They talked as they ate, talked easily, as people talk who are at home with one another; where the necessity to explain oneself is past, but where discovery still remains.

He told her of his plans for the factory, wondered if he were a fool to branch into a new line. They spoke of the book she was working on, and laughed at small ordinary incidents of their days, and he told himself that he was happy, utterly content and that this was what he asked of life . . . to be with her in peace, the day's work done.

And then, as they were drinking their coffee in the court-yard again where the blue ceiling of the sky had become painted with a few pale stars, she said, "Have you heard from Piers this week?"

The question raised resentment in him and he wanted to say, 'Why did you have to remind me of Piers? Of all of them? Of Bellhammer? Why did you have to spoil this lovely thing? Couldn't you understand that, for once, I'd forgotten them? That I was pretending, if you like, that I was free? That there was no reason on earth why I couldn't love you. And why, in particular, Piers? Why not Annabel? Don't you remember how on that other night, that first night, you said, "It's got to be this way. I couldn't meet *Piers* again . . ." Don't you understand that it wasn't even Clare you mentioned then, but Piers. Piers who became the barrier between us; the condemnation.'

He put his coffee-cup down and said, somewhat heavily, "'The usual letter. He doesn't say much. Four or five lines with 'I hope you are quite well' filling up a couple of them. He doesn't seem to have grown any more communicative."

"You think he's happy, though? Settled down, there?"

He shrugged his shoulders.

"I suppose so. One can't tell. I don't see why not."

"'They'll be coming home soon."

"Yes." They'd be coming home, both he and Annabel. And all this would end, and if it didn't actually end, the spontaneity, the ease would be gone out of it. Their very presence would remind him that he was their father; that they were his children. And even as the thought came into his mind, he sheered away from his repudiation of them. A fine father, he scorned to himself, wanting your own children out of the way. Oh God, why did everything have to become spoiled, tarnished? He wanted to reach out his hand and clutch, not only this, the present moment here with her, but, too, his fatherhood—the children—Annabel with the cloud of her hair falling about her face, David and the Baby, even Piers, poor odd little devil that he was. Suddenly, desperately, he wanted their happiness; his own happiness; Irma's happiness; longed for some quality of assurance, some certainty of a permanent beauty for all of them; for all men, everywhere. Sadness settled down on his shoulders like the memory of childhood. He thought, 'This is an end.

I know it. There is a finality, a drawing to a close. Never
again will she and I be together as we are tonight. I *know* it.'
He tried to shake the knowledge away, push it behind him,
but it remained, heightened, if anything, by the sheer quiet
peace of the place.

"Let's walk down to the shore," he said suddenly.
"Finished your coffee?"

"I didn't know we could."

"Through the cornfield. What about your shoes?"

"They'll be all right."

He helped her on with her coat.

"I'll buy you a new pair if you ruin them."

The intimacy of the little phrase was a balm to his sadness.
He remembered that as he drove to the French Embassy
he'd thought that he'd like to buy her boxes full of frivolous
clothes.

They passed out of the gardens and came to the path
through the cornfields. There was light still in the west
where sea and sky met. The corn stalks were as high as her
shoulders, heavy-eared, utterly still. In the last rays they
appeared luminous as though radiating light from within.
The path was sand-soft, muffling their footsteps. When they
reached the shore, the tide was high, with slow, rolling
waves breaking whitely, noiselessly, round the large stones
at the top of the beach. There was no one about, no sign of
man's existence. They might have been alone in the world.

"Not cold?" he asked her.

She shook her head and he tucked his hand inside her
arm.

"I do love you," he said.

She still looked out over the darkening sea.

"Yes."

"You believe that, don't you?"

"Yes, I believe it."

He did love her, she knew that, but she knew something

else—that it was Clare who was his 'woman', his life—
Clare and the children and Bellhammer and the Plantations.
Their past that had brought the present into being: the
future that would come into existence from the present.
The sheer building of it. The structure that rose, was still
rising, from the bricks he and Clare had laid. Their own
particular answer to the challenge of life. And she knew
something else, too; that, as the weeks had passed, she'd
come to love him with a depth which troubled her night and
day; not only to love him, but to depend on him, to need his
companionship, his understanding, his protection. She
looked back in astonishment to that April night when he'd
said 'Is this love?' and her own too-facile talk of 'friendship',
'devotion'. One word then and one word now and he would
become her lover. And yet that word couldn't even be
thought. She knew it, not only with her reason, but with an
intuition that was stronger than reason, stronger than any
conviction of loyalty or faith. And so, a week or so ago,
she'd decided to put forward her promised visit to her sons,
and this morning her flight reservations had been confirmed.
She was leaving London Airport in ten days, and when she
returned next year . . . If she did return . . . She couldn't look
into that future blinded as it was by these final hours. During
the day she'd decided to tell him she was going, to mention
it casually over dinner, but she hadn't mentioned it casually
over dinner, because the courage she thought she possessed,
had seen herself as possessing, had become thin as a wisp as
the day passed. It was to flay courage into life that she'd
asked him if he'd heard from Piers.

The light on the horizon was fading. It was fading slowly,
imperceptibly, becoming merged into the deep summer
darkness, as this, too, would fade, become merged with the
long night. 'You fool, to refuse life and love,' she told herself. 'Clutch your cold little morals to you! Bury yourself
away from the surge and romance and colour of life.' But

she couldn't deceive herself with that adolescent nonsense. She saw too clearly; *too clearly*. To go down to the 'surge and the colour and the romance' was too easy. To stand against it was the 'other way' which, on that night he'd brought her the roses, had seemed so clear-cut, so simple.

"I brought you here to be happy," he said. "I didn't mean it to be sad. Didn't want it to be."

"There's happiness, too," she answered, and suddenly knew that, somewhere, somehow, it was true.

"You've given me so much," he said.

"I?"

"More than you'll ever know. Sort of opened my eyes to things I didn't realise were there."

"A school-mistress?"

"Ah, no. The 'other side' of things. I can't use words. Do you understand what I mean?"

"I think I do, but . . . " Not all she had given, all she had witheld. She watched the stars taking up their stations as the sky darkened.

He pressed her arm to his side, "There are even times— now this moment I think—when, oh lord, understand me, Irma, when I'm glad it's been this way. Glad we've kept this one thing, what's the word—inviolate. What I thought was frustrating, sterile, isn't that. At least, it's not that all the time. It's as if, somehow, it's shot through with something else. A sort of strength. Peace, I think. As though we'd found a way through the woods. Do you know what I'm talking about?"

He saw her head move, but he didn't see the lids pressed down on the tears in her eyes. In this moment of the victory she had striven for was the desolation of knowledge that, in that same moment, for all time, she had lost the promise of his love.

"You can't apportion blame," said Patty.

Mark piled mashed potato on the piece of sausage on his fork.

"Yes I can," he answered, and he opened his mouth and put the food into it. When he had swallowed the mouthful he said, "I can apportion blame because I happen to know the difference between black and white. I'm one of the few people left in the world who does. The majority, you included, can only see a uniform grey because you're morally colour blind."

"I'm morally nothing of the kind," said Patty. "You've got to understand, or try to understand, the circumstances."

"Understand the circumstances! What you've got to do is look at the facts, my girl. Facts. If you go paddling about in circumstances, you'll get bogged down in a lot of excuses like the rest of this so-called civilisation."

"Yes, but you can't interfere in people's lives."

"Who can't?" Mark raised his head and stared at her, his eyes wide.

"You've no *right* to."

"I've got every right to. I've got a conscience, haven't I? A brain. Intelligence. All this passive resistance makes me sick. If they're blind, deaf and dumb to the truth, then it's time someone interfered. She's my cousin, isn't she? She's another human soul."

"They don't believe in souls."

"Whether they believe in them or not, they've got them. Are we to watch them go to the devil without raising a finger?"

"Whatever you said they wouldn't listen. People never do."

"I see! So if you saw a man walking straight into a morass, you'd merely stand politely aside and watch him do it, in case he might think you were interfering. And you call yourself a Christian! You associate your name with Peter and Paul; with little children and old men singing *Christus vincit* as they were thrown to the lions; with Saint John boiled in oil outside Rome. We're too timid, the whole lot of us, that's our trouble. The entire world's on the edge of hari-kari and the best we can do is to raise our hats and ask one another to tea. That, or organise a bazaar or a jumble sale. Good grief, a jumble sale. One of the marks of the true Church the Schoolmen forgot to take into consideration. Can you tell me of any other concern which would dare to adjust its finances by selling its clerks and typists' underpants for three-halfpence? *Can* you?"

"Yes," said Patty. "The Westmill Sports Club."

"The Westmill Sports Club! Dear God in heaven—the Westmill Sports Club! So the great Universal Church of the Incarnation and the Redemption of the human race is to be bracketed with the Westmill Sports Club."

"I didn't say it was," Patty answered. "I merely said the Westmill Sports Club had a jumble sale."

"*I am not talking about jumble sales*," Mark said. "I am talking about your advocacy of non-interference. What do you think they burned the martyrs and crucified the saints for? Not using d'oyleys? Not selling enough old hats and cheap bathsalts done up in discarded jam jars? Not saying 'Pardon me'. and 'Would you be kind enough to show me the way to the toilet?' They burned and crucified them because they *interfered*. Because they thundered and threatened and yelled blue murder at men who were committing moral suicide; killing their own souls."

"S. John didn't thunder and threaten."

"Yes he did. If anything, he thundered and threatened louder than any of them, but he did it on one note, till even his followers protested that he was overdoing it. So he wrote the Apocalypse to show them. And his one note was love, love, love." Mark stabbed a piece of bread on to his fork and mopped up his plate with it. "And he didn't say, 'Slop, slop, slop', either."

"Yes, but you're not S. John."

"I didn't say I was, did I? Why *will* you keep going off at a tangent? What I did say was that if my cousin Clare has a husband and children, then she ought to stay at home and look after them instead of running round the petticoats of that little cissy, Forest. If she'd no intention of staying at home and looking after them, then she shouldn't have had them. She's been given their immortal souls into her care and what does she do? Leaves them to the clinical admini- strations of that not very intelligent nurse, backed up by an adenoidal village girl and a soured parlour-maid, while her husband sings elderly love-songs under Irma Lovat's three- part-serial window and their marriage drifts on to the rocks. And *we're* supposed, according to my wife, to look the other way."

"Yes, but, Mark . . ."

"But. But. But. That word's done more damage in the history of the human race than any other. You *defend* her conduct. You applaud the fact that she's so busy making fol-de-rols for elderly and licensed whores that she neglects even the children she's brought into the world?"

"You *know* she's been working on the Tour designs for the last three months. And even you can't say she neglects the children."

"Yes I can. It's exactly what I do say. I don't say she neglects their bodies, but she does neglect their souls. The soul of a child needs love. It needs its mother's love. Don't look at me like that. *I* didn't create the Universe and direct the laws by which it lives."

"I didn't look at you like that. But I don't see what you or anyone else can do about it. According to Clare's way of thinking, the children are perfectly looked after. The house perfectly run. If you—"

"Then she's, as I said, a moral idiot. What's more she's a cheat. All women are cheats who cheat their children out of a home and a mother. She cheats that poor fool, Hugh, too, but he hasn't the wit to see it."

"But what can he do?"

Again Mark raised his eyes and stared at her. "I know what I'd do. I'd take off her dainty little nylon pants and put her across my knee, and try and knock some sense into her from that end if I couldn't do it by way of her third-class brains. Listen to me, Patty," he went on, "what Clare thinks or doesn't think, what she believes or doesn't believe, doesn't come into it. What I *know* is, that whether she likes it or not, whether she believes it or not, the day will come when, with the rest of humanity, she will die and stand naked and denuded of her pretty little breasts and buttocks before the face of her God to answer for the man and the children he gave into her care, and God isn't going to be a bit impressed when she answers smartly, 'Bellhammer, three cars and a television in every room.' Because there's only one answer to God's question and it's in a word of one syllable— love. And you know that as well as I do," he added.

"If you told her that," said Patty, "she'd merely write you off as a fanatic. Don't you understand that she *thinks* she loves them? As far as I can see we can only go on praying for them. Nothing else will—" She stopped as the latch clicked and the door opened and Roddy in his pyjamas, the jacket buttons undone, stood blinking in the light. "Oh, *Roddy* . . . " she ended.

Roddy came padding across the floor on his bare feet, reached Mark, climbed up on to his knee, put his thumb into his mouth and wriggled back against Mark's coat, his eyes closed. After a few seconds he opened his eyes, sat up a little and, still with his thumb in his mouth, said, "What are you having?"

"Sausages," answered Mark. "And what are you doing out of bed?"

"*Sausages?*" repeated Roddy. "Well I never did." He

leaned back against Mark's coat again. "I thought I heard Crunch. It was a noise like Crunch. A funny noise. So I camed down."

"I'll get him a drink of warm milk," said Patty "Do his buttons up. He's not hot, is he?"

Mark put his hand on Roddy's head. "Cool as a cucumber." He began to do up the buttons and Roddy squirmed and opened his eyes.

"You tickled," he said and put his thumb back in his mouth. "Can I have some sausage?" he asked indistinctly, and over his doubled fist his bright blue eyes regarded Mark hopefully.

"You can't," said Mark conversationally.

Roddy sighed. "What a cruel shame."

His lids closed over his eyes and suddenly between one breath and the next he was asleep. When Patty came back from the kitchen with the milk, Mark shook his head and nodded down at him. "He's dropped off again," he whispered.

Roddy sat up, forcing his eyes to stay open. "I haven't dropped off again," he said, but his lids fluttered. "Can I have my sausage?"

The effort was too much for him. With a sigh he leaned back against Mark's coat. His head relaxed sideways. His lashes lay lightly on his cheeks and his breathing deepened, became quiet, regular.

"I'll take him," said Mark and Roddy didn't move as he stood up.

"See the little lamp on the landing's all right," said Patty as he reached the door.

Chapter X

CLARE came down the following week-end, arriving at Bell-hammer on the Saturday afternoon. The final stages of the Tour clothes were well in hand, and next week she herself would supervise the packing. No word of the designs had leaked out. Reporters had been, most civilly, kept at bay. Daniel was on the verge of collapse and most of the staff were on edge, but it didn't matter. The thing was done, achieved, and next week she'd send Daniel off to Ischia where he could simmer his nerves away in the sunshine.

Yesterday he'd behaved quite damnably, and they'd come perilously near to a sordid quarrel. She recalled his tense figure, his head drawn back as though from a blow, a white patch round his lips, which were slightly open, cryingly sensitive.

'God, this eternal forcing,' he'd flung at her. 'You're a machine. A goad. I'll never design another thing. Let the whole concern go to the bottom. I don't care. I never wanted all this. I hate it, it's too big. Too *big*. I only wanted to be left in peace.'

Poor Daniel! He'd apologised later, but she'd come as near to anger as she'd ever done. She'd threatened to 'leave him in peace' and that permanently, and though at the time he'd hissed a 'Thank God' at her, she'd seen the fear in his eyes. That, too, he could remember on Ischia. But even as the thought of his remembering consoled her slightly, she couldn't forget the sheer injustice of his attack, hysterical though it was. Where in the name of fortune would he be without her? Still pottering about in his one room in Baker Street drawing dream-clothes which would never have reached the public—that's where he'd be. Still boiling eggs on a gas-ring and standing for hours in a queue to get into Giselle or Swan Lake.

She was relieved she was going down to Bellhammer.

Hugh was out when she reached the house, and Felton brought her tea to the loggia. The place, she thought, had never looked more beautiful, and she herself had never been so glad to be back. Down in the valley smoke was rising from The Nythe chimneys—they possibly needed sweeping, they usually did—and she thought back over the road they had travelled since those uncomfortable days in the old house. Yet, possibly because she was tired, or because of that tiresome scene with Daniel, there was, for the first time, a certain nostalgia in the memory. She brushed it aside, irritated, seeing it for what it was. To compare The Nythe with Bellhammer was absurd, nostalgia or no. To think of their financially-burdened days there, in the same breath with all they'd accomplished since, was more than absurd. She couldn't, in her way of life, afford antique luxuries like The Nythe with all its nooks and crannies and dark inconveniences. She, quite literally, hadn't the time for it. Whatever they'd done with it, bar pulling it down and rebuilding, she wouldn't have had time for it. Smoking inglenooks and bread-ovens and brick-floors and dry-rot . . . She broke the thought off swiftly, dismissed The Nythe, and concentrated instead on the swimming-pool and the dinner-party she was to give for Coré. She rather hoped he'd fix his London visit towards the end of September, after Piers and Annabel had gone back to school. Annabel's dignity would, doubtless, be ruffled if she were sent off to bed early and yet the presence of a child of her age might constitute almost an embarrassment at that kind of evening. But even if Coré was over at the beginning of the month, Patty would have the two of them for a couple of nights. There were times when, in spite of bouts of irritation, she found it not without compensation that Mark and his ramshackle brood had taken on The Nythe. Annabel and Karen were of an age and, though Bill was older than Piers and far more extrovert, Piers could usually be relied on to go down there when Annabel was going. Later, possibly, David and Roddy would overcome their present apparent loathing of one another and become less dangerously hostile.

Poor Patty—so kind, so good, so *dull*. Her life so circumscribed—Mark, the children, The Nythe. The Nythe, the children, Mark. She was happy, though, which was the main thing, and if you offered her any other way of life she'd possibly refuse it. She must make a note to bring her down a trifle from the Boutique. A belt would possibly be safer than costume jewellery, which she would either never wear or wear with the wrong things and in the wrong place. She wondered, casually, whether the Pattys of this world didn't notice, or merely didn't care what they looked like, although, on occasion she'd seen Patty herself look nearly beautiful, particularly when, on some anniversary or other, she'd worn red. The dress was a sad enough little garment, though the colour was good, and Patty with her black hair washed and, for once, no hairpins poking out of the knob at the nape of her neck, had 'got away with it'. But surely she must have realised what even such a make-shift attempt did to her? Was it that she, and Irma Lovat, for she was another of them, had an astonishing conceit of themselves? Considered themselves entirely satisfactory as they were, unadorned? If so, it was a strange form of vanity, or at least complacence. They must, she decided, slightly amused at the thought, be far surer of their attractions than she was herself. It was fortunate, she concluded dropping the speculation, that not all women were of the same mind. It would be a bleak outlook for Daniel, and for her, if they were.

She finished her tea, made some notes about lighting for the swimming-pool, saw Cook and Nanny and the younger children, had an early bath, changed into a housecoat and was going down when Hugh came in.

"Hello," she said. "You're late, aren't you?"

"I got held up," he answered briefly as he took a cigarette from the box and lighted it.

He saw himself in Irma's room, saying, 'I don't understand you. I knew there was something. That was obvious. Why couldn't you have told me? All this talk of friendship . . . '

"I came down on the three," Clare said. "I was home by half past four. I thought you'd be in for tea."

"Couldn't manage it," he said and he picked up the evening paper and glanced at the headlines.

'I can't see any *reason* why we can't go on as we are,' he'd said to Irma. 'Good grief, haven't I done everything in my power to fall in with your wishes? What more could I have done? I've behaved like a priest, never so much as kissed you, barely touched even your hand? I can't see what difference the children's coming home can make.'

"Nothing wrong at the Plantation?" asked Clare.

"Not particularly. Usual stuff," he answered. "Drink?" he asked her.

"I really think I will. Sherry, not gin. I feel I need it. Lord I'm tired."

The bleakness—a gaping hole where there had been light and warmth. He'd trusted Irma, believed in her . . . 'Oh, quit that rot,' he'd told himself, pouring out Clare's sherry. 'You still trust her, believe in her, that's the damned thing of it.' Why was she going, suddenly, like this, all arrangements made, without a word to him? It was the feeling of rejection, the bitterness of the realisation that she had got the whole thing signed and sealed before mentioning it. Didn't she realise that, whatever she did or was likely to do, he would understand as long as he was *included*. The children being home would make a difference, he knew that, but not all that difference. 'You'll make me resent them,' he'd flung at her and had been frightened at the expression that came into her eyes. 'Don't say that. Don't. You can't say it.' she'd begged. 'You can't repudiate them.' 'I'm not repudiating them,' he'd said. 'But I can't see why you say you're going because they're coming home. They've been home before. You didn't take any madly drastic step when Annabel came back at Easter.' 'It wasn't the same, then,' she'd said. 'You know that.' 'But it *was* the same.' he'd insisted. 'What's altered?' 'You've been here so much more,' she'd answered. 'And if I have, what? I haven't behaved any differently, have I?' he'd asked her. 'Good God, nobody could have been more circumspect. If I haven't broken through the iron bands you impose while they were away, I'm scarely likely to attempt to while they're home.'

He picked up the glass of sherry and carried it across to Clare. She took it yawning. "Thanks darling. Early bed. I'm dropping. Nothing on tomorrow is there?"

"I may have to see Carter for half an hour in the evening."

"On *Sunday*? He won't be very pleased, will he?"

"I wasn't thinking of his pleasure particularly, as it happens. We're having trouble with the drivers again. I don't want to face another strike."

He could run up to Carter and drop in to Irma for ten minutes on the way down. He'd got to see her again, got to get this thing right. They'd talked all round it and he'd had to leave with nothing resolved. Not only with nothing resolved, but with a ghastly twisted misunderstanding between them, which even now he could hardly believe had come about. If this were friendship, the 'other kind of love' she talked about . . . He should never have listened to all that Puritanical stuff. Life was *living*, experience, not some far idealism that sounded all right but was too lofty to be achieved. She was a flesh and blood woman as he was a flesh and blood man, and all the talk in the world wouldn't make it any different. Oh damnation . . .

"I wanted to see if I could get hold of Adams while I was down," Clare was saying. "There ought to be another couple of shelves in the cupboard in Piers' room before he comes back. I suppose Adams could do it."

Piers would be home. And Annabel would be home. And Irma would be five thousand miles away.

"He could do it," he said to Clare. "But I think he'd regard it as a mortal sin to be asked to consider the matter on a Sunday."

Clare looked at her watch. "Perhaps if I phoned him now . . . "

"You can't phone the chap on a Saturday evening. He knocks off at mid-day. Surely you can tell Johnson what you want and let him see Adams. Or else I'll get on to him on Monday."

"If I told Johnson he'd probably put the shelves in the car and wash the cupboard. His brains only function when he has both hands on a steering wheel."

"I'd like to find anyone who keeps the grass in better condition."

"Purely because he's interested in the engine of the mower. I don't think he even *sees* the grass."

"The result's the same. You'd better let me know what it is you want, and I'll either get Adams or send Meaker down from Northmill."

"I wish there were a little more time before the children come back," she said. "There are things I wanted to see to. These last three months have ripped by."

He remembered the night of Irma's birthday, when they'd had dinner at Benes and afterwards walked down to the shore through the cornfields. He remembered the quiet full swelling of the sea at high tide, and the emptiness of sea and sky. He remembered that he'd dropped in to her house two or three times a week as he came down from the Plantation. That it had become, in a manner, more familiar to him than Bellhammer. He had 'his own' chair, knew where things were kept. Once or twice, when the woman hadn't turned up, he'd filled the coal-box for her, a silly menial little job he'd not even thought about since they left The Nythe—and doing it, had felt absurdly pleased, as though it had deepened their relationship, drawn them closer. And all this, too, she was throwing back in his teeth. He'd come to believe in her talk of 'friendship', come to believe against all his experience and conviction that it was possible. Come to believe that he counted in her life, meant something. It wasn't that she was going out to Simon that mattered, but the fact that she'd arranged it without a word to him, as though he were 'outside' her life, didn't touch it at any point.

"Nurse wants to leave in September," Clare said. "She's going to marry her young man in October. I shall have to send Miss Hawkins round the agencies again. I do so dislike change. It complicates everything. I tried to persuade her to stay on till after the Coré dinner, but she was obstinate."

"What Coré dinner?" he asked.

"What do you mean, 'What Coré dinner?' I told you ages ago, darling. Coré is coming over in September and I want to give a dinner-party for him here." She smiled slightly. "You're slipping!"

"I *do* have a few other things to think about," he said dryly and he thought how odd the 'darling' sounded on her lips.

"Yes, I know," she answered reasonably. "But this is *important*."

"To you, possibly."

"Hugh!" She stared at him, surprised. "What is the matter with you? I've never heard you use that tone before. It's not only important to me, it's important to *us*. I'm talking about Coré, not Mr. Bloggs of Westmill. Do you realise," she went on, "that when Coré is in England the only private houses he even enters are Maybarne Castle or Staynes, the Maltravers' place? And that when he does enter, he's treated like Royalty? Don't you understand what it means to the House of Forest, and to me personally, to have him here at Bellhammer? In sheer hard cash, I should say it's worth thousands."

He saw himself standing up and shouting, 'Hell to the hard cash and hell to the House of Forest and hell to the whole bloody boiling of designers and clothes and Boutiques and hysterical darned genuflection to dressmakers everywhere. And hell to you and Bellhammer and the nurse and the children and the cars and the mountain of 'things' and the blasted eternal falsity of everything, everywhere. And hell to you sitting there in a forty-guinea housecoat with your face made up as though you were going to a ball and your painted nails and your latest-style hair fashion. Hell and damnation to the whole set-up . . . '

He saw himself towering over her, getting larger, beating down the blistering cool perfection in her, dominating her as she lay at his feet with her perfectly done hair wild as a witch and the forty-guinea housecoat ripped up and soiled. *Dirty*. It was what he ought to do. What he had to do. If anything were to be saved . . .

The door opened and Felton stood there, square, solid, disapproving.

"Dinner is served," she announced in her toneless voice.

'Oh God,' he thought. 'Oh *God*. There's nothing, anywhere. Nothing.'

Sunday passed uneventfully. The Mercers, an American couple they'd met in Spain five years ago, came in unexpectedly on their way from Devon to Canterbury, had drinks and eventually stayed to lunch. They were pleasant people, totally unlike the film-version American, gentle, rather shy and their admiration of Bellhammer was unbounded. Driving them up to the Plantation for a quick glimpse of the place, Hugh was thankful for their arrival, cutting in, as it had done, to the prospect of a day alone with Clare. It was odd, too, he thought, as he listened to Jenny Mercer's comments on the countryside, what a difference other people's enthusiasm made to your own mood. That's what life was like. In a split second, in the twinkling of an eye, it swung over from high tragedy to normality or even to farce. Last night in a moment of madness, he'd seen himself attacking Clare, today, after an hour or two of compliments about Bellhammer from a couple of Americans, he'd gone strutting round the place, pleased as punch, pointing out the various things of note, almost urging them to lay on the enthusiasm if they appeared to slacken. He, the man who could have left Bellhammer and never gone back, who nearly, so he thought, hated the place, was puffed up like a pouter pigeon at their appreciation of 'his' house. And that's the way it went, always. Always. You couldn't count on yourself or your feelings or your reactions for two minutes together.

The Mercers left at five, and after they'd gone he went up to see Carter, but when he stopped at Irma's cottage on the way down, she was out.

He and Clare were having breakfast on the Monday morning when Felton brought the post in and handed each of them their letters. He turned over four or five bills without opening them, slit two envelopes and glanced at the letters inside and then, with a slight frown, picked up the last of them and looked at the post-mark, ran his knife down the fold and took the letter out and read it.

"Good God Almighty," he said.

Clare, a half-smile on her face, said, "What's wrong?" as she went on reading the sheet in her hand.

"Clare!" he said urgently. "Clare!"

She looked up then and uttered a surprised "What?"

He passed the letter across to her. "Read it."

She took the sheet from him, saw the printed address and murmured, "Winton? What do they want?" When she had finished reading, she lowered the sheet and stared at him. "Whatever is Carruthers talking about?"

"I wish I knew. We shall have to go up, as he says."

"The man must be mad. What could Piers, of all children, have done to get expelled? I suppose that's what his 'immediate removal' means, doesn't it?"

"I suppose so. Oh, damnation. I'd better get on to them."

"It's probably only some nonsensical rule he's broken. You know what schools are."

"I don't like the tone of it."

"Like it! I think it's monstrous. I told you when we first went there that Carruthers was a pompous idiot. They're possibly using Piers as a scapegoat for someone else's petty default. He's just the kind to be offered up as a sacrifice."

"Don't be absurd. This isn't fiction. It's fact. A school doesn't expel a boy for no reason. He's done *something*, that's obvious." He stood up and looked at his watch. "How long will you be before you can start?"

"Start?"

He looked down at her, saw her face broken-up by surprise.

"For heavens sake Clare! Of course we shall have to go up there. You can't ignore a thing of this kind."

"I didn't intend to ignore it. You said just now you were going to telephone Carruthers."

"I am. And I shall tell him what time he can expect us."

"Hugh, really! I've never known you dramatise a situation before. You're getting it out of all proportion. Piers has probably thrown a ball through a window, or worn the wrong jacket in chapel or committed some other crime heinous in Winton eyes. I can't possibly go racing up there this morning. I simply must catch the nine eighteen and be in London by ten thirty. Piers isn't *ill*."

Hugh put both his hands on the back of a chair and leaned forward a little.

"Are you mad, or am I?" he said. "This letter states that Piers has done something so serious as to warrant his immediate expulsion. Carruthers doesn't ask, he *demands* our presence. And he doesn't ask but *commands* that we take Piers away with us, here and now, today. There's no question about it, one way or the other, we shall have to go up there."

"I tell you . . . I cannot go up there today. It's absolutely impossible. Do be reasonable, darling. You know as well as I do that I must be at the Palace by twelve, to supervise the packing of the Tour clothes. I have got to be there. No one but I, myself, can take the responsibility. If it were anything else I could possibly delegate whatever it was to somebody, but this one thing I cannot delegate. It's not just a question of a mistake, it's a question of disaster. We dare not have anything go wrong, you must see that."

"I don't see it. If you'd had an accident or been taken ill, someone else would have had to do it."

"Yes, but I haven't. I can't—"

"Oh God, this damned argument."

"I'm not doing the arguing. It's you. Piers isn't ill, I tell you. He isn't in any danger. It's all very well for Carruthers to issue his commands, but how does he know that we can drop everything and run because Piers has committed some petty child's offence? If you were in one of the Services, or if we were abroad we couldn't go rushing up there. If it's as serious as he says, he should have given us more details."

Hugh put his hand to his head.

"Listen!" he said. "Try to get this clear, Clare. Carruthers says that the circumstances are so grave that he refuses to commit them to paper, but insists on our going to Winton."

"Don't talk to me as though I were an imbecile, darling. I *read* his wretched letter. 'Grave circumstances'. What 'grave circumstances' can Piers of all people be in? It's just one of those nonsensical school mountains made out of some footling little molehill. Some of those Headmasters want a refresher course. They still behave as though they were living in the days when their schools were just founded. And when they were free at that. I don't say Piers isn't in trouble of some kind, and I certainly think we should telephone the school and make Carruthers state exactly what the trouble is, but as for rushing up there at a minute's notice as though Piers had committed murder—I think we'd just be crawling to him. And anyway, *I cannot go.* I couldn't go today whatever it was."

"Then I insist that you go."

Clare stared up at him. "Hugh, really! What on earth do you mean—you insist that I go?"

"I mean exactly what I say. I insist that you come with me to Winton. If you won't telephone Forest, I shall. You can talk all round this business, Clare, and it doesn't make the slightest difference. It's just as difficult for me to get away as it is for you, but I still say that there's no argument. *We have got to go.* I'm not thinking of Carruthers. I'm thinking of Piers. If he is in serious trouble, then he'll need us. He'll need you."

"You're merely trying to make me weaken," Clare said coldly. "I think that's a pretty rotten line to take. I keep telling you that Piers isn't ill. You really are dramatising the thing out of all knowledge. You know as well as I do that I can't possibly go up there today. Am I to let Daniel down now, at this stage? Not only Daniel, but the whole staff, everyone who's worked like slaves for three months on this supremely important order? Don't you understand the magnitude of the thing? I'm not dealing with some little local affair. I'm dealing with something of international importance, international value. These aren't just clothes that are going to be worn at a provincial party. They're English clothes that are to be worn by English Royalty abroad. This isn't only Daniel, it's England." She brought up her wrist and looked at her watch. "It's five to nine. I've got to get that train. For heavens sake be reasonable."

Hugh didn't move. His knuckles were white as he gripped the chair.

"I told you. I insist that you come with me."

Clare's face paled slightly.

"Don't use that tone to me, please, Hugh. I object to it. I know you're worried—so am I— but there's no need for hysteria. If I saw any real necessity for me to cause what might amount to disaster to Forest, I'd try and go to Winton, but I can't."

"You can't because you're blind. You're—"

"I will not brawl," Clare broke in. "And I can't stop to argue. If you choose to take this unreasonable stand—"

Hugh dropped his hands from the back of the chair. He took a couple of paces towards Clare and his right hand came down on her wrist.

"Did you hear me? I said I insist that you come with me to Winton. I'll give you one more minute to decide. I know all about Forest and the Tour clothes and all the rest of it, and I tell you they don't matter. What matters is that Piers is in trouble, That's *all* that matters. If you were any sort of a mother you wouldn't want it rammed down your throat. You'd know it. And you'd drop anything to go to him. God knows I'm not much of a father, but at least I know where my duty lies when it's thrust at me. That boy's alone up there, afraid possibly. God knows what he's done, but, whatever it is, he'll need, not even me, but *you*. For Christ's sake Clare . . . "

Clare, her head drawn back a little, stared at him from angry eyes.

"Let my wrist go at once, Hugh. All this exhibitionism. You must be mad."

"Very well then, I'm mad and it's about time someone was mad. Forest. Forest. Forest. There's never any other bloody word used in this place, morning, noon or night. What do you care about me or the children? You don't. As long as *Forest* is looked after, toadied to . . . "

"You are mad," said Clare and she tried to twist her wrist from Hugh's clasp. "*Will* you take your hand from my arm. If I didn't think you were insane, I'd—" She stopped speaking and stood quite still and the anger in her eyes became cold scorn. "You're using Piers as a shield for your own jealousy," she said. "You hate it because I'm successful, don't you? You hoped I'd fail, come crawling back to you. You hate it because I make as much, more, money than you do. You hate it because you can't dominate me and because I contribute as much to the house as you do. You hate it because I don't have to beg you for new clothes as the majority of women do. You hate it because I'm independent, because I've won my independence through hard work. Piers! You know as well as I do that Carruthers is making a fuss about nothing, and that the sane, normal thing to do is to telephone him, but that wouldn't give you any chance to dominate me, would it? You *are* insane. You're insane with jealousy and frustration. You think I haven't realised it? It's been obvious I tell you . . . " The sentence stopped abruptly as Hugh, an expression on his face which, for a moment alarmed her, let her wrist go with a sudden, jerking movement that nearly threw her off her balance. She watched him turn away, stand for a second with his head lowered.

"Go on, then," he said, without moving. "You've had your chance and you've made your choice. Go to Forest. I'll look after Piers. But don't come back here, that's all."

"Hugh!" For a split second there was fear in her voice as she used his name. She raised both her hands a little and then let them fall to her side as though stopping a spontaneous gesture before it was made. She said, "I think you forget that this is as much my house as it is yours. I shall come back to it tonight." Again she made that small halted gesture with her hands. "It's impossible," she said. "The whole thing. Impossible." She turned towards the door, but Hugh didn't move. "I shall telephone Carruthers myself from London," she said as she turned the handle.

Chapter XI

FOR another few moments Hugh stood as he was, then he put his hand to his forehead and pressed his spread thumb and fingers against his temples. What in God's name had happened? He lifted his head, felt in his pocket for his case and lighted a cigarette. He heard the snap of the door closing, and some minutes later the engine of Clare's car as she went down the drive. Let her go. Let her go and, as he'd told her, let her never come back. Let her go to Forest for good . . . He shook his head as though to free it from restriction. None of it mattered now. There was Piers to be thought of. Carruthers. Better phone. Why? No point if he was going up there. Alone? Suppose the poor little devil were 'in a state'. He wouldn't be able to manage him and the driving, too. Nanny? Impossible, with David and the Baby on her hands. Felton? Oh, lord, *Felton*. Irma . . . He reached her name as a haven, knowing it the place he had intended reaching from the beginning. She was packing for Africa. Would she be able to spare the time? Would she forget that he'd slated her? There was no question, really . . .

He picked up the telephone and called her number and, when he had finished speaking to her, he rang the Plantation. Half an hour later they were on the road.

The sky was uniformly grey. Gusts of rain lashed at the windscreen. Every now and then, where the showers were heavy, the hail bounced up from the roads or pitted the milky puddles and overflowing gutters. The cows stood miserably in the sodden meadows. Once they passed a caravan on tow, and he caught sight of a woman's fretful face peering out between lace curtains looped back with blue ribbon over the hand-painted sign "The Happy Rover" on the back door. Poor devils.

"All right?" he asked Irma and added, "Another half hour. Like to stop for coffee?"

"Not unless you want to."

"Think we'll get on." He passed a stationary lorry and said, "One can't imagine what he could have done. He's not the type to break rules."

"No. Unless——"

"What?"

"It is possible, I suppose, that someone else is involved. You don't *know*."

"I've thought of that. You mean homosex?" He laughed shortly. "Possibly have to expel half the school *and* half the staff, if they started on that from what I hear. Oh lord. I wonder. Could be, I suppose, except that I shouldn't have thought . . . " He shrugged his shoulders slightly. "One can't tell. You were right, weren't you?" he asked, "You always said he 'troubled' you."

She didn't answer that, and he thought of how he'd caught Clare's wrist and said, 'For Christ's sake, Clare . . . ' Jealousy! Good God, *jealousy*. And yet, was there truth in that? Not then, not at that moment. Dominate her! He didn't want to dominate her or anyone else. If there was one thing that was true, it was that he'd thought of Piers. Had he been 'unreasonable'? Was it 'unreasonable' to expect your wife to go to a child in need? He could picture her scorn if, when he got to Winton, the whole thing was, as she'd insisted, a mountain out of a molehill. But it wasn't. Whatever it was, it wasn't that. Expulsion wasn't 'nothing'. There must be some *reason* for it, and for Carruthers refusing to write the details. Why did he question himself? He knew well enough. It was because the long steady drive and the mechanical concentration had steadied his anger, as it always did. Had he expected too much of her? He heard her voice in his mind saying, 'These aren't just clothes that are to be worn at a provincial party. They're English clothes to be worn by English Royalty abroad. This isn't only Daniel . . . it's *England*.' He could see, now that he was calmer, that she had some justification. And yet . . . Piers, her own son, in trouble. A child's passing trouble? God knew. A child's need, to be sacrificed 'for England'? Put like that it sounded ludicrous, dramatic. And the heart of the matter wasn't *there*, it was deeper, fathoms deeper. It hung on the old eternal question which has no answer. He saw himself standing in Irma's room saying, 'Forest's partner's husband. As if I didn't know.' Irma. There wouldn't have been any question, any choice, for Irma. 'People have always seemed more important to me than things.' Even things of 'international value'? He couldn't answer that. Irma would have thrown her writing to the winds and gone to her children, but Irma's writing wasn't 'international'. A day, two days, a week's work could have been 'made up' later. You couldn't compare the two things. All this argument!

"I gave you hell, but you came just the same," he said to her

"Why not?"

"Don't be ridiculous. Why not? You could have told me to go and get myself out of my own troubles, couldn't you?"

"It didn't occur to me."

"Didn't occur to you! I bet it did. Didn't it?"

"For a moment."

Less than a moment, she thought. For the time it took for the thought to flash through the mind, the swift 'Why should I?' to attack the heart. And the following second, the in-flow of joy; the knowledge of reprieve, the age-old woman's cry 'He needs me', and everything else flung overboard because of it. But why not Clare? 'Clare simply can't do it,' he'd said on the phone. 'She's got to be at the Palace at twelve, and she can't cancel *that* at a moment's notice. On the other hand, Piers might need some comfort, one simply doesn't know. He's at ease with you.' But she had an idea that he wasn't speaking the whole truth. It didn't matter. Miraculously, she was sitting beside him as they drove through the rain towards Winton. The door, which had closed, had opened, letting in the light again. It would only be for a moment, she knew that, and the reason for it seemed frighteningly inevitable, as though odd tag-ends of half-uttered sentences were forming into an understandable message. She remembered Piers sitting on the hearthrug tossing the chestnut from one hand to another, and suddenly she thought, 'Last year they meant nothing to me, just some people who lived nearby. Now I'm caught up in their lives. One night I happened to come down on the same train with Hugh from London—just that— and now he and I are driving through the rain to his son.'

She remembered standing in Fleet Street, looking at her watch and wondering if she would get a taxi to Victoria and catch the five train, or ring through to Marda Garonne in Kensington and suggest dinner. A taxi had pulled up at her feet and a man had got out and, swiftly making up her mind, she'd decided to go straight home. The man, tall, with kind, rather tired eyes, had held the door open for her. She'd seen him going up the steps into the block of offices she had just left, as the taxi drew away from the kerb.

"That sheet of water down there to the right, is the reservoir for the coastal towns," Hugh said. "The school gates are fifty yards along here to the left."

He vaguely remembered the panelled study, the gold-framed pictures of past Headmasters, the ceiling-high book-cases each side of the fireplace; the curious part-ecclesiasti-

cal, part-board-room atmosphere. It made him feel uncomfortable, at a disadvantage, as though he were still a boy
himself. He wished Carruthers would come and get the
thing over, this hanging about put an edge on the nerves.
If only Clare had been with him . . . The thought, slipping
into his mind without volition, brought him up short. Nothing so outstanding about that, he told himself. Clare *should*
have been with him. Wasn't she the boy's mother? Weren't
they 'together' in this thing? They weren't, but they should
have been. He remembered giving Piers a pound note the
evening he left for Holland. Annabel was there and she was
wearing earrings . . . The memory shut down as the door
opened and Carruthers came in and, with a quick penetrating
glance at him as though endeavouring to assess Hugh's
state of mind, shook hands with him.

"Good morning, Mr. Eagleton! I'm afraid I've kept you.
We were rather expecting you to telephone the time of your
arrival."

The mild reproof irritated Hugh, and he answered shortly,
"I came straight up. I gathered from your letter that the
matter was urgent."

Carruthers went to his desk, sat down and held out a
monogrammed cigarette case.

"Urgent and grave," he said, and added, "Virginian are
on the right."

"I'd like you to come straight to the point," Hugh said,
lifting his head from the lighter Carruthers held out to him,
and he felt that he had equalised the rebuff. 'A pompous
idiot' Clare had called Carruthers. Was he? He tried to size
the man up—the athletic frame, just beginning to show the
usual signs of softening, the potentially heavy jowl, the
slightly too-small mouth. But his eyes were direct enough, a
light hazel, deep-set.

"The point," Carruthers answered, and he just moved
his right hand a trifle as though regretfully acceding to

Hugh's request, "since you ask me to come straight to it is this. Your son has been stealing money and other articles from boys in his house." His small mouth closed, giving the impression of a little trap closing, but it opened again as he said, "It is something that, you will understand, cannot be tolerated."

Stealing! Good grief—*stealing*. The one thing that had never entered his head. He remembered Clare saying, 'They're possibly using Piers as a scapegoat for someone else's petty default. He's just the kind to be offered up as a sacrifice.'

"Proof," he shot at Carruthers and Carruthers lowered his head the barest fraction in assent.

"Obviously. We don't make mistakes about a thing of this nature, Mr. Eagleton." His hand went out to the paper-weight on his desk, touching it as though feeling its quality. "It's a wretchedly painful business for you."

"Never mind that," Hugh broke in. "What proof have you got?"

Carruthers still looked down at his hand on the paper-weight. His head was slightly lowered, his mouth slightly pursed. "Things were missing," he said slowly. "Money, a watch, a wallet. Suspicion fell on Eagleton. Coins were marked and found in his possession—"

"You trapped him."

The hand lifted an inch from the paper-weight and returned to it again. "There wasn't much need," he said, and there was almost sorrow in his voice. "When accused, he confessed."

"Third degree? Because he was frightened into confessing."

"No. There was no question of force of any kind. We found the watch in his locker. The money he'd hidden behind some loose boarding."

"I don't believe it."

"I was afraid you wouldn't. That's why I asked you to come here."

Hugh got up from the chair and walked to the window. "What *reason* could he have for stealing?" he asked. He swung round and faced the Head again. "There is no crime without a motive, even a boy's petty theft, and there surely could not have been any reason for his taking anything. The thing's nonsensical. If he'd been short of money, short of the right things; the things the other boys have, I could, possibly, understand it. He wasn't. He had everything he needed. Everything . . . "

Still Carruthers kept his head slightly lowered, watching his hand slowly move the paper-weight.

"You are right in saying that there is motive behind every breach of law," he said slowly, "but the motives aren't always apparent."

"Apparent or not, I blame the school," Hugh shot at him. "There has never been the slightest suspicion of anything of this kind before he came here. He's always been—" he stumbled over the word 'happy' as it came naturally to his lips, but even as the word was halted, there flashed across his mind all the burden of his own thinking as he stood drinking a quick cup of tea in the hall at Bellhammer the day he left for Holland. Happy. 'He troubles me,' Irma had said. 'There's something . . . '

"I was going to suggest," he heard Carruthers say, "that you had a talk with Dr. Phillips, the school doctor."

"*Doctor*? Is he ill?"

"Naturally this has upset him. You know without my telling you that he is a highly sensitive boy. There's been a certain reaction of course. We kept him in bed in the infirmary yesterday, both because of his emotional state and also—and you will understand this, I am sure—to defend him from the other boys of his house."

"You mean you *isolated* him. The branded thief."

"That's putting another construction on our action," came back the Head's unruffled voice. "The doctor advised it for Piers' sake and I fully agreed. You know, Eagleton . . . " but a quick tap at the door cut the sentence short. "Come in," he answered. "Excuse me one minute. Yes?" he said to the uniformed porter who entered.

"Dr. Phillips asked me to tell you that he's finished his rounds, sir, and he wants to know if you need him for any other matters. If not he would like to leave."

"I see. Thanks Stevens. Ask him to wait for just a couple of minutes will you? I'll be out."

The door closed and the Head stood up and joined Hugh who had turned round to the window again.

"I'm afraid I irritated you just now, when I said this was a painful business," he said. "It must have come as a shock to you. I can't force you to see Phillips, but I do, in all sincerity, ask you to. He's a particularly good man and he'll probably make the whole thing clearer to you than I can."

"Is this some way of telling me my son is a mental defective?"

"No. Not a mental defective by any means. There are some subjects on which his masters tell me that he's particularly intelligent. I should be very glad if you'd see Phillips."

"Does Piers know I'm here?"

"We told him that it was possible you and your wife would come up. We haven't told him, yet, that he will be leaving with you." He paused a moment, and said, "I'm exceedingly grieved about this, you know. Both for your sake and the school's. It is the first instance of the kind that I myself have encountered since I have been here, and naturally I can't allow it to continue. Every chance was given him . . . " He let the sentence go and said, "May I ask Phillips to come in?"

"It doesn't appear as though I have any choice, does it?"

"You have every choice. In asking you to see the doctor, I am thinking wholly of your son's future."

His future. Yes, of course. Where could the poor little devil go? Where was the school who'd take him after he'd been thrown out of Winton for stealing? Good grief! *Was* the whole thing a 'plant'? Another 'Winslow Boy'? If it were, he'd fight it to the last ditch. Let Carruthers bring in his damned doctor and he'd hear what he'd got to say.

"I'll see the doctor," he said to Carruthers, "but I'm not accepting this situation on your proofs only. You're branding a child for life, aren't you? These stories don't lose in a boy's repeating of them. They go the rounds, get exaggerated. Neither my wife nor I are unknown . . ."

"Then if you'll excuse me a minute, I'll tell Dr. Phillips," Carruthers answered, ignoring the rest of Hugh's protest. "I don't want to keep him waiting. He's a very busy man, and," he added, "as I said just now, a very good man at his job." The small mouth closed trap-like again, and then, the lips parting, he said, "Would your wife care to come in and see him, too?"

"My wife?" The words were uttered before their implication had cleared in Hugh's mind. He remembered, with slight shock, that Irma had preferred to remain in the car. His voice was cold as he said, "My wife was unable to arrange to come with me at such short notice. A family friend, Mrs. Lovat, drove up with me in case Piers should need anything." Again he felt at a disadvantage, a boy being forced to explain behaviour.

"Ah, yes," Carruthers said. "I see. Yes. Then of course . . . Perhaps she'd care to go over to the house and my wife will give her coffee. A miserable day. I'll send Stevens out, with your permission." He reached the door with his short, controlled athlete's stride, the just-too-broad shoulders held steady as rocks. "I'm sure you won't regret seeing the doctor," he said as he put out his hand and opened the door.

Gilbert Carruthers passed across the hall and went into the small waiting-room. John Phillips swung round from the window at the sound of his step. He watched him close the door.

"It's yours," the Head said shortly. "He didn't believe it, of course. Hinted at legal action. Possibly thinking dramatic thoughts of the Winslow Boy. False accusation and a third-degree confession. Poor devil."

"What type?"

The Head's shoulders moved a fraction.

"Usual successful man. No," he contradicted himself. "I don't know that that's right. I've a notion he's got an idea . . . " He didn't finish the sentence and said, "Frankly, I don't know."

"Wife?"

"No," the Head answered shortly. "He said it was impossible for her to come at such short notice. The lady is a family friend, so he says."

Phillips let a quick glance come into his eyes, but veiled it rapidly with lowered lids. "Pity," he said and added, "They've got a glossy magazine at home with a full-page portrait of her and an article. Daniel Forest, her partner, or whatever the relationship is, landed a royal order."

"An Order?"

A slight smile touched the doctor's singularly peaceful mouth. "Oh, come, Head. Dresses, not Merit. Forest is what the women call 'the' designer of the moment."

"Really."

The smile still hovered about Phillips' mouth. "An almost judicial ignorance," he observed. "But the fact in this instance is not without relevance. I repeat, it's a pity. I'd better get in there," he added.

"I could wish," said the Head, "that I'd never heard the name Eagleton."

"May I say that you're not alone in that," the doctor

answered dryly. "I don't view my part in this with enthusiasm."

Carruthers sighed. "No. I suppose not. I got nowhere," he ended.

"It's possibly exactly where I'll get myself," Phillips answered as he went across to the door.

Hugh stood up and dropped his cigarette into the ashtray as the doctor came in.

"Mr. Eagleton? I'm Dr. Phillips, the school doctor. Shall we sit down?"

"What is all this?" Hugh asked abruptly. "Do you believe the boy's a thief? I'll tell you, as I've told the Headmaster, that I cannot and will not believe it. There's either an appalling mistake or some other solution. Beside the fact that he's more than amply provided for, he isn't the type to steal. You're a doctor. Surely you know that. And what's all this muffled hinting at 'illness'? Is he ill? I want to know."

"It's what I came to see you for," the doctor answered. He sat forward in his chair, his arms resting on his knees, his hands clasped. It wasn't going to be easy, he realised that. It was all very well for the Headmaster to wave his law of black and white like a banner, though he himself agreed with him to a certain extent in this case, but pontificating about behaviour was one thing and making the blind see another. He'd begged Carruthers not to antagonise the parents, not for their sakes God knew, but for the boy's. Besides, at a quick glance, he liked Eagleton. Possibly more sinned against than sinning. Weak? Not necessarily. Didn't look it. Simply caught up in the present maelstrom more like it. Chap was obviously under a strain, and not entirely connected with this immediate strain either. Oh Lord, satellites in orbit round the sun, cameras that photograph back into time, but man still at war within himself and without, knowing as much about the workings of his mind—and his heart—as a three-month-old baby knew of aerodynamics.

"The answer to that," he said aloud, "is that he is ill. Not physically, but emotionally."

"Emotionally! A boy of ten!"

"I'll try and make it clear," Phillips answered and he wished he were dealing with a nice uncomplicated fractured tibia. "To begin with," he said, "not every boy is a good candidate for boarding-school. He's very highly sensitive. You know that, of course."

'Did he know that, of course,' Hugh wondered. What did he know about Piers? Always the barrier, the non-response. "Well?" he queried.

"You may think that what I am going to say is obvious," Phillips went on. "But sometimes we have an extraordinary ability to miss the obvious. Every child born into the world needs three things to develop as he was meant to develop— food, air and security. The quality of the food and the air are not, in my opinion, so important as the quality of the security."

"Look here," Hugh broke in impatiently, "do we have to go into all this? Can't you say straight out what's wrong with him?"

"Yes," Phillips answered. "Yes I can. I was coming to it."

"Food, air, security," Hugh muttered. "Do you imagine the boy was starved?"

"I know he was," the doctor answered quietly, and within himself he winced at the knife going home. He waited for the outburst that didn't come and, surprised, looked up. The expression on Eagleton's face shocked him. The flesh was drawn tightly about his jaws. His head was lowered. "You know it, too, I think," he said. And he thought he was literally bearing the other man's pain.

"Why should he steal?" muttered Hugh.

"Compensation."

"For what?"

"I spent a lot of time with him," Phillips said. He drew a breath. "Your wife's away a great deal, I believe, and you're a busy man."

"There's an excellent nurse."

"I'm sure. Security is another name for love. Personal love. Parental love, when it's possible."

"And when it isn't possible?"

"Children are eminently reasonable. When it isn't possible, when a parent has been removed by death, the child is still depleted, but not injured. It doesn't suffer from a sense of injustice, humiliation. But when it is consciously deprived of a love it knows it should receive . . ."

"All this psychological stuff," Hugh broke in.

"I don't think it matters what you call it," Phillips answered. "It's as much a fact of existence as is malnutrition if you don't eat enough. Only the effects of physical malnutrition are obvious, and call forth more sentimental pity than malnutrition of the emotions—more's the pity."

"What's injured?" asked Hugh roughly. "His mind? Are you telling me this is kleptomania?"

"It could develop into it. But it won't, because you'll have treatment for him."

Hugh got up and walked to the window again and Phillips went on speaking to his back. "You asked me, just now, why he stole, and I told you that it was his compensation for inadequacy. You are a successful man, Eagleton. Your wife is a successful woman. It may be difficult for you to imagine non-success. Difficult for you to imagine the corrosion of permanent failure that eats into the heart—even into the hearts of children. You know how it goes. The child paints some daubs on a bit of paper and runs with it to his mother. The mother looks at the daubs with admiration and says 'Clever boy', or 'What a lovely picture', or some other phrase women use, and her words not only glow in the child's heart and satisfy his mind, but they are stored in his memory, so that the next time he attempts a difficult action, he calls on that memory and it gives him confidence. But the thing also works in reverse. Where there is no praise, no appreciation, no warmth of heart, the memory stored is of failure, non-confidence, fear. The child, or the adult, is thrown back on himself, his contact with his immediate world is broken. He becomes isolated." He threw a quick glance at Hugh's back, flicked his lids quickly over his eyes and up again, and said, "Piers stole because he couldn't bear the isolation any longer. He'd got to break out of his prison somehow. No man—no child—is an island. He's got to have contact with the others, got to have their appreciation for his contribution to life. Even for his very existence."

He stopped speaking and thought, 'I'm talking all round the thing.' And he remembered how twenty years ago old Milner had said to them, 'Straight to the point, be the point ulcer of mind or body. One clean stroke. Anything else is cruelty and weakness masquerading as kindness. It is yourself you are afraid to hurt, your own nice feelings. True courage is never afraid to hurt when it sees the need. The courageous man will cut clean, knowing that a clean wound heals fast.' He wished he could see Eagleton's face, wished, too, that he could be blazing angry, for the boy's sake. That his anger would obliterate the compassion he felt for this man. Why should he feel compassion? Hadn't he and the woman between them twisted the boy all out of shape? Their own son. He wondered then what the other children were like.

"You're telling me, aren't you," came Eagleton's voice, with an edge of ice to it, "that in your opinion—in *your* opinion—my son wouldn't have been a thief if my wife had given up her career and stayed at home? Do you really expect me to believe that the children of all the millions of married women earning their own livings today are potential criminals?"

"Not all of them. Some are neurotics or develop psychosomatic illnesses of one sort or another."

"I don't believe it."

"You would, Eagleton. If you'd worked in a mental hospital or a remand home." Phillips stood up and walked a few paces towards Carruthers' desk. "The phrase 'Love one another' was not," he said "as some people think, a charming little pleasantry, you know. It was not only the sternest phrase ever uttered, but also the most scientific. Had people listened to it—even the medical people—Freud and Jung would have been saved a great deal of trouble. There was no question of a Welfare State or free milk or plumbing or diet or even hygiene, if you remember. These were all secondary considerations, because, without the security, the love as I said before, they simply didn't count. They still don't count."

"You're condemning the entire social set-up," he heard Eagleton say. "What about women doctors, scientists, lawyers, all the rest of them? What about women themselves in their own right? You're throwing them back into the caves. There are women who have no gift for running homes and children. The homes and children are better off without them. You're condemning nearly the whole race of women."

"No," Phillips answered. "I'm not condemning women at all. Though taking it by and large, I can't think—at least without concentration—of any single one of them who is what one might call great in any sphere, can you? Pleasant, clever, but not great, bar perhaps Mme. Curie and possibly Boadicia. No Shakespeares, Leonardos, Bachs, Nelsons; no Fords, Nuffields, Hillarys or Fuchs; no Churchills. Not even a Joseph Lyons. How could there be? Their biological make-up doesn't give them a chance, when all's said and done. As for condemning them, God forbid. I'm not condemning them. If anything, I'm condemning you and myself and all the other males of the species. Males we may be. Men we aren't. If we were men we'd have the guts to be the heads of our own households. We'd have the guts to tell our wives that a home and a mother's love of our children were the most important things in the world. We'd have the guts to keep our women —I don't mean to earn enough money for them only, though that's important heaven knows, but to keep them satisfied, content. Thousands do. But for the most part they're the so-called 'little' men the world doesn't notice, or if it notices turns up its nose at, because they're not sensational. They're the 'little' men who, for the most part, live in Acacia Avenue and catch the eight-thirty and help bath the kids when they get home. The 'little' men who go without cigarettes to buy Johnny good strong boots and take the family down to Littlehampton in August. They aren't of any news value, and if the novelists write about them, they scald them with sarcasm or superimpose their own nasty traits on them—I tell you, Eagleton, that they're nearer manhood than . . . " He didn't finish the sentence, but said, "We're getting away from the point."

"Why don't you say it?" Hugh muttered. " 'Than you', you were going to say, weren't you?"

"Yes," said Phillips. "I was. And I dodged."

Hugh didn't even answer. Was the chap right, or was it all doctor's talk? He was sick of all this modern mental clap-trap. If a boy didn't know the difference between right and wrong . . . That line lead to confusion, his own confusion and he shied away from it.

'Isolated. Got to break out of his isolation somehow . . . '

He remembered a night when he was talking to Annabel in the loggia and Piers had come sidling up the steps and sat on the edge of a chair in the shadow, not saying anything.

'Starved of parental love. . . '

It wasn't true. Hadn't Clare been talking about shelves in the boy's bedroom only on Saturday. The new swimming-pool was ready for him and for Annabel in the long holiday, and he himself had given him a pound tip before he left for Holland. New shelves. The swimming-pool. A tip. 'Isolated. Lack of parental love . . .'

Pictures were forming down in the darkness of his memory; as though some purely mechanical process were going on quite apart from his own will—old snippets of situations, actions; colour and shapes and sizes; people; lips speaking words; an expression in eyes; morning, night.

Irma, her face half-turned to the fire so that one moment it was in light, the next in shadow said, 'If I had any ambition it was just that——that we'd be together. I felt I had to be with them myself.' Irma went and Philip Sheridan sent a cigarette curving out into the dusk. 'I was shackled by a vast accumulation of things—things, things, things. Now I'm free, bar this lot.' Annabel put the house telephone down and he saw that her nails were varnished. 'He's coming,' she said, and the light flashed on the cheap earrings she wore in her ears.

Clare, a young Clare, madly attractive with red, red lips, stepped in front of Annabel, a glint in her eyes, 'With both of us making money, we'll be able to have so much that we can't afford otherwise. I had enough pinching and scraping when I was a child.' 'We only had an old boat and an older donkey,' Irma answered her, 'but I don't remember ever being made morbid because of it. A lot depends on the parents' attitude to money, I suppose.'

'I lived for myself and worked for myself, myself and none beside; Just as if Jesus had never lived, as if He had never died,' Philip Sheridan chanted. 'We've built up a Franken-stein, a monstrous god of a thing we're chained to.' And then Clare was back again saying, 'I could never be content if I didn't have something to do in my own right. You'll make Eagletons famous and I'll make Daniel famous.' He was there himself, then, too, holding her in his arms. He couldn't see himself, but while he was wild with excitement at her nearness, another self, a thin ghost of a thing, drew away saddened, defeated, knowing something twisted, out-of-shape, *weak*, far beneath the excitement. But he obliterated the ghost and the twisted, out-of-shape thing and the weakness and kissed her red lips and pressed her so close to him that he could feel every line of her body with his own. She should have everything she wanted—the whole thundering world and the stars thrown in if it pleased her. Who was Daniel Forest anyway? His young self faded out, but *he* was still there, standing by Irma's fireplace. 'I'm Daniel Forest's partner's husband, as if I didn't know.'

'Males we may be, men we aren't,' shouted the recent voice of the school doctor. 'The 'little' men who catch the eight thirty and bath the children when they get home . . . I tell you, they're nearer manhood than—*than you, Hugh Eagleton*. If we were men we'd have the guts to be heads of our own households. We'd have the guts to tell our wives that a home and a mother's love for our children were the most important things in the world.'

The swimming-pool. The shelves. The pound note. Things, things, things. But love? 'I'm dealing with something of international value,' Clare scorned. 'English clothes to be worn by English Royalty abroad. This isn't only Daniel—it's England. You hate it because you can't dominate me; because I'm not dependent on you; because I make as much money as you do. You hoped I'd come crawling back to you.'

If we were men . . .

God in heaven what was it all? And what the solution? Clare wouldn't give it up now, on the crest of the wave. The thing had gone too far. She'd brush this trouble over Piers aside as a lot of exaggerated Public School parochialism; the doctor's opinion as a non-specialist's psychological fad. 'Thousands, millions of married women earn their own living . . . ' A mental hospital. A remand home. An injured child deprived of the love it knows it should receive . . . But she wouldn't see it. Nothing would make her see it. 'Go to Forest,' he'd shouted at her. 'I'll look after Piers. But don't come back.' And her cold voice answered, 'You forget this is as much my house as it is yours.' And it was true. It was *true*. 'If we were men, we'd be heads of our own households.' What the solution? What about Annabel; the younger children? 'Nurse is going,' she'd said. 'I'll have to send Miss Hawkins round the agencies again . . . ' The Coré dinner. 'I told you. It's worth thousands to us.' His own anxiety when he saw Annabel's varnished nails. Youth reaching out towards romance or something else, something dark, frightening? The need to *protect* her. No time to protect her. No time to question even, because he had to get off to London and catch the plane for Holland. And Piers himself? What, literally, was to happen to him? Not only in the future but now, today, when they got back to Bellhammer?

'Stealing!' Clare would scorn—if she were there at all— '*Stealing*! What a word to use for a child taking a couple of coppers. All children take one another's things. Didn't you? I told you Carruthers was making a mountain out of a molehill . . . '

"What treatment?" he asked the doctor suddenly, because he couldn't stand the noise of his own mind any longer. "You said something about treatment."

"Yes," Phillips answered. "There's a man . . . " but he let the sentence go as the door opened swiftly and the Headmaster came in, an air of suppressed urgency about him. He swung a glance round the room.

"Piers here?" he snapped at Phillips, and his small mouth clicked shut.

"No?" answered the doctor on a query. "He's across in the infirmary. Or he was the last I saw of him half an hour ago."

"He isn't now. Matron went down to have her coffee and when she went back he'd gone."

"The car?" suggested Phillips. "He's possibly slipped out to it."

"I thought of that. Stevens has already looked. Neither is he with my wife and Mrs. Lovat."

The doctor's brows were drawn together. He gave a sharp glance up at Hugh, then turned to the Headmaster.

"I'd better go over and see Matron," he said.

By squeezing up to the corner of the window, standing on tip-toe and squinting sideways across the Quad, Piers could just see the bonnet of the car standing outside the main building.

They'd come. He couldn't see them get out, but he just did hear the door click shut. Now they were going up the steps and through the arched doorway into the hall and turning left into the study. 'Ruthers' would be sitting at his desk as he was on that day when they'd taken him in there. He couldn't 'see' his father, but he could see 'her', although it wasn't possible to interpret, even to himself, just what he saw, for there was no figure with face and features, but rather a 'knowing' of her, a recognition of the person she was, of the image of her that he held deep within himself.

And 'Ruthers' would tell her that he'd taken the money and the other things. He would tell her that he would be charged and sent to prison. He knew that they intended to send him to prison, although Dr. Phillips had denied it. The doctor, he knew, had thought that he believed him; and he let him think so, but he hadn't believed him, because he was quite certain in his own mind. He was quite certain, too, that the doctor had denied it out of kindness, but he had seen through him.

He told himself that he would rather go to prison than stay at Winton. The barred windows, and the warders stand-

ing guard outside the three-tier lines of cells with pistols in
their belts, would be better—much better—than school.
The deepest dungeon where they chained him to the slime-
green walls would be better. Neither in the cell nor in the
dungeon could Harris get him down on the floor and
straddle his naked body as he whispered terribly, in case the
prefects heard, that he was riding a donkey. Neither in the
cell nor the dungeon could Merriman and O'Brien hold him
down while Manning screwed his arm back and twisted
pieces of his flesh between his thumb and fingers. There
wouldn't be cricket balls crashing into his face till the blood
poured down his nose and seeped into his throat so that he
had to swallow it, all warm and sticky from himself. He
wouldn't have to run over the fields in the pouring rain till
his thin shorts and shirt were spattered with mud and stuck
to his body like another, saturated skin, and his aching legs
could hardly move, and Harris turned and flung a clod of
wet earth at him because he couldn't keep up. Even if they
sent him to the Chair, there wouldn't be anyone to blindfold
him and flick him round the dormitory with their dressing-
gown cords.

It wasn't the thought of prison that tortured him, but the
thought of 'her'. 'Piers, I'm so proud of you . . . '

He saw himself, then, walking beside Bill up through the
fields to The Nythe on that Sunday afternoon when, for the
first time in his life, he knew what it was to row. He remembered, with a strange far-off joy, the sensation in his arms
and shoulders when at last the oars had obeyed his will and
the boat slid along between the banks with indifferent ease,
very fast, quite straight, as though dancing along the water.

Down in another part of the building a door slammed,
and he forgot the boat and thought of the day he'd taken the
half-crown out of Harris's pocket. At last there was something he'd done that Harris, none of them, knew about; his
own secret act. He remembered the pleasure of the dark

smile in his mind and how, during the history class, he'd put his hand into his pocket and felt the half-crown warmed by contact with his own thigh. And *Harris didn't know.*

But 'she' would know, because 'Ruthers' would tell her. What would she say? What would she do?

With a suddenness that drained the blood from his lips, leaving them stiff and awkward, he knew, quite certainly, what she'd do. When they sent for him to go to the study, she wouldn't look at him. She would turn her eyes away—he could see the movement of her head on her neck—and then she'd say, 'Don't let him come near me. Don't let him touch me. I never want to see him again.'

There was almost a sense of release in knowing, at last, as though after a long journey he had reached an end. But hard on release came fear, and the fear spread over him till his whole body seemed to be trembling with the knowledge that he couldn't endure that moment.

He must get away. This time he must . . .

He didn't see the rain pouring down, didn't give a thought to where he'd go, or in what direction. Only one urgent, terrified need was in his mind, the need to get out of the building, to get *outside*, before they sent for him to go to 'her'. It didn't take long. Out of the infirmary door—there was no one about—along the corridor, down the back stairs that led to the games room, through the games room to the far side door that opened on to the nursery field . . . and then the school was behind him, the squelching grass beneath his feet as he ran, head down, into the rain.

He'd got to keep running. Got to. Whatever happened, he mustn't stop. Keep running. Keep running. The rain was stinging his face, dripping from his saturated hair and running down inside his collar. He could feel the cold of it penetrating through his jacket on to his shoulders. Keep running. Keep running. The sodden grass dragged at each foot as he put it down, but the boundary of the field was in sight and the 'out of bounds' wood was ahead. Under the wire and into the wood, but keep running. You aren't safe yet. The slither of leaves blown down in the gales. The sharp crack of twigs beneath his feet. The trees swaying high above the wet darkness where he ran and stumbled and ran on. A low branch whipped at his face. A blackthorn reached out and slashed down his leg, biting into his sock, clinging to it, trying to hold him. His left shoe-lace was undone, but he couldn't stop to do it up. He'd got to keep running.

'God sees all the bad things you do and writes them in a book so that He can punish you for them.' God's got little tiny eyes that watch and great blunt hands that reach out for you. He's peering down through the trees at you with his little goddy eyes, watching you running away because you took Harris's money. He will send you to prison . . .'Don't let him touch me. Don't let him come near me. I never want to see him again . . . '

The breath was tearing up into his throat, and his ears were full of the noise of beating drums, but the wood was thinning. He could see the sky out beyond the trees, and the slashing rain slanting down. He ducked under the wire at the edge of the wood and was out on a narrow lane. Water ran down it in little rivers, and here and there lay on its surface in milky puddles. Over the other side of it were some iron railings and, beyond them, a steeply-rising bank. There were iron gates with a notice board on them. He splashed across the lane, crawled under the railings and began to climb the bank. His feet slipped and he went down on his spread hands. He'd got to get up the bank. Got to. They were behind him now—Harris and Manning and 'Ruthers' and the police and the warders. He could hear their feet crashing in the wood. They might have the tracker dogs with them. He must get to the top and over the sky-line. If he didn't God would write it in the book with his great blunt hands, and Harris would ride him like a donkey and Manning would twist his skin.

He slipped and sprawled downward, but pulled himself up and on, crawling now on all fours, his wet hand clinging to the tufts of grass, his knees sliding and slithering backwards.

It was no good. He couldn't go on. Couldn't get there. He was too tired. He couldn't keep his eyes open. He hadn't been able to keep his eyes open before, that other time in the chapel, when Mark . . . He didn't know, quite, what it was that he was trying to think, but there were flowers there, because God liked flowers, great splashes of blue and gold and white, white lilies. And then Roddy had come running down from the altar and the Robinsons were there, outside, in their tank. 'A safe lodging'—that's what he'd been trying to think. 'A safe lodging'. He followed Annabel out of the loggia into the house and as he went he passed his fingers over a chair-back. 'A safe lodging'. 'Tread softly, because you tread on my dreams.'

With his last strength he pulled himself to the top of the rise and tried to stand, but his unlaced shoe twisted away under his foot and, as his ankle took the strain, he stumbled again, lost his balance and fell forward and, unable to stop himself, sprawled and rolled down the steep, sharp drop the other side of the bank.

As he went, the water came up to meet him.

Chapter XII

THE rain-belt had at last passed on. In the clear evening light, Bellhammer became once more a pattern of white walls and dark shadows, faintly reminiscent of Andalusia.

Johnson, seizing his opportunity, had spent the day cutting the grass, and the lawns appeared as new and shining as though every cropped blade had been oiled. The river, swollen from the rains was high and, as Johnson walked home to his cottage, he saw the swans go up-stream, the male first, followed by the five cygnets, with the female bringing up the rear.

Clare saw the swans when she left her desk in the morning-room and stood by the window. She saw, too, the newly-cut grass and, down to the right, the acquamarine oval of the swimming-pool with the clean white lines of the changing-room and sun-trap on the bank. Once more Giles Roache and his genius had translated the idea, indefinite even in her own mind, into a living reality.

Tonight, though, the awareness of achievement was dulled by fatigue that was near exhaustion, and, for the first time for years, she felt confused, as though her brain were incapable of its usual swift action, and she had to flay herself to do even the small amount of necessary work she had done. That was hardly surprising, for no one could endure the turmoil of the last week without some reaction, and, although she had commanded herself not to look backwards, memory was too strong for her and before she could put up any defence, she was going over the whole dreadful thing again, and again the same questions were hammering at her.

Piers was dead, but why had Hugh been so weak? The school and Carruthers had beaten him. He ought never to have consented to their demand to try and hush the whole tragic affair up. What did their precious school matter beside Piers' life? She didn't believe now, and she never would believe, that he had stolen anything. There was no *reason* for him to steal, and even supposing for one moment that he had stolen, then the school itself was entirely responsible. Just as it was responsible for his running away and the accident that caused his death. And Hugh, instead of what more or less came to siding with the man Carruthers, should have blazoned their false accusations and neglect in every newspaper in the country. But he had refused even to listen to anything she'd had to say, going through the whole ghastly business of lawyers and inquest, police and press in a strained white-lipped silence, almost as though she herself had not been concerned; as though he alone had suffered grief. His attitude was bitterly unfair, and stemmed from the sordid scene they'd had the morning of that dreadful day. Though he had never spoken of it, he still in his heart blamed her for not going with him to Winton. He hadn't understood then, or since, that it had been *impossible* for her to go. If it had chanced that it was he who'd had some vastly important work on hand—work affecting hundreds of other people—would he have left it because of what, at the time, appeared a child's trivial misdemeanour? And, at that stage, it *was* only a child's trivial misdemeanour. Blame or non-blame was beside the point now, but if there were blame, then she, too, could blame him for his handling of the situation and of Carruthers when he did get there.

She put her hand to her head for a moment. All this argument. And yet—would it have made any difference if she had gone to Winton and dealt with Carruthers? You couldn't tell. No one could tell, now. There was only one thing that was certain—that she wouldn't for a moment have allowed Carruthers to shift the responsibility on to *their* shoulders as Hugh had so passively done. Was he himself, now that it was over, touched with remorse because of that weakness? Was that the reason for the terrifying change in him? Or, in spite of all that had happened since, was he still silently harping on that impossible quarrel they'd had that morning? She'd said some bitter things to him, but the chief bitterness was that he had made her lose her temper, lose control of herself, become, in her own eyes, a slut. But many of the things she'd thrown at him were true . . his jealousy of her success, his jealousy of Daniel, and his sheer male fury at being unable to dominate and ride rough-shod over her, the old Adam-hatred for Jill being as good, even better, than her so-called Master. Her mind ceased its chatter as she entered deeper into memory and relived the moment when she'd said, 'I will not brawl, and I can't stop to argue . . . ' And then, most unexpectedly, he had stormed across the room and grasped her wrist in a grip that really hurt, that even made her force back tears at the sharp physical pain of it, and his face had been white with anger, his eyes blazing down at her . . .

She lifted her wrist then and looked at it, as though the mark of the bruise were still there. In all the years, she had never known him to be violent, had never suspected that he had violence in him. And yet—she turned away, nauseated, from the memory . . . nauseated because, crawling on the very ground of herself was a woman who even now, in retrospect, knew a fierce, unexpected joy in that blazingly angry man who towered over her, twisting her wrist till she bit back tears. Like any little cheap man-worshipping masochistic adolescent . . .

Swiftly she forced that memory down, too, unable to tolerate it, and her brain got to work on the thousand things piling up for her in London; on remembering that she must get in touch with the agencies to engage another nurse; that yesterday Annabel had come home, her school coat woefully short and tight, the sleeves half-way up her arms. She made a mental note to engage Miss Kimmins, the village dress-maker, to go through the trunk and make repairs and let down hems.

Piers was dead, but life went on. Grief and shock had to be borne, and yet put behind you, as the wave of life rolled forward.

For the first time since his death she thought about the Coré dinner; the American orders; the rush of work result-ing from the Tour designs; but in the corner of her mind, she was aware of the unopened trunk in Piers' bedroom; the neatly-made unoccupied bed.

The door opened and she turned from the window, and for a shocked second she didn't recognise Annabel in the figure which drew back and said, "Oh sorry, I didn't know you were still working in here. I thought you'd gone upstairs."

Annabel! Her hair was taken up into an Edwardian swathe on her head. Cheap glass earrings were in her ears and a double rope of beads round her neck. She had used lipstick on her mouth and pencilled her eyebrows. As she took her hand from the door-handle she saw her scarlet nails.

"Annabel!" she exclaimed. "What have you done to yourself, darling?"

Annabel's pencilled eyebrows were raised, a surprised query entered her eyes.

"Done to myself?"

The undercurrent of childish insolence irritated Clare, already off-guard by the accumulated grief and conflict resulting from Piers' death.

"Don't speak to me like that, darling," she answered shortly. "I really don't like it. And I don't like—" she lifted her hand—"all that either. I know you've only just come back from school and want a change from uniform, but I can't have you going about with quite so many decorations. Where did you get the earrings?"

Annabel lowered her lids.

"In Westmill."

"Strattons? I thought so. And the nail-varnish, I expect, is mine."

"No, it's not yours. It's my own. I bought it with my own money."

"I hope you bought some remover, too. Go and take it off, there's a good girl. And the earrings. When you're old enough for jewellery I'll bring you something a little more suitable from London. And take your hair down and give it a good brush."

Annabel didn't move. There was not a trace of a change of expression on her face. Her large eyes alone held a glint whose hardness struck at Clare with sharp, swift fear.

"Annabel!" she said again. "Did you hear what I said? Don't be tiresome, darling. I really don't feel that I could stand it. You're quite old enough to realise what a strain we've been through this last week, and I don't want trouble the first day you're back. Go upstairs and take it all off as I ask you."

There was a vulnerable sensitiveness about Annabel's mouth.

"No," she said. "I won't take my earrings off. Or undo my hair. Why should I? I'm tired of being treated like a baby."

Clare's irritation flamed to astonished frustration. The dull headache she'd had all day gathered about her right temple.

"You know, you'll make me angry in a moment," she said. "And I don't want to be angry. For the last time, please do as I tell you."

"I won't do as you tell me," Annabel answered and there was a break in her voice. "Why shouldn't I wear earrings? Everyone does in the holidays."

"Everyone may do. You will not. Darling, do be sensible. Do you think I'm going to let you make yourself a laughing-stock in front of Cook and Felton?"

Colour rose in Annabel's cheeks, her eyes brightened to a vivid blue and Clare, on a swift wave of panic, thought, 'She's beautiful. Annabel—that child.' But the moment of beauty had gone. The colour receded from Annabel's cheeks, her eyes became cold again.

"I'm not a laughing-stock," she said. "You only say that to make me afraid. You don't want me to grow up, do you? You want to keep me dressed in those stupid baby clothes because you're jealous. You're . . . "

Clare was angry now, angry and bewildered, for she had never known Annabel in such a mood. "How dare you say such a thing to me?" she said. "You're an uncivil, ignorant little girl . . . "

"No, I'm not," Annabel interrupted. "I'm fourteen, nearly fifteen. I–I–" She drew a shaking breath and said, "What do you care what I am? You don't care. You don't. You don't care that Piers died. I expect you're glad really. Piers waited and waited for you to come so that he could show you how he could row, but you never came. You didn't mind that he waited and waited. And he *could* row. He did it, and he wanted to show you. But you didn't come. You promised and then you broke your promise, like you always do. And now he's dead . . . " Her voice trailed away, and Clare took a couple of steps forward and raised her hand as though to slap her as she might have slapped David. But she lowered her hand again and said coldly, "Try to control yourself, Annabel. I know Piers is dead, and his death has brought great grief, not only to you, but to us all, but there is no reason for you to be insolent to me. Go up to your room and wash your face and when you come down you can apologise."

The tears were running down Annabel's face, and she brushed the back of her fingers quickly over her cheek. "I won't apologise. Because it's true. You don't care that he's dead. You don't care about any of us. Mark said you didn't. He said you only wanted us to add to yourself, like you want new clothes. He said . . . No!" she ended on a cry, for Clare had come right up to her and her hand was gripping her arm.

"Will you control yourself," Clare said. "What is all this —'Mark said'? What did Mark say? What are you insinuating? Come along, Annabel. I want to know. What did Mark say?"

But Annabel's brief spell of courage was over. Clare's very nearness, her hand gripping her arm, had tipped the seesaw of adolescence on which she balanced back to childhood. Even her angry tears had ceased.

"No," she said again. "No. I didn't mean it. I—"

"*What did Mark say?*" Clare repeated. Tired and confused as she had been when Annabel came into the room, she herself felt, for the first time for years, as though her own control were at breaking point. "You will tell me what Mark said," she insisted.

"I can't . . . " Annabel began. "He didn't say anything. Oh, I didn't mean it. Really I didn't. Please, Mother."

"Then if you won't tell me, I shall go and ask him," said Clare in the same tone. "Are you going to tell me, Annabel?"

"You *can't* go and ask him. You *can't*. Honestly, you can't. Oh, please . . . " Clare had dropped her arm and was at the door. "Mother! No. *No* . . . "

But Clare took no notice. With an expression on her face which Annabel had never seen on any face before, she went out of the room, passed rapidly through the hall, swung open Giles Roache's copy of the Andalusian wrought-iron screen doors and was gone down the steps. A few minutes later Annabel heard her car go down the drive.

She had never been so frightened in her life, so frightened that she stood quite still, hardly daring to breathe. What had she said? What had she done? And what would Mark say to Clare? What would he *do* to her? He appeared in her mind then, enormous, bearded, his voice thundering out. Suppose he . . . but suppositions went streaming behind her into the evening air as she ran out of the house and across the fields, climbed the stile where, so long ago—so long ago—she stood looking down at Adrian and on to The Nythe. What she was going to do when she reached The Nythe, she had no idea. She only knew that she must get there, must stop Mark from—she didn't even know what it was she had to stop Mark from doing, except that there was some danger in it to Clare. And as she ran she clung to the thought of Patty. Patty would be there. Patty would do something. Patty always did something. Patty, Patty, Patty, her feet called at each swift stride.

She came to The Nythe by way of the paddock and the kitchen door, but, though the door was open, the kitchen was empty and she ran on through it into the empty dining-room and across the hall to the seldom used drawing-room, but there was no sign of Patty. No sign of anyone. Through the drawing-room windows, she saw Clare's car drawn up on the drive. She swung out of the room again, and in the hall, sitting on the third stair up, dressed in his pyjamas with his blue dressing-gown half-on, half-off, the collar all tucked in and the girdle hanging untied, she saw Roddy.

He was bending over at a perilous tilt examining his left foot, below him on the next stair. He glanced up at her and then continued with his examination.

"I got a onion," he said. "Like Dad's. Look at my onion, Anna." He bent over even further and raised his foot in both hands. "Look, Anna."

"Roddy," she said, and she dropped on to her knees on the bottom step. "Rod, where's everyone?"

He lifted his head and his big eyes accused her with a terrible accusation.

"You aren't looking at my onion," he said. "I asked Jesus to send me a onion like Dad's and he has. My nice onion. Look at it, Anna."

She threw a glance down at his small pink foot.

"Yes, darling. It's lovely. But where's Patty, Rod?"

"Gone to get Bill and Karen," he answered. "And d'you know what?" He opened his eyes wide and dropped his voice to a loud whisper. "They won't be home till it's *pitch dark*. Dad thinks I'm in bed," he added. "And then Crunch comed up and he got on me and whew! he ponged, and I put the pillow on him and he still ponged so then I heard a car and I got up. Have you come to supper?"

"Is he in the studio, Rod?" she asked him urgently as she stood up again. "Is he? Dad, I mean."

He must be and Clare . . . She ran down the hall again, but stopped abruptly in the kitchen and turned back when she heard Roddy pattering along behind her. "Rod. Go back to bed. You must. You can't come. Really you can't. You'll get into trouble. Go on." She bent down and gave him a little push, but he refused to budge.

"Let me come, Anna. I got my dressing-gowd on. Be a sport."

"No, you can't. Really, Rod. They'll be angry. Do go back."

"*They* won't be angry!" scorned Roddy. "I bin out in my dressing-gowd before."

The minutes were ripping past. She must get to Clare. "Oh, come on, then," she said, and remembered, on a new anxiety, the days of rain and Roddy's bare feet. And even then, in the deep centre of all the turmoil and panic-fear, almost unformed, came the thought, 'One day I shall have a child.'

"I'd better carry you," she said to Roddy, but he jerked away from her, his dignity bitterly offended, "I'm not a baby," he said. "I don't be *carried* no more. Where we going, Anna?"

"I don't know," she said. "Look, Roddy, you must be quiet if you come. You mustn't talk. Come on. We've got to hurry."

"Is there a sosserous?" Roddy asked. "Bill said he saw one. He said it snuffed at him."

"Hush," said Annabel. "Don't talk. Come *on*. Quick, Roddy."

The door and windows of the studio were open. With her hand on Roddy's shoulder to keep him quiet, and with her own heart thumping, she crept up to the west window which was screened by the lilac-bush and crouched beneath it. She couldn't see inside the studio, but she heard Mark's angry voice quite clearly. "And I say you're a cheat," he was roaring. "A cheat. You've cheated from the beginning and you'll go on cheating to the end. You're cheating your husband out of his wife and your children out of their mother."

Roddy squirmed beside her, and she touched his hand to remind him to be quiet. "Well I never did," he whispered into her ear, and he leaned against her and put his thumb in his mouth, swaying slightly against the pivot of her shoulder.

Clare was speaking now and she strained her ears to hear what she said, but Clare must have been standing at the other end of the studio, for though she could hear her voice she couldn't distinguish the words. Then Mark began a second time.

"Yes, I did say it and I'll say it again and go on saying it. And I'll say something else as well—that you and you alone are responsible for that child's death. If you'd no intention of giving your husband and your children a home and love, then you'd no business to have married. Love! You don't know the meaning of the word. Because loving is giving, sacrifice, and you don't give, you only take. You're a thief as well as a cheat because you stole Piers' birthright—his right to be loved·by you, cared for by you. You think you'll get away with it, but mark my words, you won't. There'll be a reckoning and—"

For a few seconds their two voices were confused, then once more she heard Clare's voice only and she knew by the tone of it that she was angry, but Mark broke into whatever it was she was saying and drowned it.

"It's no use your looking like that. I tell you, you are. You had the physical pleasure of conceiving him, you bore him—and then you tossed him over body and soul to some total stranger who had no more understanding of his sensitive mind than a bar of soap. That boy had your father's sensitivity Clare, a palpitating sensitivity that breeds genius or failure, and only you, *you* could have understood it because, though you've killed it stone dead by your tearing ambition and greed for money, you had it once, yourself. Your father, God rest him, was in·the world's eyes, a pitiful failure, though the angels may take a different view of the matter, and you made quite certain that your son would be a failure, too. You didn't give the poor little devil so much as half a chance. Dear heaven, a neurotic bundle of phobias at the age of ten.'' His voice dropped and became even more frightening. "You didn't want him did you, Clare? He came at an awkward time for you, and spoiled the shape of that nice flat stomach you doted on. That nice flat stomach that looked so delicious in a Daniel Forest creation. If you could have done it, you'd have murdered him before he was born, wouldn't you, only you were just a little too afraid of Hugh, because Hugh still had some humanity left in him? It would have been so much simpler, wouldn't it? So much less trouble. And no one would have known . . . "

Once more there was the confused jumble of the two voices together, and Annabel, crouching in the shadow of the lilac-bush, trembled. What could she do? *What*? If only Patty were here to go in and stop them. Mark's half-understood words were seething in her head. There was something so dark and terrible in them that she felt numbed, not with fear, but with some other wordless emotion which made her feel physically sick. Roddy shifted his position against her shoulder, and she saw that his eyes were closed. She made to move, to get up, to rush in through the open door and go and beat at Mark to make him stop, but the movement was suspended as she heard him speaking again.

"You *have* no excuse. You were baptised into the Church of Christ, as I was, as Philip was. You knew the truth. But the truth got in your way, so you turned your back on it. There wasn't enough cash in Christ, was there? No dividends, no snob-value. So you couldn't be bothered with Him or His truth. But you made one mistake, Clare. You imagined that the mark of your baptism, because it didn't show outwardly, didn't matter, didn't count much. You fool! I'll tell you this. Though you deny it and tell yourself it's nothing; though you think you've drowned it with gins or obliterated it with lies and neglect, though you think you've got your little hands round its throat and throttled the life out of it—it's still there. And nothing you can ever do will erase it from your soul, because it's the mark of love—the love you sold, not for thirty pieces of silver, but for Bell-hammer and Daniel Forest's dresses and your three cars and your swimming-pool and Piers' young life and your husband's love affair with Irma Lovat. Why don't you let the poor devil go to her? Why not let *her* care for the children you condescended to bear and can't be bothered with? Marriage! Yours is no marriage. It's nothing but a shrewd business arrangement contracted in a civil servant's office. One hundred per cent profits for Clare Eagleton. Winner takes all and gives bloody nothing. But you're too mean-hearted even for that, aren't you? *You* won't give them the love they need, and you'll take good care no one else does. Irma . . . "

The word hung in the air, for a second, then there was another sound, the sound of footsteps, rapid footsteps—Clare's footsteps on the wooden floor of the studio. Five, six paces, and then the sound changed as she reached the flagstones on the path, faded as she went across the grass and passed into silence, broken seconds later by the whirr of the self-starter of her car.

And still Annabel crouched beneath the window, shaken, bewildered, and confused with this thing she half understood and wholly feared. No longer able even to think nor take any action, yet desperately in need of some contact with another soul, she let her head drop on to Roddy's head and lie there against his hair. The movement woke him and he edged nearer to her, and she heard the little sucking noise he made on his thumb.

"Can we go in now?" he whispered indistinctly over it, "I'm cold, Anna. Why you crying?" he ended.

She ought to take him back to bed. He might catch a chill and be ill. But where was Clare? Had she gone home? She must get to her. She hated Mark. Hated him. He was a liar, a beast. She'd like to kill him . . .

Carefully she stood up and eased herself forward so that she could see into the room. Mark was there. He was standing quite still, his shoulders hunched, his head lowered into his curved right arm flung across his eyes.

Clare got into the car, backed, turned and went off down the drive. At the gates she slowed up, swung left towards Bellhammer, stopped, backed again and repassing The Nythe gates continued on down the lane. Her head was now all pain, spreading from both temples and meeting at the back on a throbbing pulse. She could no longer think with any coherence, for thought was overridden by the sound of Mark's voice. 'You and you alone are responsible for that child's death.' 'You didn't want him.' 'That boy had your father's sensitivity.' 'The love you sold, not for thirty pieces of silver but for Bellhammer.'

He was a fool. A fanatic. An exhibitionist. Dramatising every situation and shouting like an Old Testament prophet. And it was all lies. Exaggerations.

'There wasn't enough cash in Christ, was there? No dividends. Thirty pieces of silver.'

He *was* mad. Raving.

'You fool, you *knew*. You were baptised. Nothing will erase it from your soul.' 'The nice flat stomach you doted on.' The vulgar beast. As though . . . It wasn't true. It wasn't.

Why take any notice of him—a raving lunatic? Even when they were children he'd been an exhibitionist. So had Philip. Philip—a Carthusian monk! *Philip*. But he hadn't come out though. He'd stayed. What did it matter what Philip had done. It wasn't anything to do with her. With this. They'd had their first Communion on the same day. The priest had bent down very low to them. Afterwards Philip had said, sanctimoniously, 'I shall be a priest.' And he'd become an actor! Now he *was* a priest. *What did it matter what Philip was or wasn't?* It had nothing to do with her. 'Pray for us, sinners, now and at the hour of our death.' 'Pray for us.' Those were the last words he'd said to her on that Sunday night at The Nythe before he left for the mona-stery. 'Bye, Clare, I'll pray for you.' And, he'd added, with a queer, half-troubled look in his eye, 'You need prayers.'

Stop remembering. Command yourself to stop. You can, if your will's strong enough. Shut out memory. Don't listen.

'The love you sold for Piers' young life and your husband's love-affair with Irma Lovat.' *Your husband's love-affair with Irma Lovat.* It's a lie like all the rest. *Irma Lovat.* Hugh barely knew she existed. She'd come up to Bellhammer the night they were going to the Embassy. Yes, and then as they were driving to London he'd defended Irma and she'd teased him. But wait a minute! That night when they'd got home, he'd taken her own arms from his neck and politely rejected her. And another time she'd suggested, half in fun, that he asked Irma to lunch when she was held up in London and he'd shied away from it. Too quickly. Much too quickly. Of course, *much* too quickly. But *Irma Lovat!* Those awful jumpers and skirts. And she must be nearly fifty. While she'd been working like a slave on the Tour designs. It must be nonsense. And yet Hugh . . . So altered. But that was because of Pier's death. No, it was before, earlier, back in the spring. 'Why don't you let the poor devil go to her?' But Mark was mad. Unbalanced. When he lost his temper, he said the first thing that came into his head. He always had done and he always would.

She'd been driving fast, mechanically, knowing only that she'd got to get to Hugh now, at once. Got to get the one question answered. Because though Mark was a lying exhibitionist he'd spoken those words *as though he knew,* as though he thought she herself knew. 'Your husband's love-affair with Irma Lovat.' Something generally accepted. Hugh. *Her husband.* That faded little novelist creeping about after him while . . . She winced away from the spontaneous jealousy, furious with herself. Like any little shop-girl . . .

Straight to Hugh, to Northmill. 'I shan't be in till eight or so, get them to make dinner half past, will you?' he'd said when he left. But she couldn't wait. She'd got to see him now.

The thought of him, then, and the image that came before her mind was not that of the man she knew as she knew herself, but of the figure that had stormed across the room and gripped her wrist. And she hated herself because of that image.

She came to the intersection of the lanes and turned right to head for the main road. The lane ahead was narrow, winding, and she had to slow down. It wasn't until she came to the second bend that she remembered, with a sense of shock that was queerly inevitable, that Irma Lovat's cottage was round the third and last bend, and even as she did remember, as the sense of inevitable shock flicked down into her hands on the wheel, she rounded the bend and saw his car, not outside the house, but off the road drawn up in front of Irma's own garage, the bonnet facing the garage doors and only the back of it unobtrusively visible.

Roddy was half-asleep in her arms as Annabel crept away from the studio and up to the house, but, once there, he woke again and demanded biscuits and milk. While, under his direction, she was finding them for him, she was afraid that Mark would come in and want to know what she was doing there, but, although Roddy took ages to drink the milk and eat the biscuits, Mark didn't come, and immediately Roddy had finished she hurried him back to his bedroom. Even then he insisted on going down on his hands and knees and peering under the bed to look for Crunch.

"I can smell him, I know I can," he said, sniffing. "It's a Crunch smell." He climbed into bed and said, gloatingly, "If Mum sniffs him up here, my word!"

Annabel drew the sheets and blanket over him and he lay looking up at her.

"Will you stay till I drop off?"

"Oh, Rod, I can't. Really I can't. I've got to get home. I just must."

"What a cruel shame," he murmured and he turned his head on the pillow and his eyelids closed.

She drew away from the bed, wondering if she ought to

leave him before Mark came in, but he heard her and murmured sleepily, "I haven't dropped off, yet. You didn't kiss
me," he added accusingly.

She bent down and kissed him and he rubbed his cheek
with his fingers.

"Your hairs tickled," he said and quite suddenly he was
asleep, and she crept out and ran swiftly down the stairs and
on through the hall and kitchen to the back door where
Crunch had taken up his position and was meditating on the
sunset, an air of un-sweet innocence about him, as though he
had no knowledge of decomposed fish-heads, nor even the
most remote awareness that the architecture of the place
included two bedroom floors.

He turned his head when he heard her, and looked up at
her with his zany smile, his tongue lolling, but he was too
fatigued after his day's toil to rise and she had to step over
him.

"Gosh you do stink," she told him, and with a quick
glance towards the studio ran across the flagged yard and
through the gate to the paddock.

Once out of the shadow of the old house, all the anxiety
and fear came crowding back again, churning in her mind
with its half-understood implications. What did Mark *mean*
when he said Clare was a thief and a cheat. What did he
mean when he said she would have liked to murder Piers
before he was born? The very thought of that, fraught with a
sickening horror, made her tremble again, as she groped out
after some dimly-apprehended knowledge that eluded her.
Her mother . . . doing that. That dreadful thing. *Killing Piers
before he was born.* While he was still inside her. While he . . .
she stumbled, afraid, in a fog of terrifying innuendo. Dark,
shameful acts came flickering before her mind. Dimly-lit
rooms and things being done in silence. Queer satisfied
faces, figures holding something in their hands, going away
with it to somewhere outside. Someone lying on a bed. A

skirt over a chair-back. Her bruised mind turned away, unable to look, unable to bear the nightmare. 'The flat stomach you doted on . . ' She hated Mark. Hated him. He made her feel sick. *Sick.*

She had reached the stile, breathless, and she put her hands on the cross-bar and lowered her head into the curve of her right arm. 'I can't bear life,' she cried within herself. 'I thought it was lovely, but it isn't. It's—filthy. I hate it. Oh, why did I think it was beautiful? Why did I? I don't *want* to live.'

Over the fields a gun cracked, and the little echoing sound ran through her. Someone had shot a bird, a pigeon possibly. One moment it had been cooing away on the tree, the next it was fluttering to earth, a red stain spreading on its blue-grey feathers.

'No,' she cried. 'I can't bear it, any of it. I hate it. I don't want to live.'

The warm tears fell on to her arm and ran down it. She was aware of her own flesh pressed against her eyes in the darkness, a darkness that was the deep purple colour of her bruised mind, too tender for even the lightest touch, too palpitating and painful for any consolation.

After a while she lifted her head again and brushed the tears from her face. The sky was bannered with rose and gold clouds as the sun went down. The trees were still, drawn against the flaming west. High overhead some rooks went plodding home. She looked down at the stile and drew her hand across the wood of the cross-bar, as though it enshrined something precious, a faint memory which, in spite of present anguish, pointed towards some far hope of permanence; of beauty that ran through the ugliness; of joy that was part of pain. For a moment she looked down at her hand on the grey wood, then she climbed over and ran on towards Bellhammer.

The screen doors were open, and she hurried through the

hall, but there was no sign of Clare in the downstairs rooms. For a moment of acute fear she felt giddy, and she put her hand to her forehead. Suppose Clare had gone for good? Suppose Mark . . . She let that go and ran up the stairs, too frightened to call Clare's name in case there was no answer; in case there never would be an answer. Clare's bedroom door was closed. She swung it open and drew back.

Clare was there. She was huddled on the easy chair by the window, and her right arm was flung over the chair's arm and her head was lowered on to it. She was crying, not quietly, but with long-drawn sobbing breaths that shook her shoulders.

"Mother!" She closed the door, ran across the room and dropped on her knees beside Clare. "Oh, Mother don't. Please don't. Don't cry."

Clare raised her head slightly. She pressed a handkerchief to her eyes. "Annabel, you'd better go. I—I must be alone. Please leave me alone."

For a moment obedience struggled with some newer emotion, a strength born of that moment when out of her own awakening to pain, she had raised her head and seen the trees drawn against the sunset.

"I can't go. Really, I can't. Please don't send me away. I . . . " She put her arms about Clare's body and lowered her head down on to her knees for a moment. "I didn't mean to say that. Oh I didn't. I didn't want you to go down there. I tried to stop you." She lifted her head and said, "Mark's a beast. I hate him. You didn't want Piers to die before he was born, did you? You *did* want him, didn't you? It's so lonely without him and . . . "

Her words penetrated Clare's misery, sharply, like a thin probe going into her mind.

"What do you mean?" she said. "How do you know what Mark said. Annabel, you . . . "

"I ran across the fields," Annabel broke in. "I couldn't

bear it. I thought he might . . . oh, I don't know. I was afraid. I thought he might . . . might *hurt* you, might . . . oh, I don't know. And then I heard. I was kneeling down outside the window and Roddy came and . . . " She brushed her hand across her face, smearing the lipstick on her mouth, leaving a streak of it, a little red scar, down her chin. "He's a beast," she said. "I can't bear him. I wanted to . . . " She didn't finish the sentence. "All those dreadful sickening things . . . They aren't true, are they? You do want us. You don't want us to go to Irma, do you?" Again she lowered her head and drew a long sobbing breath. "We shan't have to, shall we? I couldn't bear it, really I couldn't. I want to stay here, at Bellhammer. Don't make us go to Irma . . . Please . . . Please don't, Mother . . . "

She raised her head again and Clare looked down at her. The Edwardian swathe had tumbled and was tilted sideways on her head. One thick strand of her hair fell over her shoulder and her face was dirty with her crying. The livid little scar of the lipstick stained her chin, and her mouth was a grotesque smudge of bright pink. Her eyes . . .

"Of course you aren't going to Irma," Clare said, though her voice wasn't steady. "Nobody's going to Irma." But in her mind she saw Hugh's car, not drawn up outside Irma's cottage, but turned off the road its bonnet against the garage doors.

"Do you mean . . . " Annabel was saying. "Shall we be able to stay here then? And Daddy? I couldn't bear it if . . . "

"You won't have to bear it," said Clare. "Mark . . . " She steadied her voice. "Mark talks a great deal of nonsense. Why do you imagine I'd let you go to Irma? You're my daughter, not Irma's."

"Yes, I am. And you want me, don't you? There won't have to be a divorce, will there? Ann Grant had one and she said it was awful. They had to give her sleeping pills."

"Don't be ridiculous," Clare answered. "I tell you Mark

talks a great deal of nonsense." But the car had been *there*, outside Irma's cottage, drawn off the road. Hugh had lied to her.

Annabel turned her head slightly. She saw her profile and again the little stab of fear went through her. Even now, with her hair half-down and the smudged eye-brow pencil and smeared lipstick—beautiful. No longer with a child's beauty, but with an indistinct yet certain promise of adult beauty; a woman's beauty.

Annabel turned to her again. Her arms were still round her, but loosely. She sat back on her heels. "Mother?"

"Yes?"

"I . . . " Annabel began and she hesitated, groping after something which, though she realised its import, yet remained out of reach. "Mother," she said again. "Couldn't you—Must you always have to work? Couldn't you ever be just at home, like Patty?"

Clare didn't answer. She sat very still, and even her breathing became almost silent. To be just at home. To be like Patty. It wasn't possible. It simply wasn't possible. All that she'd striven for, built up. All the excitement, success. All that she and she alone had achieved. Her life. Not only her life, but her talents, her initiative, drive, personality—all to be buried, stultified, frustrated. Annabel was a child, with no experience, no comprehension. But one day she would be adult. One day she, too, would realise.

"You don't understand," she began. "It's not . . . "

"I do try to," Annabel broke in. "Really I do . . . And I suppose if Daddy can't earn enough money—"

"Of course Daddy can earn enough money. That's not the point at all. It's . . . "

There was a slight frown of concentration on Annabel's forehead.

"You mean you—you don't want to be home? You *want* to be at Daniel's? I always thought . . . "

"Listen Annabel. You're only a child and you don't understand. You *can't*. You're not old enough. One day you will. Patty *likes* being at home. She'd hate not to be at home. Some women do, because they haven't the . . . the brains, the ability, to do anything else. They love cooking and running a house and pottering about with the children. They . . . " She saw the expression on Annabel's face and broke the sentence short, realising with sudden clarity the effect her words were having. "It really wouldn't make much difference to you, you know, even if I were here. You're away at school so much," she ended.

"Oh but it would, it *would*," Annabel said, and the tears started in her eyes again. "It's so awful without Piers, really it is. I–I used to grumble at him but . . . " She lowered her head. "I miss him so. And I loved him, really I did. He used to make me cross, but . . . I never thought of him dead. And now it's so–so *lonely*. I know there's Karen and Lyn over at Westmill and people, but—oh I don't know, it's not the same. If you were here, we could do things together, couldn't we, like Karen and Patty do? We could go to London, and if I had people to stay you'd be here. And you could take us out in the car, like Lyn's mother does, and it would be—" She didn't finish the sentence, but said, "I suppose it wouldn't be any good if you want to be with Daniel in London, though."

"It's not so much that I . . . " Clare began, and then the impossibility of explanation striking her again, she said, though more to herself than to Annabel, "It's not enough. It's simply not *enough*."

The littleness. The restriction. The broad sweep whittled down to a thin daily monotony. Independence, her own way of life, her own income. She had won through to those things. They were hers, hers by right of conquest. She couldn't give them up. Not even to keep Hugh? The question came cutting through her mental protests, riding on

Mark's shouting voice, 'Your husband's love-affair with Irma Lovat. You won't give them the love they need and you'll take good care no one else does.' But the car was there. She'd told Annabel that there'd be no divorce, but suppose he really was in love with Irma. Suppose he asked her to free him? She threw a quick glance at her watch. It was just after eight. He'd be back within the next half hour.

She looked down at Annabel again. Annabel's head was lowered and she noticed, for the first time, the lovely line of her neck.

"Annabel," she said, "I—Darling it's such a big question, such a very big question. It wants thinking about. Nothing's very easy at the moment. I know you miss Piers, we all do, and—"

"Yes, but you weren't here, were you?" Annabel broke in. "You weren't with him. I–I keep thinking he's there, in his bedroom, and then he isn't. I can't bear to think of him *alone*. He hated being alone, except in his 'place'. And now he is alone. So *alone*. Out there somewhere."

"Listen darling, you're tired out," Clare said. "We all are. And things always look so much worse when one's tired." She put her hands on Annabel's shoulders. "Go and have a bath and get into bed, and I'll send you some dinner up on a tray. We'll talk about it in the morning. Come along, now."

Annabel got up slowly and slowly walked to the window. There was no more light in the sky. The purple dusk had obliterated it. The rose and the gold had gone.

"Yes, all right," she said, indifferently.

Clare walked to the window and stood beside her. "Everything will be better tomorrow," Clare said. "It will, you know."

"Will it?" Annabel answered in the same indifferent tone.

"Oh, darling, of course. It's been a dreadful day. Everyone's nerves on edge. Everyone losing their temper. And then you rushing down to The Nythe and hearing all that raving nonsense of Mark's—dreadful. We're both exhausted. It will all look so different after a night's sleep."

"Will it?" said Annabel again.

She half-turned from the window and looked at Clare, a long considering look, adult, remote. There were dark circles under her eyes. She looked desperately tired. But it wasn't the tiredness stamped on her face and burdened on her drooping shoulders that brought a swift panic-fear to Clare's mind, but the realisation, cold-clear as steel, that between one moment and the next, some warm, living relationship which had been between them when Annabel knelt on the floor at her feet, had died.

"I'll go and have a bath," Annabel said. "Goodnight Mother."

Chapter XIII

'RELAX' Clare told herself, as she lay in a hot bath in her own bathroom. She stretched her long straight legs, feeling the muscles become taut and loosen again. She drew a deep breath and let it out slowly and the tension went from her shoulders, though the pulse still beat its aching rhythm at the back of her neck.

Quarter of an hour. In a quarter of an hour Hugh would come back from 'Northmill'. In a quarter of an hour . . . Would he lie the whole thing out? Brush it aside? Pretend there was nothing in it? If only she knew, were certain, she could handle the situation with a firm touch, coolly, as she'd so often handled Daniel's 'temperament'. But suppose it were true? Suppose . . . No, she wouldn't even consider the supposition again. To do so was to flay herself; weaken herself and she needed all her strength. All her balance. She stepped out of the bath and wrapped the warm bath-sheet round her.

She was sitting at her dressing-table powdering her face when Felton knocked and came in. She saw her reflection behind her in the glass, the disapproving lips and slightly-protruding eyes—envious eyes, wary.

"Yes, Felton?"

"Will you have your dinner on a tray?" Felton asked. "The master telephoned while you were in your bath and he won't be back till half-past nine or ten. He said not to wait as he'd have something out. He's been delayed."

The dull, unemotional voice droned its message into the

gold-lit faintly-scented bedroom. The shell-white draped walls gathered it up and tossed it back to the crystal bottles on the dressing-table. Clare's right hand holding the powder-puff, lowered slightly, her lids flicked down before Felton's reflected stare, then she raised them again and met the wary eyes in the glass.

"Thank you, Felton. Yes, a tray will do. I'll have it in the morning-room. Has Cook sent something up to Annabel?"

"She's having it now. Chicken salad and some raspberries and cream."

"Yes. Not too heavy. Right, Felton. And just some chicken salad for me, too, please. No soup. You might open a half-bottle of Liebfraumilch, will you?"

The wary, envious eyes were watching her, she knew that, watching for the slightest sign of weakness, the slightest clue to the 'trouble' which more than possibly she already knew all about.

She raised the powder-puff and laid it meticulously against her forehead with a steady rocking movement, pressing the powder into her skin. Then she put it down and picked up her eyebrow brush and bent forward towards the glass.

"Thank you, Felton. I'll be down in five minutes."

She watched the squat back with the thick buttocks in the glass, as it receded out of the circle of the dressing-light, saw the door open and close again. She put down the eyebrow pencil and sat very still. Very still indeed.

She ate the chicken salad and drank the wine. Commanding herself to swallow the food, clamping down on thought, pushing the clamour of it back beyond the barrier of her mind, beyond the throbbing insistence of the pain in her head.

"I'll have my coffee in the loggia," she told Felton, when she came for the tray. "Has Annabel finished?"

"Finished and fast asleep," Felton answered shortly.

"Worn out," she added, her mouth tightening into little vertical lines.

Clare didn't answer. She left the morning-room and walked across the hall into the loggia. Felton had switched on the small table-lamp. It lighted one of Giles Roache's chaise-longues, the table itself and a wrought-iron magazine-stand, but beyond the radius the loggia was in shadow; shadowed pillars twined with the Clare Eagleton climbing rose, framed a sky-full of stars.

She stood at the top of the steps looking out over the dusky garden till Felton brought her coffee, then she returned and lay back in the chaise-longue and, as though Felton's disappearing back were the signal for release, the barrier in her mind went down.

So it was true. Now, when Piers had only been dead a week. The humiliation. Easier to bear had Irma been young, beautiful. She wasn't young or beautiful. She was middle-aged, nearly old. There was something sordid about it, an elderly woman's desperate, final grabbing at youth, entangling a man younger than herself; battening on him. Mark had been right. He'd *known*. Possibly they all knew—Felton and Cook and Johnson. Everyone, but she herself. The bitterness. You could almost taste it on the tongue. 'A cheat!' It was a lie. She'd told Hugh from the beginning that she intended to have her own career, that the little round of a house wasn't enough. He'd known it. Understood it. They'd been partners. Or so she'd thought. But he'd failed her. So *weak*. The same weakness that had let him toady to Carruthers. Piers' death. 'Alone out there somewhere.' Annabel had knelt at her feet, crying. Pressure on pressure. Day after day of it. No wonder control snapped. Alone 'out there'. Where? Oblivion? The mind shied away from that. 'In the sight of the unwise they seemed to die, but they are at peace.' The Convent. The Rev. Mother marshalled the blue-uniformed line of them into the chapel. It was

Easter and there were lilies on the altar. 'Now is Christ risen from the dead.' Sister Philomena sat in the garden, all billowing habit and clicking rosary underneath the apple-blossom. 'He conquered death and is alive for evermore. His undying life flows through His Church as the sap flows through the trees and brings the blossom. Through you, Mary. And you, Catherine. And you Clare.' 'Tell me about S. Clare, Sister.' 'She was the friend of S. Francis of Assisi, the Little Poor Man of God. And she gave up riches to become poor, too.' 'Why did she?' 'Because she loved Our Lord so much that she couldn't be bothered with a single thing that came between her and Him. And like S. Francis, she spent her whole life loving God's children.' And then Sister Agnes chipped in with her Irish brogue to say, 'And haven't they given you the grand name to live up to—and you always admiring yourself every time you pass the pane of glass in the garden door, as if I hadn't seen you with my own two eyes.' You would be holy, like S. Clare. You would be poor. You would become a nun and have a gentle smile and your eyes would shine with love. Oh, *childhood*. Piers. My son. 'Sensitive, like your father. Only you could have understood.' Hadn't Mark created enough havoc? Annabel in tears, shocked by his raving. Annabel. There was a new vital relationship between them—and then, change. 'I'll go and have a bath,' she'd said. 'Goodnight Mother.' Don't go, Annabel. Don't leave me. Don't . . .

The headlights swept over the loggia as Hugh's car came up the drive, passed and left it in shadow again. The engine beat ceased. She heard the low grind of the doors on the rollers as they swung together, heard his footsteps coming along the path, then his figure blocked out the pillar-framed stars as he walked up the steps.

"Hello. Lovely night," he said. "Sorry I couldn't get back for dinner." He sat down, but got up again and said, "Think I'll have a drink. You?"

"No, thank you."

He went over to the tray and she heard the fizzing of the soda-water. "Felton give you my message?"

"Yes."

He came back into the circle of the light and shot a look at her. "Thought she might have forgotten," he said as he sat down. "Lord, I'm tired. I don't know what's the matter with the men these days. One trouble-maker and—"

"Don't go on, Hugh."

He was lifting the glass to drink, but he checked the movement and looked across at her, frowning. "What is it?"

"I hate pretence," she said. "Hate it. I know it all. I know where you've been. There's no need to lie."

He drank then and said, "And what is it you know? Or think you know?" he asked.

"I know that you've been with Irma Lovat," she answered. "I know that you're having what's called an 'affair' with her. I know . . . " She stopped and he lowered his head a little and said, "I see. May I ask who told you I'd been having an 'affair'—wretched word—with Irma?"

"Does it matter who told me? Everyone knows. Felton, Cook, the whole village. And I have the evidence of my own eyes. I saw your car outside her cottage this evening."

"I see," he said again.

"I trusted you," she went on. "I believed in you. I . . . " her voice trembled, but she recovered her balance and said, "While I was working to the very limit of my capacity in London, you were . . . " The sentence went unfinished and she said, "There's something so distasteful in it, a woman older than yourself. A woman who was supposed to be our friend."

He stood up and went across the room, out of the radius of the table-lamp and she saw his shadowed figure against the night. He hadn't denied it. She felt suddenly cold. She closed her eyes.

"Let's at least get the facts in proportion," she heard him say. "You were working to the limit of your capacity in London because you wanted to work to the limit of your capacity in London. It's not like you to fog the issue."

"So that's the line it's to be," she said. "I'm the culprit. The scapegoat. You're going to blame me, as Mark blamed me. If I hadn't . . ."

"Mark? What's Mark to do with it?" he broke in.

She hadn't intended to bring Mark's name into it. She was too tired.

"Because it was Mark who told me. What does it matter? They all know. And you're going to swing it back on to my shoulders aren't you, Hugh? You're going to twist out of any responsibility as you twisted out of your handling of Carruthers. You didn't defend your own son. And you aren't going to defend your so-called love for Irma."

She thought that it was as though she were beating with impotent hands on a locked steel door. Beating to make some impress. To break through.

He didn't answer, and as the silence increased she tensed her hands on the chair-arms. Involuntarily she recalled the morning of Piers' death when he had come across the room and gripped her wrist. She tried to obliterate the memory, but it was there now, part of the pattern of her life. Whatever she did, whatever happened to her, it would still be there, filed away in its place, one of the sequence of acts of which her life was composed. He had been half-turned towards the garden, now he moved and faced her.

"It's time this thing was thrashed out," he said. "I shouldn't have brought it up tonight, but you have. Now we'll have to go through with it."

There was sadness underlying his words which shocked her more than the anger she had expected, as though the steel door on which she'd been beating had swung open at a light touch.

"There are some things about Piers' death that you don't know," he said. "I hadn't told you, because I thought we'd have both been through enough for the time being." He came forward a couple of steps and laid his hands on the back of an upright chair. "There was no doubt, Clare, that Piers had stolen. No doubt at all. You've imagined that I accepted the school's ruling without question. I didn't." He stopped speaking for a moment and then said, "That morning at Winton, I didn't only see Carruthers, I saw Dr. Phillips. I didn't know then, but I do know now, that Phillips was a specialist in child psychology. He had to give up his London practice for his own reasons—I believe his wife had polio and is a total invalid, something of the kind. It doesn't matter. Carruthers consulted him about Piers. Phillips had spent some time with Piers, Clare. He knew him. He knew him better than we did, because neither of us had the time to know him. We were too busy with our own lives. No," he said, as Clare began to speak, "don't say anything yet. Let me finish." He rocked the chair towards him, then set it back to stand on the floor. "To begin with he told me that Piers should never have gone to a boarding-school. He assumed I knew it. I didn't know it. I knew, you knew, that he was—different. That there was 'something' wrong, but we didn't want to know it. To know it would have been an inconvenience to us. When he was born—" he stopped and sent her a swift glance, then said, "There's no point in speaking of that, now. It's too far back. What Phillips said to me was this 'You're a successful man, Eagleton. Your wife is a successful woman. Possibly neither of you can imagine failure—a permanent failure that eats into the heart, even into the hearts of children.' Piers was a failure, Clare. He was a failure because neither of us had the time to give him the understanding and encouragement he longed for. Oh yes, I know we had nurses. The present nurse. The one before her, Nurse Dickson. The one before that, Rogers or whatever her name was. Five altogether wasn't it? Good enough, all of them, but *changing*, nothing secure. All right for the others, perhaps, though . . . I don't know. I . . . "

But Clare had had enough. She swung from the chaise-longue and came towards him.

"So you *are* blaming me!" She raised her hand and let it fall again. "The injustice . . . " she began, but that sentence, too, was broken. "You think I didn't love Piers, don't you? You think I didn't care that he died? I did care. Because I don't show my feelings, don't cry and make a scene . . . And now you swing the whole burden on to me. It's so unfair. So bitterly unfair."

"You're wrong, Clare. I told you what Phillips said, because, ever since Piers' death, you've believed that I went hand-in-glove with Carruthers to keep the whole thing as quiet as possible. I did. I did because I knew the kind of horror that could be made of it if the thing became a press story. There wasn't any question of my shielding Carruthers. I was shielding myself. And you. There was nothing to shield Carruthers from. Winton can't be condemned for our handling of Piers. What Piers was, he was before he went to Winton. He stole because he had to break out of his isolation somehow. The isolation we, God help us, had forced on him. But I don't blame you." He lowered his head and raised it again. "You say I was weak with Carruthers. No. I . . . " He lifted his hands from the chair and half turned away from her, then swung round and faced her again. "I'm going to tell you something else. When I married you, I loved you to the point of idiocy. You know that. My one thought was your happiness. I wanted to give you every-thing. Nothing was too much. We lived at The Nythe. I hoped you'd love the old place as I did. You didn't. That didn't matter so much. But soon after Annabel was born you told me you wanted to go back to Forest. You wanted to make money so that we could leave The Nythe. You wanted your own career. You said, 'I've got to have something in my own right.' You've possibly forgotten that night long ago. I haven't. Because I knew, even as I agreed with you, that I disagreed. Inwardly, another man in me was saying, 'We're married now. W've got a child. We'll possibly have other children. What's the size or shape of a house matter beside a home. A proper home where the children grow up in peace?' That's what the other self said. But I hadn't the courage to stand by what I really thought. I was afraid you'd despise me, think I was old-fashioned, a lagger in your swift world. You went back to Forest. I let you go back to Forest and gradually Forest and all his concerns absorbed you, as my work absorbed me. When Piers was coming, it went through my mind that you'd give it up, but by then you'd got back into that world and you couldn't leave it. You took a month off. It was long enough because Piers was put on a bottle immediately so that you could get back in record time . . . " He lifted his hand and let it fall to his side again. "I'm not blaming you. You'd got on a line and you were stopping on it. And I hadn't the guts to say, 'You're my wife and that's my son and I intend to have him fed naturally and Forest can go to hell.' Perhaps if I had said it Piers would be alive now."

"Hugh! What are you saying? All this—this—"

"Yes, and I'm not done yet," he broke in. "I told you when we started that we'd go on to the end—and we're going on to the end. The time for pretence and hedging's gone. The time for saying one thing and thinking another's gone. It went the day Piers was drowned. When I came in tonight you accused me of having an 'affair' with Irma. I had no 'affair' with Irma—though God knows it wasn't my fault that I didn't. She—" a twisted half-smile touched his lips—"she didn't see it that way. A year, eighteen months ago, Forest became news. You, as you said you would, had made him famous. By that time even your week-ends—most of them—belonged to your work. Oh, I don't deny that you still ordered the material side of the place by a species of remote control, plus Cook and Felton and Johnson and Nurse and the adenoidal child from the village and the daily. We still got meals and the bath was cleaned. One night I came down from London with Irma. I drove her back to her place and I stopped for a drink. I got to know her. You said at the beginning of all this that there was 'something distasteful' in our relationship, because she was 'supposed to be' our friend. There wasn't much supposition about it. She was my friend, But she was yours, too. Oh yes, there was a time when I first got to know her that I'd have been her lover if she'd have had me. She wouldn't. She wasn't even remotely 'in love' with me. And even if she had been, to her I was married to you—and that was that. You said you saw my car outside her place this evening. Maybe. I didn't happen to have driven it there. Two days ago Irma flew to Nairobi, to Simon. And when she leaves Nairobi she's going on to Philip in India. Don't get it into your head that she's going 'because of me'. She isn't. She'd fixed it long before I knew anything about it. She's going simply because she'd promised she'd go this year. Tonight Harcourt took my car down there to pick up a lawn mower we'd lent her when her's went wrong. He would have gone in a van but there wasn't one available." He drew a breath, then said, "And that's Irma disposed of."

Clare was staring at him, her lips pressed closely together.

"What is all this?" she asked again. "What are you saying? What are you . . . ?"

"I'm telling you the truth," he broke in. "All the truth. About everything."

"It's not the truth. You're exaggerating. Dramatising the whole thing. All this masochism."

"There's no exaggeration. No masochism."

"You say you blame yourself, but in your heart you blame

me. You're inferring that if I hadn't gone to Daniel, Piers . . . " She let that go and said, "It's not *true*. You're inferring that if . . . " she raised her hand to her forehead. "How could one go on living if . . . "

Behind her hand raised to her eyes, the clamour of her mind was unendurable, a churning sea of voices shouting at her, crying to her, hammering at her with cold reason. They were trying to break her because she was a woman in a man's world. Because she'd succeeded in her own right. All down the centuries the twisted injustice was there. The child-bearer. The vehicle for the production and care of the next generation. Nothing, nothing but that. From the beginning of time till now, today. 'The woman tempted me . . . ' Always the shame, the blame, the burden. Women thought they'd escaped, but they hadn't. The centuries-old chains were still shackling them to the earth. Child-bearer. Mother. Home-maker. And all the fighting and strife were futile. It hadn't got them anywhere. It never would get them anywhere, because life itself, the sheer biological facts of it always threw them back again. Oh, yes, they were let out of their prison to play a little, to dance on the edge of the male world and pretend to themselves that there were no barriers, no differences, but nothing in heaven or earth could alter the fundamental fact. Mother. *Mother. Mother.*

"I don't blame you," she heard Hugh say. "God knows I don't, Clare. I tell you, I blame myself. I wanted to give you 'everything', but the one thing I didn't give you was . . . content."

Content. He didn't understand. The divide between them was too deep the life-divide of the man and the woman. The two points of view that could never be bridged. Never? Or was there some way across? Blindly, she groped for that way.

"You're condemning half the world," she said.

"Is the action of the masses always the right action?" she

heard him say. "It isn't, Clare. Are women dressed up in Daniel Forest's creations of more value than our children's lives?"

The child-bearer. The home-maker. The mother.

She raised her head. "You're telling me to give up my career, aren't you? You're telling me to leave Daniel, now, when all I've worked for, all I've fought for, is achieved. You're telling me to throw away my brains . . . Haven't I got a right to life, too? *Your* life will go on. You'll still have your freedom . . . "

She saw the white pain stamped about his mouth and her heart sickened.

"Have you had so much freedom, Clare?" he said. "For the last five years, you've been chained hand and foot to designing. You haven't even had freedom for your own family. Aren't we all shackled always, all the time to one thing or another? To our cars, our amusements, our comforts, our very way of life. Freedom? With Eagletons to run? Ah, no. As for your brains, your talent—couldn't you use them for us for a bit? For your family. The children. Even for Eagletons if you saw it that way. And Annabel needs you, Clare. That night back in the spring when I was going to Holland—the last night I saw Piers alive—she came to say goodbye to me. She'd decked herself out in cheap glass earrings and nail-varnish. She looked like a prostitute. I know I ought to have said something to her but I hadn't the time. All the way to London it troubled me, because I couldn't make up my mind if it were just a child's dressing up, or something else, something—frightening. And after I'd been to Hinton's and was crossing Leicester Square . . . " He didn't finish the sentence, but said instead, "You've never seen Annabel looking like that. You'll say I'm exaggerating again. I'm not."

But she had seen Annabel looking 'like that'. Today. This evening. It had been the start of it all—of all this piled-up avalanche of grief and bewilderment and injustice and fear; of old forgotten things storming into the mind; of Piers and Mark and Daniel and Annabel and Hugh and life and death——an avalanche which even now was sweeping towards her, to engulf her, carry her away. She lowered her head again.

"And I need you," she heard him say. "I need you so desperately, Clare."

Silence closed round his voice. She heard the sound of the last London train going down the line the other side of the river.

"Is it such a terrible thing for a man to ask his wife to come home?" he said, as the bumpy noise of the train was swallowed up by the night. "Is it, Clare?" he said again. "Is it?"

Mark lay beside Patty in the four-poster they'd bought for a song at the second-hand shop in Westmill when they first came to The Nythe. The windows were open, and every now and then the curtains blew forward into the room, just as they'd blown forward on summer nights when William Eagleton lay in bed in that same room, the dream of a flame-coloured rose in his eyes.

"I lost my temper," Mark said. "I said the most awful things to her. I vowed last week that I'd never lose my temper again, and then, when she came in, I did. Oh lord, Patty."

"I don't suppose she'll take it seriously," Patty answered. "She knows about your temper. A bit of temper doesn't hurt all that."

"You don't understand," Mark said. "You weren't there. I accused her of killing Piers."

"Oh, darling! Oh, poor Clare! That was dreadful. He's only been dead . . . "

"Don't tell me. I'm not a fool. I know. And that's not all.

I told her that her husband was running after Irma Lovat, and why didn't she let him go to her and take the children with him if she couldn't be bothered with any of them."

He felt Patty's body become still. He could hardly hear her breathing.

"There you are," he said, "Even you bludgeoned into silence. Oh lord. *Why did I do it?* I'd just stubbed my bunion on the corner of the cupboard and it was all red-hot wires, and then she came prancing in decked out in the latest Daniel Forest, and I thought of that child sitting beside me in the chapel asking me if God wrote all the bad things you did in a book so that He could punish you for them, and I let fly."

Patty groped for his hand and held it. She tried to feel out into what he'd told her, to assess it, find some centre in it. There was a centre. There must be, because he hadn't said those things to Clare maliciously. In a way, he was right. But the wound to Clare! The hurt. Coming so soon after Piers' death. How would it affect her? Affect them all? If, because of what he'd said, there were a l reak in their lives, he'd never forgive himself.

"I had to be Almighty God and judge them," she heard him say. "I had to list all their faults and sins and point them out to them in case He couldn't manage the job. Oh, *lord*, Patty. Suppose she does leave them . . . "

"She won't leave them."

"How do you know she won't leave them? You don't know."

"I'm sure she won't."

"Sure! You can't be sure. No one can be sure, How can you be sure?"

Patty didn't answer, and again he said, "How can you be sure?"

"Because I think I understand Clare," Patty answered. "A bit, anyway. She's played straight as she sees it. I'm sure she has. And, in her way, she's loved them. She has, Mark. She's honest. But I don't think she's realised . . . " She didn't finish the sentence and said, "It's hard, sometimes, to be a woman."

"What's hard about it?"

So many things, Patty thought. The strange, deep burden of motherhood. The lives given into your care. The demands made on you. The sacrifices. And yet there was a kind of hidden glory in it, too. And there was love. The love of the children. Their dependence on you when they were small. Their companionship when they grew older.

"What's hard about it?" Mark said again.

"Perhaps," said Patty, "you don't know, God sent Clare in just when you'd stubbed your bunion and . . . "

"Bunions!" Mark scorned. "Good grief, *bunions*. I am not talking about *bunions*."

"After all," said Patty, "if we believe that He arranges all things and is in all things, always, all the time . . . " She suddenly stopped speaking and raised herself on one arm, "Was that Roddy?" she said.

Mark lifted his head six inches from the pillow.

"No. The wind getting up."

He lay back, but Patty still listened.

"Are you sure? I thought he was a bit restless when I went in just now. You put him to bed all right, didn't you?"

"Of course I put him to bed all right. He tucked down at once. Didn't hear another sound."

"I thought I smelt Crunch up there."

"He was draped over the kitchen step when I came in from the studio."

Patty lay down again.

"I suppose it was the wind getting up," she said, and added, "It's only because we can't *see* what God's doing with everything that it looks all fogged-up and nightmarish."

Oh, for her simple trust, thought Mark. No threshing of

self. Hardly a thought of self. Never blame. He wondered sometimes if she ever saw anything but good, in anyone. Not because she was stupid, but because she hadn't anything in herself to see evil *with*.

He thought of Piers again, sitting beside him in the chapel, his blistered hands twisting between his bony knees. Oh Christ, the pain of the world! The pain of children suffering, dying. Man's inhumanity to man; the eternal crucifixion. The eternal death of love killed by selfishness, blindness. By—oh dear God—by evil temper. He lay staring into the shadowed, familiar room. The curtains eddied out from the window and flapped back again with a little shudder of the rings. The smell of the grass he'd cut earlier in the day drifted in as the dew rose.

'Don't let me have done them any damage,' he cried silently. 'Don't let them be hurt again through me.'

He heard the bumpy rattle of the last train running down the line the other side of the river. Twenty-five past eleven. He remembered the light on the delphiniums as he'd gone across to the studio before breakfast.

'Lord support us all the day long,' he began, but sleep clouded his mind. He sank into the darkness of it for a moment and returned to brief consciousness again. 'Till the fever of life is over and our work is done . . . ' He heaved round in the bed and lay on his side, one arm resting across Patty's already sleeping body. 'Then in Thy mercy grant us a safe lodging. In Thy mercy . . . A safe lodging . . . '